# Remember
# Me

# Also by Mario Escobar

*Auschwitz Lullaby*
*Children of the Stars*
*The Librarian of Saint-Malo*

# Acclaim for Mario Escobar

"Escobar's latest (after *Auschwitz Lullaby*, 2018) is a meticulously researched story, recreating actual experiences of the 460 Spanish children who were sent to Morelia, Mexico in 1937. Devastating, enlightening, and passionately told, Escobar's novel shines a light on the experiences of the victims of war, and makes a case against those who would use violence to gain power. Although painful events in the story make it hard to read at times, the book gives a voice to so many whose stories are often overlooked, while inspiring the reader to never give way to fear or let go of one's humanity."

—*BookList*, STARRED REVIEW, ON *REMEMBER ME*

"In *The Librarian of Saint-Malo*, Escobar brings us another poignant tale of sacrifice, love, and loss amidst the pain of war. The seaside town of Saint-Malo comes to life in rich detail and complexity under German occupation, as do the books—full of great ideas and the best of humanity—the young librarian seeks to save. This sweeping story gives us a glimpse into the past with a firm eye towards hope in our future."

—KATHERINE REAY, BESTSELLING AUTHOR OF
*THE PRINTED LETTER BOOKSHOP*

"Luminous and beautifully researched, *Remember Me* is a study of displacement, belonging, compassion, and forged family amidst a heart-wrenching escape from the atrocities of the Spanish Civil War. A strong sense of place and the excavation of a little known part of history are reverently handled in a narrative both urgent and romantic. Fans of Arturo Pérez-Reverte, Chanel Cleeton, and Lisa Wingate will be mesmerized."

—RACHEL MCMILLAN, AUTHOR OF *THE LONDON RESTORATION*

"An exciting and moving novel."

—*PEOPLE EN ESPAÑOL* ON *RECUÉRDAME*

# Remember Me

*A Spanish Civil War Novel*

## MARIO ESCOBAR

THOMAS NELSON
Since 1798

Published in Nashville, Tennessee, by Thomas Nelson. Thomas Nelson is a registered trademark of HarperCollins Christian Publishing, Inc.

Thomas Nelson titles may be purchased in bulk for educational, business, fund-raising, or sales promotional use. For information, please email SpecialMarkets@ThomasNelson.com.

Publisher's Note: This novel is a work of fiction. Names, characters, places, and incidents are either products of the author's imagination or used fictitiously. All characters are fictional, and any similarity to people living or dead is purely coincidental.

ISBN 978-0-7852-3661-0 (trade paper)

### Library of Congress Cataloging-in-Publication Data

Names: Escobar, Mario, 1971- author. | Abernathy, Gretchen, translator.
Title: Remember me : a Spanish Civil War novel / Mario Escobar ; [English translation: Gretchen Abernathy].
Other titles: Recuérdame. English
Description: Nashville, Tennessee : Thomas Nelson, [2020] | Originally published in Spanish as Recuérdame in 2019 by HarperCollins Español. | Summary: "From international bestseller Mario Escobar comes a 20th-century historical novel of tragedy and resilience inspired by Spain's famed Children of Morelia and the true events that shaped their lives"-- Provided by publisher.
Identifiers: LCCN 2020015430 (print) | LCCN 2020015431 (ebook) | ISBN 9780785236580 (hardcover) | ISBN 9780785236597 (epub) | ISBN 9780785236603 (downloadable audio) | ISBN 9780785236702 (international edition)
Subjects: LCSH: Spain--History--Civil War, 1936-1939--Fiction. | Children and war--Fiction. | Political refugees--Mexico--Fiction.
Classification: LCC PQ6705.S618 R4313 2020 (print) | LCC PQ6705.S618 (ebook) | DDC 863/.7--dc23
LC record available at https://lccn.loc.gov/2020015430
LC ebook record available at https://lccn.loc.gov/2020015431

Spanish Editor in Chief: Edward Benitez
English Editor: Jocelyn Bailey

English translation: Gretchen Abernathy

*Printed in the United States of America*
21 22 23 24 25  LSC  10 9 8 7 6 5 4 3 2 1

To my children, who are around the age of the Children of Morelia; may life never lead them into exile, and if it does, may they be as brave as the Republican children during the Spanish Civil War.

To Elisabeth, my beloved wife, my mother country, my flag.

To my grandmother, Ponciana, and my grandfather, Tomás, who endured the ravages of war and the hatred between brothers and sisters.

To my mother, Amparo, who shed countless tears for lost dreams and sowed stars in my heart.

*I weep because, since I'm fully a Spaniard and fully a Mexican, I feel like, when it's all said and done, I've got no identity at all.*

Emeterio Payá Valera, one of the Morelia children

# A Note from the Author

The Spanish Civil War was a river of tears and blood. All war is terrible, of course, but when it occurs between brothers, the violent conflict becomes tragedy. The wounds stay open for decades and never fully scar over. There are no just wars! The victims were the same as always: the civilian population, the bystanders who never wanted to fight yet were obliged to pay with their lives or lose their loved ones in the cruel barbarity of the conflict that was a training ground for World War II.

The coup d'état of July 17, 1936, which led to a long and brutal war, started off like a party. That is how the Spanish poet Juan Ramón Jiménez described it in a letter that sought to raise support for the Republic's cause. The letter was read aloud in New York that same summer:

> I've seen it with my own eyes: During these first months of the war, Madrid has been a tragic, crazed party. The jubilation,

a strange joy of a bloody faith, rebounded on all sides; it was the joy of being convinced, the joy of willpower, the joy of a favorable destiny—or not.[1]

The party came to an abrupt end as the people learned from the harsh lessons of bombs and bullets that what was being ripped away was the future.

Antonio Machado realized at once that the civil war was much more than a conflict between Spaniards. He said:

> The civil war, so ethically unequal but, in the end, between Spaniards, ended a few months ago. Spain has been sold abroad by men who cannot be called Spaniards . . . Such that now there is nothing but a Spain invaded . . . by foreign greed.[2]

For me, writing this book has been a long, difficult, internal, and external journey. The civil war has marked my life since childhood. My parents were children during the war, and my grandparents endured great hardships throughout the conflict, especially my mother's parents. My grandfather, Tomás Golderos, fought and went missing on the front, leaving behind four children and a wife who suffered the harsh Francoist repression. The conflict's fallout made such a big impact on me when I was younger that every year on Christmas Eve I would pray that Spain would never experience another civil war.

*Remember Me* is the story of three siblings who are sent to Mexico in hopes of being reunited with their parents after the war

---

1  Juan Ramón Jiménez, quoted by Antonio Machado in his prologue from 1937 to J.R. Jiménez, *Guerra en España. Prosa y verso (1936-1954)*, rev. and expanded, Madrid, Point de Lunettes, 2009, 7. (Translated from original Spanish.)
2  Antonio Machado, *La Guerra. Escritos: 1936-39*. Ed. por Julio Rodríguez Puértolas y Gerardo Pérez Herrero. Madrid: Emiliano Escolar Editor, 1983. (Translated from original Spanish.)

and who must face the dangerous journey of exile. It is the story of thousands of children who left and would never return either to their homeland or to their homes, to the true mother country of family. And it is the story of children who found themselves lost and alone in the world, with no one to embrace them or point out the way they should go.

*Remember Me* is the collective story of the Children of Morelia. Some 460 children between the ages of four and seventeen were sent from Spain to Mexico in an attempt to escape the terrible ravages of the war. The children traveled under very difficult circumstances to Veracruz in the summer of 1937. The Ibero-American Committee for Aid to the Spanish Peoples oversaw the logistics of getting the children out of the country. Carmela Gil de Vázquez and Amalia Solórzano, the wife of President Cárdenas, were the driving force behind the effort.

The adventures of Marco, Isabel, and Ana Alcalde are of course a tribute to the Children of Morelia, but they are ultimately a tribute to all the children of the Spanish Civil War who were sent to safety in exile in the Soviet Union, Belgium, the United Kingdom, France, Argentina, and Chile. They had to leave behind what they loved most—their parents—and, in many cases, they were exiled forever.

My hope is that *Remember Me* pays homage to the exiles of all wars—to those who have lost their homelands to the brutality of human violence.

# Prologue

My hands shook with the letter I had just received, postmarked from Mexico. The memories of the sad, exciting journey of my childhood returned to remind me that, at the end of the day, I belonged nowhere. I wiped my tears with my shirttail and studied the sender's name: María Soledad de la Cruz. That girl had stolen my heart nearly forty years earlier. For a long time I had tried to convince myself I was a Spaniard, that my time in Mexico had been a kind of daydream. I had awoken from that dream as abruptly as the bombs had started falling over Madrid in the summer of 1937. I had gotten used to the black-and-white city Franco's followers ran like military barracks for nearly forty years—so used to it all that the memories of life in Veracruz, Mexico City, and Morelia were no more than distant, imagined ghosts. They were Don Quixote's loquacious deathbed visions after the entrance to his library had been sealed shut. I had spent the intervening years remaking my life, and I had a job I loved. I had inherited my father's printing press. For so many of us, the civil war had taken health, property, and existence itself. For me, it had also ripped away the future.

I thought about María Soledad de la Cruz's eyes, which still shone out bright from those eclipsed years. They were so black the light disappeared in her pupils but came back out through her thick lips in the first stolen kiss there in Cointzio.

I opened the envelope and read the short letter with a lump in my throat. Then I looked at the small black-and-white photo hidden in the mustard-yellow envelope. It was the same girl with black braids and pearls for teeth, the one who had taken up shop in my heart and who reminded me yet again that, being fully Spaniard and fully Mexican, I could lay claim to no homeland. I still could not forget it. It was my bounden duty to remember, like my mother told me that day in Bordeaux, the last day of my old life and the first of a journey I never could have imagined.

Part 1

# Bombs All Around

# Chapter 1

# The Search

For children, war feels like a game at first. They have no idea that behind the gunshots and uniforms, the marches and rallying songs, death clings like mud to shoes and leaves footprints of blood and flesh, forever marking the lives of whoever falls into its infernal clutch.

The Spanish Civil War began long before soldiers took up arms on July 17, 1936. At least it had begun for us, the children of poverty and misery.

First thing that morning, I heard someone beating on the door of our house in the La Latina neighborhood. We were still in bed: my two sisters and I, my parents, and the girl who watched us while my mother worked in the theater. Instinctively, my sisters and I ran to our parents' room. Isabel, with her white cotton nightgown, trembled and shrieked as she clung to our mother. Ana sobbed in my arms while our father masked his fear behind a smile and told us nothing was wrong.

María Zapata, the girl who helped around the house, also started to cry as she followed my father like a scared puppy to the door. The rest of us hunkered down in the main bedroom, but when I heard the shouting and skirmish in the hallway, I left my little sister in our mother's lap and headed for the door without a second thought. While not particularly brave, I wanted to help my father. I was still young enough that my dad was the invincible, mythic hero I longed to become. I stood trembling at the doorway of the small room we called the study, which was just a six-by-nine-foot room stuffed with books and papers. The walls were caving in and the shelves bowed, but to me that room was the hallowed halls of wisdom. However, right then it felt like the entrance to hell itself. Papers flew about as the gloved hands of the Social Brigade tore brightly colored spines from books yanked off the shelves. Nearly all the books were from Editorial Cervantes, a publishing house in Barcelona for which my father's printing press sometimes did work. My father raised his hands in despair, each ripped spine and crumpled page falling like the lash of a whip on his back.

"We don't have any banned books here!" My father's strangled shout interrupted the chaos of military boots and police barking. The sergeant turned and punched him square in the mouth. Blood gushed from my father's busted lip, and I, horrified, saw a terrified look on the face of the man I had always believed to be the bravest soul on earth.

"You piece of red trash! We know you're one of the leaders of the printers' union! On October fifth your people attacked the State

Department, and you're part of the Revolutionary Socialist Committee. Where are the books? We want the union's papers and the names of everyone on the committee!"

The sergeant was shaking my father, who, in his silly striped pajamas, looked like a marionette in the man's hands. I knew the books they were talking about were not in the study. A few days before I had helped my father hide them in the dovecote on the roof of our building.

"I'm an honest worker and loyal to the Republic," my father answered, more calmly than I expected. His collar and the front part of his shirt were red with his blood, but his eyes had recovered the courage that always guided his steps.

Yet he doubled over when the sergeant punched him hard in the stomach. The officer shoved him, and the guards fell upon him with their nightsticks. My dad sank to the floor, screaming and flailing his arms like a drowning man grasping for oxygen at the bottom of the ocean.

"Boy, come here!" the sergeant barked at me, and for the first time, I looked him full in the face. He was like a rabid dog with spittle flying from his mouth. His thick, black mustache made him look even wilder. He grabbed my shirt and yanked me out of the study to the living room and threw me into a chair. I landed abruptly, and the man crouched down to get his face right in front of mine.

"Look, kid, your daddy is a red, a communist, an enemy of peace and order. If you tell us where the papers are, nothing bad will happen. But if you lie to us, you and your sisters will end up in the Sacred Heart Orphanage. Do you want them to shave your mother's hair and lock her up in the prison of Ventas?"

"No, sir," I answered. My voice shook, and I nearly wet myself from fright.

"Then come out with it before my patience runs out," he spluttered, more foam gathering at the corners of his mouth.

"These are all the books my dad has. He's a printer, you know . . . That's why we have so many."

The sergeant lifted me up by the folds of my shirt and shook me with violence. My feet flailed aimlessly in the air until he dropped me onto the floor. Then he turned and raged back to the study with great strides.

"Let's go! We're taking the adults with us!" he snarled.

"What do we do with the kids?" one of the guards asked.

"The orphanage. Let them rot with the lice and bedbugs."

I ran to the door of the living room. One of the police officers was dragging my mother out of the bedroom, and I threw myself upon him, grabbed his neck, and bit one of his ears. Bellowing, the officer let go of my mother and tried to shake me off.

"Marco, please!" my mother yelled, terrified at seeing me on the police officer. The officer wrestled me off and threw me against the wall. He pulled out his nightstick and raised it to strike, but my mother grabbed his arm. "Please, he's just a child. Don't hurt him," she begged through her tears.

The sergeant appeared in the hallway. Two of his men were hauling my father off. His face, nearly purple, was covered with blood, his eyes swollen. He groaned in pain. My little sisters ran to him, but the sergeant shoved them back. Moving forward with the rest of the group, he called out, "Grab the brat!" But before the other guards could reach for me, I opened the door to the hallway and tore down the stairs.

The last thing I heard as I raced away was the voice of one of the policemen and my mother's screams as they flooded the entry stairway. Her voice swelled like thunder and lightning until it broke into muffled sobbing. Pain seared my chest as I raced down the street. I did not stop until I reached the Plaza Mayor, where the street cleaners were hosing off the cobblestones. I leaned against one of the columns in the plaza and wept bitterly.

The war started a long time before 1936. By then it was already coursing deep in the blood of the entire nation. That day I understood that people can be right and still lose, that courage is not enough to defeat evil, and that the strength of weapons destroys the soul of humanity.

Chapter 2

# María Zapata

Madrid
November 14, 1934

I don't remember how long I walked. I was cold, but I hadn't even
noticed I was wearing my pajamas and some old canvas shoes. I
felt like I was in a nightmare I couldn't wake up from. The scenes I
had just witnessed at home repeated themselves endlessly before my
eyes: my mother screaming, my sisters clinging to her nightgown and
crying, my father's lip split open, the blood dripping down his stubbled
chin. I couldn't shake from my mind the image of the policemen with
their nightsticks and the sergeant who threatened to take us to an
orphanage. When I neared University City, I finally noticed where I
was. It was my first time in the northwest corner of Madrid, but I had
heard about the redbrick buildings and well-tended lawns. I raised

my eyes and studied the snowcapped mountains in the distance. They seemed close enough to reach out and touch, yet somehow so far away, like the peace that had reigned in my home until that morning. I slumped down beneath a statue of a horse. My head dropped to the side, and I fell fast asleep.

I have no idea how much time passed like that before a female voice and a soft hand woke me. "What are you doing here? Are you all right? Are you lost?"

Just inches from my dirty, tearstained frame, a girl with green eyes and a lovely oval face was smiling. I had no idea how to respond. Of course I was not all right. I was terrified and half crazed, but at my age it wasn't easy to express my feelings, much less explain them.

"Do you want me to walk you home?" she asked. "Where do you live?"

A group of girls was waiting for her a few yards away. A couple of them told her to come back and to leave me alone. "Sorry, I can't just leave him here," she called back to them. Her waist was barely covered by a short purple jacket, and her loose hair streamed around her face but could not hide her beauty. "I'm Rosa," she said. "Rosa Chamorro. What's your name?"

I looked up at her and started to cry. It felt like a cowardly thing to do, just like it was cowardly to run away and leave my family in the hands of the savage police, but I couldn't help it. Tears are sometimes a child's only option for relief. As we grow up, crying becomes taboo. We're told not to show our weaknesses but, instead, to endure pain, loss, and sadness without letting tears wash through our hearts and clear away whatever is constricting our souls.

The girl helped me up with her left hand. In her right, she carried a notebook and a pair of black gloves. Her friends went on, exasperated with her, and she and I walked a mile or so back toward central Madrid.

"I'll get your trolley ticket, but you have to tell me where you live. Your parents are probably worried about you."

The pain in my chest intensified at the mention of my parents, but I held myself together. In a voice raspy from crying, I told her I lived in La Latina neighborhood, near the San Ildefonso school.

She nodded. "I live . . . well, not close to there, but it's not out of the way."

We waited at the busy stop crawling with college students. In my neighborhood there were no college students. Laborers' children learned a trade, and at twelve, thirteen, or fourteen we were apprenticed out to start helping support the family.

As I looked at the law textbook pressed against the girl's notebook, someone approached. He wore a striped suit, like a gangster in the movies, with his hair greased back and a short little mustache that contrasted with his childish facial features.

"What are you doing with this rapscallion?" he asked, nodding to me. "I didn't know you were babysitting vagabonds these days."

"He's not a vagabond. He's a lost child."

We got on the trolley, and the guy turned his nose up at me as if he were dealing with a pest. He positioned himself next to Rosa and continued, "He'll be the son of some red, I just know it. The police are flushing out everyone who participated in the strike last month. These people are destroying Spain. They're like rats. We've got to get rid of them before they become a plague."

The girl pursed her lips. "It's none of your business, Fernandito," she said. Fernandito was one of her older brother's friends. A diehard Falangist, he was repeating his first-year classes for the third time.

"Hey, but you're my friend's sister, and I've got to protect you from riffraff. It's not a good idea for you to be traveling alone on the trolley. It'll be dark before long, and Madrid is crawling with crooks and criminals."

Rosa sniffed. "I can watch out for myself. I don't need you to protect me from anything."

Fernandito rolled his eyes. "Girls these days think they're so independent. You can go to college and wear your little miniskirts, but things are about to change. This sacrilegious, atheistic Republic won't last long," he said, regurgitating what he had learned in meetings with José Antonio Primo de Rivera, a silver spoon Andalusian who tried to copy Benito Mussolini's fascist ideas but had been upstaged by a certain Austrian named Adolf Hitler.

My father would tell me about all of these things after listening to the radio in the afternoons after work. I loved listening to him. Huddled up next to him on the rug, it was the only time in the day when we were alone together. Then he would stretch out in our one shabby recliner and motion for me to crawl up next to him. I loved resting my head on his chest and hearing his heartbeat while the radio played songs by Gardel, one of my dad's favorites. My mother listened to the radio in the mornings, but she preferred Imperio Argentina.

Fernandito gave me a shove right as we rounded a curve, and I nearly fell out of the trolley.

"Leave him alone!" Rosa snapped.

A man in a worker's uniform turned and pierced Fernandito with a cold stare. "This guy bothering you?" he asked Rosa.

Fernandito dropped his thuggish posture and skulked away to another part of the trolley.

The trolley reached Plaza de España and then kept going along Gran Vía to Plaza del Callao.

"I know my way from here," I told the girl when the trolley paused in front of the Callao theater.

"Don't worry. It's still pretty early, so I can go with you." We walked along Preciados Street, but she stopped in front of Café Varela. "Let's go in and get a bite. I imagine you haven't eaten all day."

We went in, and the warmth brought me back to myself after all day on the cold street. People stared at us. No one failed to notice that a kid in dirty pajamas was spending time with a pretty college girl, though it was hard to say which stood out more in that provincial Madrid environment.

A waiter wearing a white jacket more decorated in braids than an army general's greeted us ruefully, not wanting his other tables to be disturbed by our presence. Interest waned, however, and within a few minutes the restaurant's customers had returned to their monotonous lives and I was eating a delicious, steaming steak sandwich.

"I take it you were hungry?" Rosa asked, bathing me in the angelic glow of her smile.

I nodded, my mouth full. "Thank you for everything."

"Don't mention it. Sometimes a chance meeting is a gift from heaven, if you know what I mean."

I did not know what she meant. The only heaven my parents believed in was the one that could be "stormed." I knew that phrase from the philosopher Karl Marx because my dad had used it once when the neighborhood priest upbraided him on his way home from work for not taking us to church.

"I don't know what's happened to you," she said, "but I assume it was something terrible. Leaving your house in your nightclothes and wandering all that way . . ."

I wanted to trust her, but my father had told me we could never trust anyone outside our class. I still had not learned that sometimes children have to show the way when their parents get turned around.

"The police came and took my parents. They were looking for some papers because my father is a printer. I mean, he has a little workshop near the house. My mom is an actress. She works for the Jacinto Guerrero troupe."

"I've never been to the theater," Rosa said. "My father's modern,

15

but not *that* modern. He lets me go to the movies some Sundays, but doesn't the playwright you're talking about do musicals and revues?"

I nodded and wiped some of the steak grease off my chin. "I've been a lot. My mom takes us to the rehearsals and sometimes there are snacks. The actors are really picky, and there's always chocolates and treats."

Rosa took the napkin and cleaned off the rest of my face, then paid for the meal. It was even colder out on the street when we went back out, the day darkened by gray clouds that threatened snow.

"Brrrr!" she squealed. Then she opened her coat and used it to shelter us both as much as she could.

Before long we were at the entrance to the building where my family had lived until that morning. Few people were out in the streets, and I hesitated, unsure of what to do. The police had taken my parents and probably my sisters too.

"It's been nice to meet you, but you still haven't told me your name," Rosa said.

"Marco Alcalde, at your service," I answered, just as my mother had taught me.

She reached out her hand and shook mine, fragile and cold. "I hope things work out for you, Marco. I'm going to leave you with a quote. I memorize one every day, to help me learn how to live. People think that existence is just one big improvisation, but really it's a rehearsal. The phrase is from the philosopher Jose Ortega y Gasset: *Loyalty is the shortest path between two hearts.*"

Rosa turned and walked back to Mayor Street, and I stared after her retreating figure. She had kept the pain and terror at bay and helped me do something other than obsess about what had happened that morning, but as I walked up the dark stairs, my mind replayed it all again. I was trembling as I reached the landing at our door, more from fear than from cold. With not even a whisper of hope,

I knocked. I kept knocking, then pounded the door in desperation. Our apartment was my refuge—the thing that separated me from the savage world outside. Finally, I heard footsteps. Someone opened the peephole, but it was totally dark where I was on the landing.

"Who is it?" the nervous voice of María Zapata asked.

"It's me!" I answered, surprised and also hopeful. Perhaps I was not wholly alone after all.

María timidly opened the door, as if she could not actually believe it was me. She pulled me to her in a tight embrace and caressed my hair. "Oh, my boy, I was worried sick for you!" She brought me inside, heated water in a big pot for my bath, and gave me clean clothes.

"Have you eaten?" she asked. "The sergeant let me keep your sisters here, but they're asleep. The poor dears have had a terrible time of it today. I didn't take Isabel to school because I was too afraid. They've whimpered in bed all day, like the grief has gotten all balled up in their throats and can't move an inch."

That day I learned two lessons I will never forget: No matter how bad things get, someone is always willing to lend a hand; and sometimes you must lie to the villains. My teachers had always taught me that lies limp along for a short time while the truth takes long, confident strides. But I had to protect my family, the most important thing in the world to me. And my father had already warned me that the people in charge of keeping the peace were often the lackeys of the powerful.

# Chapter 3

# Victory

Madrid
July 18, 1936

I remember it was a Saturday. I didn't usually keep track of the days of the week when we were off school and had nothing to do but laze about and play outside. A year and a half had passed since the terrifying morning when the sergeant hauled our parents away. For a full week my sisters and I hunkered down in fear with María Zapata, and then one day, with no forewarning, our parents appeared at the door. They had been released without explanation. Their bodies healed, and we slowly returned to our normal routines as a family, though we never forgot that violation of our peace.

I had turned thirteen a few weeks before that day in July 1936, and my parents faced the dilemma of wanting me to stay in school yet not having the funds to pay for it. They could perhaps ask for help from the party, as it was always in need of lawyers and other professionals, or perhaps I could be apprenticed to Dad's workshop once summer was over. My mother wanted me to continue my studies. She was as committed to the party as my father, but she was unwilling to reject her troupe director's offer to pay for my first semester of high school. Mom always said that pride was a luxury poor people couldn't afford. On the other hand, my father surveyed my sisters' worn-out shoes and the scant food he managed to bring home and preferred to set me up at the printing press so I could learn a trade or to take me to work sites to learn construction, which earned decent wages.

The heat was unbearable that summer in Madrid. The trolleys sped along Mayor Street, and people meandered, trying to stay out of the sun in the hottest hours of the day. There was a war going on, but no one seemed too concerned, perhaps because bloody party infighting had been happening for so long. On July 14 the funeral of the leader of the extreme right, José Calvo Sotelo, had been held, and tensions were as high as the summer temperatures.

Just a few weeks before, the city had smelled of winter's hot chocolate and churros. Now the aromas of frying lamb intestines—our beloved *gallinejas* and *entresijos*—and of Spanish tortillas and freshly sliced hams filled the streets. Older men sat and lingered over conversation at their customary cafés. They rambled about a little girl who had been run over the day before; the actress Tina de Jarque, star of the Teatro de la Zarzuela, and her fine pair of legs; and the murder of "Pepe el de los perros," a young man found dead on the road between Húmera and Pozuelo. Pious women gathered at the doors of the church of Jesús de Medinaceli to ask for three wishes. There were no strikes in the city that day, which was noteworthy given how often anyone and everyone—from woodworkers to government clerks to elevator operators—marched and went on strike in recent months over the slightest provocation. By the afternoon, rumors were spreading that a military uprising had occurred in Ceuta or Melilla, but this news was far away, no cause for concern.

That night as we sat down to supper, someone knocked at the door and shouted, "Francisco, the workers are taking up arms! The prime minister has resigned. The Civil Guard is loyal to the Republic, but the governor is afraid the military will attack the capital tonight."

My father was wearing breezy pants and a sleeveless shirt, so he went to the bedroom for his short-sleeved shirt and hat. Then he took his pipe from the shelf and kissed my mother on the forehead.

"Francisco, please be careful," my mother pleaded. I could see she was trembling, despite the heat.

"Don't worry, darling. This'll be over after maybe four gunshots. There's nothing more cowardly in this world than a fascist."

Before my father realized it, I was following him down the stairs.

"Where do you think you're going, little shrimp?" my father's friend asked, gently pulling me back by my collar.

"I want to go with you. I'm practically grown now."

"And you think killing a man is a game?"

"We're not going to kill anybody," my father interrupted, sliding his arm around my back. "Don't you remember what happened in Africa? Those cowards at the military base are all full of talk about the fatherland and honor, but they're a bunch of traitors. Besides, Marco is thirteen years old now, almost a man. He should see with his own eyes how the fascists are gift wrapping the revolution for us that we've been awaiting for so long. They've choked at the ballot box and know we're for real this time. We won't let them steal our liberty again."

The three of us headed for Monteleón Station, where some activists with the National Work Confederation passed out guns and greeted workers with raised fists. Excitement sparked in the air even though it was nearly eleven o'clock at night. With the guns, we headed to Luna Street, where most of the union headquarters were located. I was surprised to see a boisterous multitude coming down the street with arms raised high, begging loudly for weapons.

"Let's head to party headquarters at the Segovia Bridge. They'll know what to do there. These anarchists are incapable of organizing things," said my dad's friend.

We spent most of the night walking through the city, which seemed to be one big street party. Sunday dawned as we made our way down Segovia Street into the socialist sector. People were running this way and that, and the general jubilance seemed to celebrate the military uprising rather than fear it.

"Where's Largo Caballero?" said my father to a girl who held an armful of folders and documents.

"In a meeting," she answered, not pausing.

My father had known Largo Caballero since they were kids, when they lived near each other in Madrid's Chamberí neighborhood. Father walked into the meeting room without knocking, and we followed. Half a dozen men were deep in discussion around a table.

"Mr. Alcalde, come in; don't be so calm about it," Largo Caballero goaded. Then, lifting his fist into the air, he said, "Comrades!" to which everyone responded in kind. "The fascists have opened up the doors of paradise for us. We failed in '34, but this time no one will stop us. We'll flush the cowards out of government and get someone with guts. It's time for the brave to step forward," he continued.

I did not understand why everyone was so happy, but their optimism was contagious. People were hugging and singing, speaking of how they would create a new world, a world without classes or injustice, a world where all men were equal and those who did not want to be part of it would meet death.

# Chapter 4

# The Montaña Barracks

Madrid
July 19, 1936

I eventually fell asleep on a bench. Someone threw a blanket over me, and before it was even light outside, my father was shaking me awake. I looked at him blankly, trying to remember where I was and what had happened during that strange night.

"Go back home and let Mom know I'm all right."

"Where are you going, Dad?"

"To the Montaña Barracks," he said. There were circles under his blue eyes.

"But Mom, she—"

"Women have the gift of creating life, which is why they always protect and care for it as the most sacred thing that exists in this world. War is for men. We must destroy the world to build a new one. Do you understand? It's either them or us. There are only two realities: the one that wants to impose fascism, or the socialist paradise. Now, head back home."

I left him and was surprised to find the trolleys running at that hour. I hopped on the first one that arrived, and it was obvious that the city had stayed up all night. People walked along the streets in near hypnosis. On one side were the workers in armed groups and on the other, the remaining inhabitants who didn't have to work since it was Sunday. People meandered along the streets and parks, and all the cafés were open because it was too monumental a moment for normal business hours. The city seemed to be split between those who felt the war to be a grand adventure and everyone else, as impassive as always and heedless that everything was about to change. On my way home, I passed a few trucks dragging cannons toward the Montaña Barracks, as well as groups of civil guards running toward the improvised front.

My mother was waiting for me though the rest of the house slept peacefully. When she saw me, she burst into tears and hugged me so tight I could barely breathe. "Oh, thank goodness nothing happened to you. I waited up all night, listening to the radio. Things have gotten ugly. The military has won in Seville, Zaragoza, and other posts, so this is more than a coup d'état." She led me into the kitchen and started fixing me some breakfast. "But where is your father?"

"They're surrounding the Montaña Barracks."

My poor mother covered her face with her hands. Yet she maintained control of herself and managed to warm the milk and pour some into the coffee she handed me. Then she sat beside me. "Men think they can change the world with bullets, but the only thing that can transform our planet is tenderness. If children were left with their mothers when they start to really discover life, we'd teach them that the only way to be brothers and sisters is to soak in tenderness. Hatred has never changed anything. The cemeteries are full of hatred and greed. Humanity's real problem is in our hearts. Do you understand me, Marco?"

"I don't know. How can we convince a fascist that he's supposed to love? That's impossible. They want to kill us. What really matters is who kills first and who dies first." I was reciting from memory the things I had heard my father say hundreds of times at party headquarters or over card games in cafés.

She clucked in response. "Go on, go to bed. You probably haven't slept all night."

I washed my face and was about to crawl into bed when I noticed my mother from across the room. She was taking something out of the dresser, a little piece of paper. I did not know then that it was a holy card with a picture of a saint. She kissed it and whispered something with her eyes closed. Then she put it back and called my sisters to come to breakfast. That little ceremony frightened me more than the guns and war cries from the night before. Because if my mother was harkening back to the old god of her ancestors, I knew she must really believe that the jubilance would not last and that the streets would soon be stained with blood.

I have no idea how, but the next day I convinced Mom to let me take some food to Dad. The workers had kept watch on the Montaña Barracks all day, and the besieged military inside showed no signs of giving up. Rumors that rebel reinforcements would come from Zaragoza, Valladolid, or Burgos encouraged them to hold out.

I headed for the barracks in one of the crowded trolleys and listened to all the news and gossip. Apparently, the coup d'état had failed nearly everywhere in Spain, especially the big cities, except for Seville and a few provincial capitals in Castilla la Vieja.

I jumped off at a stop on Gran Vía and walked with my hands

in my pockets to Príncipe Pío hill. I had never paid much attention to the huge, squared building up there. It looked modern, more like a hospital than army barracks. As I drew closer, I found myself surrounded by more and more people, as if I had walked into a market or fair. Yet a hundred yards ahead, a mix of workers, soldiers, and civil guards were crouching behind improvised barricades. Artillery and machine guns were aimed at the building, but if not for the weapons and cannons, no one would have guessed that one of the first battles of the war would start there.

I spotted my father stationed at one of the cannons with other socialist workers. Each union group and political party had its own emblematic paraphernalia which its members wore on their necks or arms. As I walked toward my father, one of his friends slapped my neck down, and I cried out in surprise.

"Get your head down or they'll take it off with a bullet. What do you think you're doing here?" the man demanded.

I could not understand what he was angry about. War seemed like a grand game to me. I had no inkling of the danger and suffering it could leave in its wake.

"I brought Dad some food," I said, taking care to crouch low.

"Your dad is up there at the cannon. Deliver it and then get out of here. This is no place for kids."

I walked along, crouching down among the men. A few kept their sights aimed at the barracks, but most were circled up together talking, smoking, or drinking cold beer.

"Marco, what are you doing here?" Dad asked in a wearied tone when he saw me. The bags under his eyes had grown deeper, and his summer tan contrasted with his gray hair and black hat.

"I brought you some food."

His initial frown faded when he saw the white bread, chorizo, and sausage rounds. When I pulled out the bottle of wine, several of his friends gathered around with keen interest. My father elbowed them away good-naturedly and went up to a dark-haired man. "Here, Orad, this will help us regain our strength."

The man smiled and stretched out his hand to take a slice of bread with chorizo. He savored it as if it were the finest delicacy and washed it down with a long swallow of wine. When a round of shots rang out, everyone dove to the ground except for this man, Orad, and my father, who both seemed immune to fear. "Just like a fascist to ruin a good meal," my father growled, turning, aiming, and firing a few rounds.

When the air had calmed, he sat beside the cannon and continued to eat. He offered me a bit, and I felt like the happiest person in the world.

Just then, airplanes flew overhead. Everyone ran around in confusion, expecting a bomb to fall, but the sky grew strangely clouded as thousands of pieces of paper rained down. My father grabbed one as it floated, and I saw it was a warning pamphlet for those who resisted in the Montaña Barracks. In the name of the Republic, the papers formally discharged any soldiers who rebelled and disobeyed the Republic's orders.

I stayed with the men for a few hours. Many of them killed time by playing cards or singing, until a group of soldiers approached the barricade and spoke to Orad.

"We have to attack. We can't let night fall," one of the soldiers said.

"I doubt that a few blasts will drive them out," said an artilleryman.

"In a few minutes, we'll bomb them from overhead. That will be the signal."

Once the soldiers left, my father turned to me. "Get out of here before things heat up."

I agreed to leave and had just picked up the empty wine bottle when the sound of airplanes pierced the sky. I heard a whistling noise, and then I instinctively covered my ears at the sound of an unbearably loud explosion. Bombs were hitting the ground around the barracks, but one struck the front of the building, which then crumpled over the double staircase.

Orad gave the order to load and fire the cannon under his command. The explosion threw me backward to the ground, and I balled up with my head between my legs, as if doing so could protect me from the blast. The machine gun shots sounded over our heads, and for a few minutes chaos reigned. A wounded man fell down beside me, and when I glanced over, our eyes met. He seemed more like a scared child than a militiaman.

Soon another soldier fell down near me, and his rigid, bloody body left me no doubt that he was dead. I had never seen a cadaver before. His face was disfigured and had lost its human factions. He looked more like a scrap of meat lying forgotten in an alley.

I felt strangely alert. The smell of gunpowder and the blast of cannons sent the adrenaline racing through my veins. I decided to look up. My father was firing nonstop and shouting for his men to do the same. A group of men sitting on the ground continued to load the guns and hand them to the shooters.

We heard machine-gun fire coming from one of the rooftops of the building behind us. The windows of the barracks in front of us shattered in response.

I do not know how long the shooting lasted, perhaps only a few minutes, but it was an eternity to me. We saw a white flag in the building, and the militiamen hurried toward the stairs. Most of them had their guns raised high in victory. My father's group was about to join them when Dad waved them back and shouted for them to get down.

The burst of machine-gun fire from the fascists fell like hail on the militiamen advancing toward the barracks. Dozens fell, and those who managed to escape retreated to the barricades. Our group held nothing back in response. My father was enraged by the fascists' deceit and the naïveté of his comrades. It had been a dirty coup, not a gentlemen's agreement.

At noon, when the sun was beating down hard, we saw white flags again. This time no one moved until the doors of the barracks opened and the first soldiers threw down their guns. Some of the barrack defenders ran out, throwing down their helmets and guns and shouting, "Long live the Republic!" The assault guards advanced first, and a mass of militiamen from the gamut of political parties and labor unions followed. Everyone cheered, and some belted out battle songs. My father turned and ordered me not to move an inch.

While I waited, I heard a few shots. Later I heard the shouts of some officers who were dragged out of the barracks and beaten with sticks before the crowd. Blood flowed everywhere, but what stood out to me was the fear on the prisoners' faces.

I disobeyed my father and snuck up closer to the building out of curiosity. I had to pick my way around bodies lying on the cobblestones and step over more covering the stairway. I saw a boy my age pointing a pistol at an officer who walked down the street with his hands above his head.

A journalist took photographs nearby, and curious bystanders had gathered to watch as the militiamen collected all the guns. When I tried to get into one of the barrack yards, I was blocked. Cadavers were lined up in groups of ten. Some officers who had committed suicide still held weapons in their hands. To one side, groups of men shot the Falangists who had joined the rebel soldiers.

Some of the assault guards were forcibly removing General Fanjul, the rebel leader. No one else got close to him, though they spat on him and mocked him from a safe distance.

Then I spied my father, sitting alone on a stone bench, his gun draped over his back. His face was dark with sadness. I thought he would reprimand me for disobeying and leaving my post, but he hardly reacted when he saw me. I sat beside him in the middle of that field of death, and he put his arm around me.

"I've always heard that a few deaths are necessary to create a world without violence. Wanting to kill is not the same thing as actually killing. Until today, I'd never fired a shot or killed anyone. I believed getting rid of those fascists would bring me some degree of pleasure . . . You know by now that it's either them or us. But now I feel it. Killing someone is not defending an ideology. I've killed a person, people. These men were my brothers. There's nothing worse than a civil war. Maybe the bloodbath will end and we can return to fistfights in the streets or in parliament, but not like this . . . No, not like this," he whispered.

I saw the pain in my father's anguished face and jaded gaze, heard it in his feverish words. That one day, which in many ways provoked one of the worst wars in history, was over for him. He would remain an idealist who longed for the triumph of the proletariat revolution, but something broke apart in his soul that hot July day. He could not have named the sadness any more than I could have right then, but it was without a doubt the grief of a broken heart that discovers there is no ideology on earth worth killing for.

I looked up and studied the bodies. Nearly all of them were young men. I understood they had been robbed of something more precious than mere breathing: the right to a future.

Chapter 5

# In the Trenches

Madrid
October 9, 1936

I woke up from a dream about my father. We were walking through the Casa de Campo city park on a Sunday and around the lake toward the boat rental stand. My mother carried my sister Isabel; my youngest sister, Ana, still hadn't been born. I looked up at my father, who was to me a giant capable of anything. I spent most of my time with my mother, who wasn't then working in the theater. On Fridays, payday, she used to take me and Isabel with her to the market to do the week's shopping, or she'd take us to a park to play. But I didn't often walk around in public next to my father, which is why this dream, this day, was so special to me. That spring day the sky seemed especially blue, as if it wanted to swallow us up in azure infinitude. Reflected sunlight shimmered like polished gold on the water. Hand in hand with my father, I felt safe. Nothing bad could happen because I knew he would protect me from every danger and show me the right way to go.

On happy days, like that spring Saturday when we didn't look up at the sky in fear, I learned how wonderful it was to walk along holding hands with my father. I remember he bought me an ice cream cone as we waited for the boat to come to the little pier. My mother was happy and smiling. We didn't have much. We lived in a tiny house in Lavapiés, with only two dark, dank rooms and no bathroom or heat or running water, but my father's love spilled through every look and touch.

That day we rented a canoe, and Dad let me help him row, though he was the one who moved the paddles and steered. His face oozed joy.

We took a long, meandering walk on the way back home. Isabel slept in my mother's arms, and I held on to my dad's hand. I could not put it into words, but what that day ingrained in my little mind was that safety lay between the fingers of those calloused, scratched hands.

❧

I once thought that growing up meant getting married, starting a family, finding a good job, and waiting for life to pass one by without struggles or distress. But on one autumn morning in October 1936, with the sky a dull gray and as I walked beside Isabel and holding Ana's hand, I started to wonder if getting older meant learning to take care of yourself and the people you love. We got to the trolley that would take us to Casa de Campo. The huge expanse of forest was no longer the haven of peace it had been when I was younger, when cyclists meandered down the dusty trails or Sunday visitors picnicked beneath the centuries-old oaks that had stood watch as kings, ambitious courtesans, and even Napoleon's troops passed them by.

The trolley car clacked louder than in years before, rickety now from overuse and neglected maintenance because of the war. We could see some of the ruins from the bombings, though most had hit public buildings and the Cuatro Vientos airfield. We stepped off near the Line 25 stop in Puerta del Ángel Plaza, then walked to the entrance of Casa de Campo. Militiamen came and went from all directions. They weren't wearing uniforms, but there was no mistaking their armbands, military hats, and rifles. The color of the bandannas around their necks indicated the party or union to which they belonged. As we neared the lake, they greeted us with raised fists, surely because we were all three dressed like them, with little hats and the socialist party bandannas around our necks.

Since taking the Montaña Barracks, my father had supported the city's assault guard. He spent most of his time in Salamanca, one of Madrid's most well-to-do neighborhoods. My mother, along with most of her theater troupe, had enlisted in a militia that defended the capital. She rarely carried a weapon since she and her colleagues mainly focused on keeping morale high among the volunteers by dancing, singing, and performing satirical skits about the enemy and priests.

My sisters and I reached the improvised camp, barely a dozen tents where food was distributed and the volunteer army received instructions. Most volunteers showed up in the mornings, joined their units, then went back to their homes at night.

We searched for our mother among the tents and finally found her rehearsing with some of the other actors. As soon as she saw us, she left what she was doing and smothered us in hugs and kisses until I turned red with embarrassment.

"Come on, Mom," I said, wriggling away and wiping her lipstick off my cheeks. "I'm not a little kid anymore."

"What time did you leave school? You're here earlier than I expected."

"There's a procession this afternoon. The International Brigades are arriving," I said, turning my head to get a better look at the cannons just beyond the tent.

Mom nodded. "Go on, you can go look at the weapons. I know you're interested."

I was already outside next to a cannon by the time she finished speaking. It was enormous, much bigger than the one I'd seen at the Montaña Barracks.

"You like it?" one of the artillerymen asked. I nodded. "Want me to show you how it works?" He smiled when he saw my eyes light up. He nestled his cigarette in one corner of his mouth, then heaved up a missile, loaded it into the cannon, shut a little door, and pushed a lever.

"These models are old, but they've promised us the Russians are bringing us newer weapons. The Soviet comrades will help us win this war and bring the revolution. Father Stalin is keenly interested in what happens in Spain. The German fascists won't quit bombing us, and I've heard they're sending tanks and new arms to the rebels."

I paid much more attention to the cannon, the missiles, and the nearby machine guns than I did to his words.

"You're old enough to fight, you know," the man said. "You should enlist in one of the militias. We need every hand we can get."

I studied his black hat and matching black bandanna. He was an anarchist with the National Work Confederation—a leftist organization like the one to which my dad belonged, but in many ways at odds with it.

"León!" my mother's voice rang out. "What ideas are you putting into my son's head?" She was coming out of the tent with my sisters.

"I'm just telling him the truth. That he's old enough to fight against the fascists."

"His father and I are already helping in the struggle. His job is to study and become someone useful to our cause."

"What cause? You socialists have always been sellouts," the anarchist spat out.

"Stupidity can't grasp nuance," my mother said, grabbing my hand and pulling me back to the tent. We were barely inside when we heard a loud explosion, quite nearby. Mom's face grew tense. She grabbed her purse and made to leave the tent, but another explosion, even closer, put her on alert. She looked around wildly but saw nowhere to take cover. "We have to get away from here."

We went outside and saw airplanes flying low, as if the sky belonged to them. Bombs fell on the camp, and the cannons I had just been admiring moments ago flew through the air. We ran toward the lake. Ana screamed and cried as Mom dragged her along, and I had Isabel, who cried like a much younger child, by the hand. When we managed to get beyond the park, we saw a column of smoke rising, darkening the sky even more. The airplanes flew back over the city and disappeared on the horizon.

We walked up the hill to the Segovia Bridge. My father would be waiting for us near Puerta de Alcalá. We were worn-out and very scared by the time we got there, and when he saw us, he could tell right away that something had happened. Mom threw her arms around him and began to cry. We went to a café to regroup, and my parents drank coffee while my sisters and I had orange juice despite the chill in the air.

"Francisco, it's getting too dangerous," Mom whispered. "We have to get the children out of Madrid."

"But the war can't go on much longer. The fascists have hardly advanced, and we're holding the fronts. Largo Caballero says the tanks from Russia are coming any day now. Plus, we'll have new airplanes to stop the German attacks."

My mother shook her head. "I don't believe Largo Caballero. We've known him since we were kids, and we both know he lies through his teeth. We don't have a proper army. The militiamen are brave, but wars aren't won with volunteers."

My father glanced at the tables around us. What my mother had just said about the war could get us in trouble. A few weeks prior, groups of militiamen had started hunting down traitors in the capital and taking them "on a little walk." It was known they were being executed, a practice becoming more and more indiscriminate.

"Any negative comment could be construed as treason," my father warned.

"I know. Since that load of fascists was massacred at Modelo prison, the political commissioners aren't letting even one woman sneak by," Mom said.

"That was for the bombing of Argüelles and in retaliation for the fascists' killing spree in Badajoz."

"No, it was because the government doesn't have control. Prieto was horrified by the massacre at the jail, and so was Manuel Azaña, but the communists and Largo Caballero know how this increases their power. It's the heyday of the radicals. This war won't be over until they exterminate anyone who disagrees."

My father frowned. "What are you saying?"

"Well, that if our own people don't kill us, the opposing party will. There's no place for moderates, and—"

"I've been in the party since I was fourteen."

My mother rolled her eyes. My father's innocence drove her crazy, but in that moment one thing was clear to me: Mom would get us out of Madrid the very first chance she got. My sisters were still slurping their juice, and a light rain had begun to fall. The monotonous silence of the street was interrupted when what started as a murmur gradually grew into the clamor of a thousand voices.

"Look, the International Brigades have come!" my father said, beaming.

"There won't be enough shrouds to go around," my mother said, lighting a cigarette and looking out the window at the idealistic young men that had left their countries for the Republic. Her admiration for them was soaked in pity.

They seemed so young and determined, and I was jealous. Right then growing up seemed to mean getting my hands on a gun and killing the fascists. Only later did I understand that maturity means protecting your own and holding their hands until you discover safety.

# Chapter 6

# My Friends Aren't Going to Heaven

Madrid
November 18, 1936

Humans are beings that suffer. This may not seem like a very optimistic definition, but as soon as we come into this world until our inevitable departures, pain is a significant part of life. War is a grand cause of this terrible suffering. Besides death, hunger, fear, and the wounds opened in the hearts of those who endure it, war brings out the worst of humanity and dehumanizes us to the point of monstrousness.

Five months into the war, we had grown used to the routine of emergency alarms telling us to seek bomb shelters and the concerning food rations. No one failed to notice that the government had moved its headquarters to Valencia, which led to widespread fear that Madrid could not hold out much longer against the fascists. The traitors of the Republic pressed in from south and west of the capital. They had taken Navalcarnero, Illescas, and Alcorcón, and in the north were approaching from Casa de Campo and University City. The war was no longer miles away from the capital but on the outskirts. We could get there on a trolley and be back by lunchtime.

A few days before, the fascists had bombed the Prado Museum and the National Library. My father, who had changed regiments, could no longer abide the indiscriminate executions that included everyone the militiamen considered suspect. He had managed an assignment defending the Prado, and I often joined him so we could spend some time together. The war meant he rarely had time with us at home, and we all missed him terribly. That afternoon the fallout from the museum bombings was still evident and painful. Part of the building's roof was on fire, though somehow none of the paintings had been critically damaged.

We were sitting in one of the museum's halls sharing a bite to eat. Despite the war, the museum continued receiving visitors, though many of them came to see the art with their rifles at the ready.

As we sat in front of a painting called *The Garden of Earthly Delights*, one of my dad's favorites, we ate our sandwiches slowly. The bread was very bad, all black and splotched with heaven knows what, but at least we had something to chew. Everyone was nervous about the winter to come. There was no coal to be had, and it was harder and harder to find the basics for life.

"Marquitos, don't forget: When museums become targets of war, take it as a sign that civilization is ready to disappear. Same thing goes for ransacked churches. This is why I detest ignorance. It's much more dangerous than fascism."

"Maybe they bombed it by accident?" I suggested innocently.

"And was the National Library an accident also? Do you know what the rebel factions fear most about the Republic?"

I shook my head.

He continued, "What they fear most is culture, that people know things. Of course they know that people can read and write and do math. What I mean is, they're afraid of people thinking for themselves. Though, to be frank, I've heard something similar is happening in Russia."

His words took me by surprise. Until recent years he had been an ardent admirer of Lenin and always talked about how Spain needed a revolution like Russia's of 1917. In a way, their revolution was the model that the left in Europe was following.

"The proletariat revolution is liberation," I answered. It's what I'd learned at school. Anywhere I looked I saw Soviet symbols, and people said that for the twentieth anniversary of the revolution a monument to Stalin would be erected in Puerta de Alcalá.

My father didn't answer. He just took another bite and then a swallow of wine.

"What do you think of that painting?" he said, pointing to the wooden panels of the triptych.

"I don't know. It's weird," I said. I knew he loved teaching me things and loved how I would eat up his lessons.

"It is a strange piece. One time the poet Rafael Alberti explained it to me." I knew my father had been friends with the poet, though it had been some time since they'd seen each other. "He told me that Bosch, the Dutchman who painted the work, unlike most artists, tried to express what was inside a man's heart, not what could be perceived with the human eye. This is how we really are: vengeful, prideful, insatiable."

"So then what good is utopia?" I asked, somewhat fearful of his answer. I had heard him talk hundreds of times about the need to believe in and fight for utopia.

Dad was thoughtful, as if he had wondered the same and still had not settled the matter. "You ask hard questions. Your mother has always said your mind is an anomaly. But anyway, utopia is the perfect society: a just society, in peace, that strives for the common good—"

"But it doesn't exist."

"No, utopia is always our goal, our objective. And the closer we get to it, the further away it inevitably moves. That's why we always have the sensation of dissatisfaction. We move a few steps forward, and utopia retreats as if hoping to escape our small, selfish desires. The moment we make utopia fit our plans and schemes, it disappears. It never serves individualistic interests because there's always something to improve, something else to fight for." His gaze now bore into mine as he spoke. His own eyes, worn-out and tired from so much pain and suffering, held melancholy.

"But if we can never reach it, what good does it do?"

"True, we'll never reach it, but that's exactly what it's good for— to push us forward so we don't lose hope."

That I could not understand my father's words was my only surety. After a few more minutes, we stood up and went to look at *The Surrender of Breda*.

"Look at the battle, all those spears, the governor handing the keys to the city over to the enemy army," my father said. "Velázquez is trying to show us that war has a meaning, a point . . . that everything boils down to victory and defeat, but at the core that's a big lie. So many times what we do doesn't end up bringing us happiness. But the paradox is that if we sit here twiddling our thumbs, we'll never reach the perfect world, that utopia, we long for. Each generation believes it's destined to change the world. It's fallen to our generation to keep fascism from subjugating us, but without even realizing it, we've turned into destroyers."

I stared at him, hypnotized. He was giving me a lesson I would never forget, but I could barely understand it at the time. His words were seeds that would take years to bear fruit.

"I've learned a lot over the past few months," he went on. "I'd been taught that individualism was a bourgeois principle, that a man is only truly human when he's among the masses. I thought war was the end of loneliness, that by joining my comrades against a common enemy and with a single purpose all the loneliness would dissipate like fog. Instead, war has made me feel new depths of loneliness. The one thing I know for sure is that if I have to choose a side, I can't be allied with those who write history from their offices or studying a map. My place is with those who suffer, who endure history. But sometimes your enemies are enduring and suffering as well. Everyone's shouting for liberty now, but if there's no justice, liberty has failed."

"Who are our enemies? The fascists, then?" I asked, dizzy with confusion.

"When I was younger, I was told we would have to kill in order to create a world in which nobody would kill anybody else. It's not true." Tears formed in my father's eyes as he spoke. "For every free man who dies in this war, five slaves will be born. The world will lose hope, lose its utopia."

We trudged out of the building with low spirits. It was dusk, but the streetlamps were dark to make it harder for the fascist bomber planes to see their targets.

Then we heard the roar of the bombers. The alarm rang out, and we ran to the metro, though my father was apathetic about the whole thing, as if death were the only gift a desperate man could hope for. As we descended the stairs, surrounded by the crowd, the bombs began to whistle overhead. Then the explosions shook the ground, making us feel insignificant and small.

We stayed underground in the dark for almost an hour, listening to the cries and groans of the crowd that jostled and pressed in from all sides. The dust falling from the ceiling choked us as we struggled to breathe, but no one talked, until one girl began to sing:

> *Through Casa de Campo,*
> *little mama,*
> *and over the Manzanares River,*
> *the Manzanares River,*
> *the Moors want to pass,*
> *little mama,*
> *but they shall not pass,*
> *but they shall not pass,*
> *Madrid, how well you resist,*
> *little mama,*
> *the bombings,*
> *the bombings!*
> *The citizens of Madrid,*
> *the citizens of Madrid,*
> *little mama,*
> *laugh in the face of the bombs.*

The song had a calming effect on the crowd. When we returned up to street level, the courage the song had given us was enough to face the fires resulting from the bombing and the stench of death. My father and I had walked less than a mile when we passed my school. There were no classes at that hour, but a group of boys played ball and girls always skipped rope in the front yard. Smoke rose from inside the main building, and a few trees were burning like torches illuminating the dark city. We heard the strangled cries of women before we saw anything more. And as we drew close to the fence, what I saw reminded me of Bosch's inferno: amputated limbs, destroyed bodies, mothers clinging to what remained of their children. My father ordered me to look away, but the images were seared into my soul forever.

"Dad!" I cried out, clutching his arm. It was all I could say. If I hadn't joined him that afternoon on his watch in the museum, I would've been there, playing with my friends in the schoolyard.

He had no words either. We walked, downcast, back to our apartment—relieved and grateful to have survived, but also full of guilt. Nothing is more absurd than death or more terrible than war. From that day on, I understood that the most important thing we do every day is to fight to live, even though life may be unbearable.

# Chapter 7

# My Grandparents and the Trip to San Martín de la Vega

Madrid
November 25, 1936

Hate is the fuel of war, and the two sides must continue to feed it. The local newspapers focused on the atrocities of the enemy but hid our own. Attacks, rapes, robbery, and death were the daily fare of the papers and radio broadcasts. I didn't have to work hard to learn to hate. That autumn we had no time for tears, only enough time to despise the enemy and wait for revenge. The city was under siege on the west and part of the south, but the northern limits were also pressed. The citizens of Madrid were under no illusions. From Valencia, the government kept sending instructions, but the government officials were not there with us in the city holding out against the siege.

My mother had decided we children should go to her parents' house in San Martín de la Vega, a town along the Jarama River. It wasn't much safer than Madrid, but she hoped that at least there would be fewer bombings and a bit more to eat. Her parents always kept a well-stocked pantry, as well as a half-dozen hens, some rabbits, and a cow—all of which provided most of what they needed. This trip was the cause of a heated argument between my parents. I had never seen them so angry with each other. The emotions of war were affecting their nerves.

Escaping the city was not easy, especially in the direction of Valencia. There were no trains and hardly any buses. The only vehicles that continued to circulate were delivery trucks and those transporting troops, but my mother, who knew plenty of people in government headquarters, managed to convince an old friend of my father's to take us in his truck. The four of us sat in the back while the driver sat up front with an armed escort in case we were assaulted on the road. Pillaging and rape were constants in those days when nothing was safe.

"What is it, Marco? You've been so sad lately. Are you still thinking about what happened to your schoolmates?"

I shook my head, though Mom knew very well that their murder had infuriated me. A few days afterward, I had tried to enlist in the army, but my parents wouldn't allow it.

"You want to go to the front to kill the fascists? You think that'll make you feel better? That's like swallowing poison and hoping it'll kill your enemy," she prodded.

I looked at her out of the corner of my eye. I couldn't understand her attitude. The fascists deserved a horrible demise, just like what they'd given my friends.

"You think I don't hate? Yes, son, sometimes hatred slips into our souls and corrodes them from within. But you know what I do? When I find hatred inside me, I try to defeat it with the invincible love you three give me. Women are capable of producing life. Men seem only good at destroying it."

"I don't want to love those people," I spat out, furious.

"I'm not asking you to love them. I'm just begging you to not let the hate overcome the love you hold in your heart. In the midst of all the tears and suffering, I've discovered an indestructible joy inside myself. War has led to the greatest disorder of all, robbing us of the life we had. But inside I possess a peace that no one can take away from me. This cold winter will pass, spring will come, and that makes me happy. I want you to learn something."

"What, Mom?" I was paying more attention now. Her words were clearly coming from a heart of pure love.

"It doesn't matter how hard life pushes. The love I have for you—the love you must store up so hate won't control you—will be stronger than anything that ever comes against you. When I go back to Madrid, you'll have to take care of your sisters. You'll be alone, but my heart will stay with you. What are you going to teach them? The strength of hate or the power of love?"

"I'll try my best," I said, unconvinced. But she knew I really would try. No one in the world knew me like my mother.

"Marco, darling, when your heart gets used to suffering, you forge a very deep connection with tragedy. Don't feel sorry for yourself. You're a very fortunate child."

The trip was too short. Once we arrived in town, the truck took us to my grandparents' house on the outskirts. The small farm seemed older and more run-down than on our last visit. I remembered

swimming in the river, and the smell of oranges sprinkled with sugar—
the way my grandmother would fix them for me.

Benito and Sara, my grandparents, stood in the door to receive
us as soon as they heard us pull up. My mother looked so much like
my grandmother, though her face was both more lucid and sadder.
Grandma and Grandpa smothered us in hugs and kisses. We went
in and sat down in the warm living room. The heating element my
grandparents used, called a *gloria*, had always captured my imagination: they kept a fire going in a cavity beneath the floor, and the
heat was pumped throughout the house through pipes. For a moment
I forgot about the war and ran around rediscovering the farm with
my sisters, life once more a game.

The time spent in San Martín de la Vega was no country holiday.
On the contrary, it felt like exile to me—the first taste of orphanhood, which would follow me the rest of my life. I had to care for
my younger sisters and help them stay calm and show them they
could trust me. None of us had ever been away from our parents. We
had always been a very tight-knit family and spent most of our time
together. The war hadn't managed to ruin our ability to enjoy life
and each other, and we were lucky enough that all five of us were still
alive. I could understand why Mom wanted us to be farther from the
bombings and the dangers that stalked us in the city, but I doubted
we would be much safer in the country.

As soon as Mom left, winter fell hard like a bad omen. We weren't
used to being so cold, and despite the good coats and shoes Mom had
found for us, we came home from school chilled to the bone every
day. Plus, we struggled to fit in with the other kids in the village. The
school was small, and boys and girls were separated. My teacher was

named Germinal, and my sisters had a young woman named Teresa. Both teachers worked hard to educate us, but the local boys missed a lot of school. The farms needed them to work since most young men were fighting on the front.

The morning of November 25, we arrived early at school before the sun even came out. The classrooms were freezing. The teachers had no wood to start a fire in the stove, and we kept our coats and gloves on all day. Yet when Germinal began to speak, I forgot about the cold and listened with rapt attention.

"The great philosopher José Ortega y Gasset, the brightest mind to come out of our country, taught us we cannot live as islands. He said, 'I am myself plus my circumstance, and if I do not save it, I cannot save myself.' We are part of the world, dear students. Everything that happens around us affects us. We live in times of opposing factions, of brothers fighting brothers. Some say that the important thing is morality, something perverted by revolutionary ideals. Others talk about proletariat love and the brotherhood of all people, but the truth is that with morality we restrain the errors of our primal instincts. However, love is capable of tempering the errors of morality. The left and the right are diametrically opposite realities—but, as the philosopher said, they are two ways for humans to be imbeciles. Surely some will declare that their ideologies are what make the world go 'round, when actually ideologies are what destroy it."

I raised my hand timidly, and the teacher motioned for me to speak. His gray beard and white hair gave him the friendly look of one of the three wise men.

"I disagree. The fascists started this war, and you're making them equal to those who are saving the Republic," I said, both confused and angry. I admired Germinal a great deal but thought he was wrong and that maybe somewhere in his mind he remained unaware of the magnitude of what was happening.

"I think you've misunderstood me," he said patiently. "The biggest crime, as always, does not lie with the executioners, in those who kill for fanaticism or disdain for life, but in those who allow them to kill. Right here in our little town several good people have been shot. When I say 'good,' I don't mean they're saints. I mean that they were as good as those who killed them."

"But it's them or us," I answered. I knew that innocence was always relative and that those who seemed incapable of doing us harm were often the most dangerous.

Germinal walked up to my desk. His hands were large and thick, and the frayed edges of his shirt peeked out from the sleeves of his corduroy jacket. His tie was off-kilter, and his round glasses looked as though they might fall apart at any moment.

"You think I'm just a poor teacher from a small-minded little town, right? People from the big city believe they alone have figured out how the world really works, but that's not always the case. It's true that I was born in this town and that I'm a child of its dry, fertile lands. Just like the fields, I need the freezing snow of winter and the spring rains to draw out the life in me that is about to crumble and die. But I was once young and ambitious. I studied education at Central University and worked at the ministry of education. I fell in love with a young woman from a good family, and we were going to get married, but I was drafted by the army and went to fight in Africa. That's where my idealism disappeared.

"Humans are the worst predators on earth. Those poor, uneducated people defended themselves with teeth and fingernails, but we used civilization to massacre them. One day we went into a village we'd gassed a few hours before. The women, children, and elders— all that was left of the population—ran out of their huts screaming in pain. The gas was burning their eyes away, and their lips were oozing pus and blood. Limp children whimpered as their mothers wiped their eyes with contaminated water. Old people dragged themselves through the mud. And we, the civilized men, finished them off with bayonets so as not to waste bullets. I had thought that the most important thing in war was to stay alive, but the only thing that truly matters is maintaining your humanity. When I got back to Spain, I walked away from everything and came back to this town. I hoped that if I could at least teach a few children and share what I had learned, then my life would have some meaning. I learned a long time ago that to see what's right in front of us requires enormous effort, because there's no man so blind as the one who doesn't want to see."

Germinal's words floated through the freezing air of the classroom and fell upon all of us, the absent, indifferent faces of the rest of the class. The other boys seemed immune to his words. I didn't know if it was because they'd heard it all before or because their difficult lives did not afford them enough margin for thought. But I was not unaffected by his story.

The mood changed when it was time for recess, and we scrambled outside with commotion. It was the only time of day when the other students seemed happy. My sisters were sitting off to one side of the schoolyard while the other girls laughed and played. Meanwhile the boys had invented a game with a partially deflated ball.

"Can I play?" I asked, my hands stuffed deep in my pockets. I hoped to look like I didn't much care what the answer was.

"No, sir, little gent," said the head boy, Óscar. I always tried to avoid him, though a few times I'd been tempted to wring his neck.

I threw out a defiant question. "Is the ball yours?"

"We don't like foreigners here! City people are nothing but trouble," the bully shouted before shoving me.

I lost my balance and fell into the mud. The boy jumped me, and I tried to get up, but he clobbered my face until he gave a sudden cry and covered his head with his hands.

My sister Ana, the younger one, was yanking his hair from behind. Isabel seized Óscar's momentary distraction to help me get up, at which point I socked him hard in the face until blood dripped from his nose. Just then the teacher showed up and pulled us apart. "Have you learned nothing? Isn't it enough that half the country is killing the other half?"

"He started it," Óscar lied, and all his friends agreed.

"You'll have detention after school," Germinal told me.

My sisters led me to the side of the yard and tried to calm me down. "Don't worry about it. Mom will come get us soon, and then we can go home," Isabel said.

"Don't count on it," I said, wiping off my wounds.

The next two hours of class seemed eternal. When the other boys finally left the classroom, Germinal motioned for me to follow him. Then he put on his coat and started walking up a path toward a house that looked abandoned. He unlocked a great padlock and lit an oil lamp. To my surprise, the light revealed a huge library. Germinal hung up his coat and began to organize books that were on top of the table.

"Do you want to know what all this is?" he asked. When I nodded, he smiled. "They're books from the town hall and from the school. We've brought them here to protect them. The mailman, who's been in occupied territory several times, has helped me hide them. When the fascists get to a town, they ransack the libraries and burn all the books they consider dangerous. It doesn't matter if they're poetry, fiction, or essays—they don't care. These people want a return to the Dark Ages and the Holy Inquisition."

"But weren't you saying in class that the left and the right are all the same?" I asked, thinking he was contradicting himself.

"Yes, but I was referring to fascism and Stalinist communism. Totalitarianism always acts the same way; it enslaves the people and leaves them in ignorance."

"This is a lot of books," I said, looking around.

"This includes the books from Morata de Tajuña and Chinchón. We need to save all the books we can. If the fascists win, we must protect the books through the regime change."

His passion to rescue the books lit a spark in me, though I doubted that once fascism was established it would be easy to drive it out of power. My father had told me how the traitor Mussolini, who used to be a communist, had been ruling Italy since 1922.

"Don't tell anyone about this place," Germinal warned as he led me to one of the shelves and took out a book. It was *The Quest*, by Pío Baroja. He held it out. "Take it if you'd like."

I held the book in my hands and flipped through the pages.

"My dear student," Germinal continued, "don't ever stop reading. The fascists seek to base their power on fear, cruelty, and hate, but that can never last long. Humans always seek out love, truth, and compassion. Don't ever forget that."

I walked out of the secret book repository heavy with the weight of a secret. This old, abandoned shack was the refuge of reason, so hotly pursued and despised. I walked along the banks of the Jarama River until noticing the buildings of the town brought me back to the brutal reality of war, which my mother worked so hard to keep us away from.

Chapter 8

# Words Rain Down

San Martín de la Vega
February 11, 1937

Christmas came and went, and my mother did not come get us. Grandma and Grandpa tried hard to make us happy and even gave us a present on Three Kings Day, knowing full well that my parents didn't celebrate religious holidays. Ana and Isabel cried their way through Christmas break, but the hardest part was yet to come. The war had been lying in wait for months, and it finally pounced in the early days of February 1937, in the middle of winter.

That morning seemed like any ordinary day. We went to school like normal, and by then I was really enjoying classes with Germinal. Since the day he showed me the hidden books, we spent many afternoons together in the repository. My sisters didn't know what I was doing, though I had let them read a few stories. They assumed the teacher was taking me to a library of some sort.

We were all trying not to think about the border of occupied territory, which was now just on the other side of the river. Gunfire rang out and the missiles roared, but after each explosion Germinal resumed his lectures as if nothing were amiss.

"Many believe that fear is bad, but they're wrong, my students. Fear is very useful; cowardice is not. If we didn't have a certain degree of fear, we'd be capable of the most imprudent actions. In contrast, cowardice is the attitude we take toward fear. Do you hear the bombs? You do, right? It's normal for you to be scared. I am too. But I hope this doesn't fill you with cowardice. The fascists are very close to us. As soon as they cross the river, nothing will be able to stop them. They need only occupy the bridge and secure their position, as most of the soldiers defending us have died or fled."

Just then the explosions sounded much louder, along with the sound of a big machine being dragged. My classmates couldn't hold out any longer and ran to the windows. I joined them with reluctance.

"Look at that," Óscar said, pointing to what looked like an armored German car. The Republican soldiers were trying to stop it, but it was relentless in its advance. The fascists crouched behind it and shot continuously at the defenders.

"Get away from the windows!" Germinal warned. But we paid no attention, hypnotized by the crossfire. Eventually we watched our men fall back and retreat up the road that led to Morata.

"Please don't leave the school building," the teacher said.

By noon we were ravenous, but the teachers were too scared to send us home. Then some soldiers approached. They stood in front of the school and yelled for everyone to file out. A colonel stood at the door and ordered us to make a line of boys and a line of girls, so our teachers led us out to each side.

"I am Colonel Asensio," said the man in charge. "You have nothing to fear. We have driven the reds out of the town. Peace will soon come, and the communists will harm you no more. Viva Spain!" he shouted at the top of his lungs, and we all echoed in chorus. He turned to the teachers.

"You are Professor Germinal Fonseca?"

"Yes, colonel."

"And you are Miss Teresa Agudo?"

"Yes." Her voice trembled. She was hugging the youngest girls to her, including my sister Ana.

I'd never seen fascists up close this way, except on the day of the Montaña Barracks siege the year before. On the one hand, they looked like normal soldiers. Yet their cold, mocking air did not foreshadow anything good.

"We were told by members of the town that you two belong to the teachers' union and that you defend the reds. Is this true?"

Germinal, showing no fear, answered, "All teachers belong to the teachers' union." Here, his lesson on the difference between fear and cowardice continued.

The colonel turned toward the students and looked us each up and down. "You, his pupils, you'll know better than anyone whether this old fop is lying. Has your teacher spoken out against the Nationalists and our caudillo, Francisco Franco?"

At first there was a deafening silence. Then Óscar stepped forward, wagged his finger at Germinal, and said, "He's a red. They both are."

Germinal looked at him with more pity than hurt. After so many years, his students betrayed him the first opportunity.

"And what do the rest of you say?" the colonel asked.

All the bigger boys started talking bad about the teachers, but the littler ones began to cry, confused by all that was happening.

I didn't know how to respond. I was afraid the soldiers would do something bad to me or my sisters, so I mumbled along with the chorus of accusations. Germinal looked at me with tenderness, his look saying he was proud of me despite my betrayal. Eventually he managed to make his voice heard over the shouting.

"Love is the strongest force that exists. You may have the power of weapons, but I serve a stronger god: the truth," he said.

The colonel frowned, took out his gun, and hit Germinal on the head. Blood gushed out, and Germinal lifted his hand to his forehead. "I forgive you. Weak men cannot forgive, but—" The colonel didn't let him finish. He hit him and threw him on the ground. Germinal's glasses were broken, and blood flowed from his split lips.

"Grab some rocks!" the colonel ordered us.

The boys picked up a few rocks without complaining, but the rest of us were terrified. I held a couple loose in my hand and stood behind the rest of the boys.

"Make a circle around him! Now you'll see the power of death," the colonel said, stepping aside. "Aim well! Today you'll kill your first red."

Óscar went first. His rock hit Germinal in one eye. Then rocks rained down on him from all sides. Germinal groaned a few times, then curled up in a fetal position.

"Throw!" the colonel growled from behind me.

With tears in my eyes, I threw a rock and missed; then a second, which hit his arm. Germinal was covered in blood. Finally the colonel went up and shot him in the head, and we all screamed in fright.

"Today you've learned the most important lesson of your lives. The strongest always have the right to do what they want. Viva Spain!" he shouted, beaming.

We all answered in kind, though all we wanted was to run away.

The soldiers led Teresa away brusquely but left Germinal's bloodied body in the schoolyard. I took my sisters' hands and led them as fast as possible back to our grandparents' house. We shook the entire walk home, and I thought about how being an adult meant feeling tremendously alone.

"What's going on?" my grandmother asked when she saw us.

My sisters began to wail, and it took Grandma a long time to calm them down. Grandpa came up to me and put his hand on my shoulder. My grandfather was a man of few words, but that day he broke his habitual silence.

"There are some things a child shouldn't see. But this war is doing away with innocence."

❧

My grandmother managed to get in touch with my mother. They had to get us to Rivas, and then she'd take charge of us.

School was henceforth cancelled, and no one dared leave home. That was the last afternoon we would spend in that town. Then I remembered the secret library. What would become of it? When my grandparents were busy with something, I took a little backpack and headed for the abandoned house. I hadn't gone far when I sensed someone was following me. I hid behind a tree and jumped out at my pursuer. I was surprised to find it was Ana.

"Why are you following me?" I asked. "Don't you see how dangerous it is?"

"Grandma told us to stay home. I don't want to lose you too," she said, her eyes full of tears.

"I'm never going to leave you and Isabel," I said, taking her hand.

We walked along the river through the thicket and reached the old house. The padlock was locked, but I slipped in through a window. I lit the lamp and looked at all the books. Who could say what would become of those cheap, poorly bound volumes? Yet here they were, nearly all the books from the surrounding towns.

We both flipped through some volumes, and before we knew it, night had begun to fall. The next day we would set out to try to rejoin our mother. I was starting to put a few books in the backpack when we heard voices outside. I snuffed out the light, and we slipped back out the window.

"This is where the books are. I've seen Marco and the professor come here a lot. I'm sure they're communist books," said a voice I recognized all too easily: Óscar, the bully from school.

"Break down the door!" the colonel barked. The soldiers kicked the door in, then shined their flashlights inside. The colonel passed his white gloves down a few spines and began throwing them to the floor. "Communist garbage. Burn the whole lot!" he ordered, piling the books up in the center of the room.

Through a small window we watched as the soldiers doused the books with gasoline and then threw a match on the pile. The paper caught fire easily, and the room lit up with a *whoosh*. The colonel's gaze was far away, as if entranced by the spectacle.

"Marco and his sisters are the children of a union man in Madrid. Their mother brought them here to keep them safe from the bombing," Óscar said.

My blood froze at this. I grabbed Ana's hand, and we ran across the fields in the dark. We fell often but were soon home. My grandparents had been terrified during our absence and were relieved yet more frightened still to see us bruised and covered in mud. We told them what had happened, and Grandpa prepared his wagon. He loaded our cardboard suitcases, and we went out to the road trembling with cold and fear. Grandma waved to us from the door. She couldn't leave the animals to their fate, knowing the fascist soldiers would rob everything they could eat.

Watchfully, Grandpa steered the wagon through the streets before heading down the road toward Rivas. The journey would take all night, but we needed to reach the other side of the front before the colonel's men found us.

My sisters fell asleep in the back part of the wagon, curled up among the blankets. The night sky and the gray clouds foreboded impending snow. Amid the quiet, my grandfather cleared his throat and spoke.

"I never could understand your mother. I was so angry when she went to Madrid. This town was too small for her, and she dreamed of being an actress. For people like me, the city is dangerous, even more so for one's only daughter, but you can't hold back such water—it'll just flow right over the dam. Your mother always did whatever she pleased. She was like a wild mare, though I have to admit she has raised some very brave children. I don't know how this war will end, but the poor people—we've already lost. What the soldiers don't steal, their masters will, and whatever we manage to hide away will soon be smoke and ashes." He didn't look at me as he spoke, gazing instead at the beautiful sky and the road lit dimly by the moon peeking through the clouds.

"Thank you for taking us to Rivas," I answered. My grandfather and I hadn't spoken much in the few months my sisters and I had been living in his house. It seemed like everything had already been said and there was nothing more to add.

"I'm not afraid of dying. Maybe I'm short on brains, which your father has in abundance, but I just don't want anything to happen to you three. By God, that's the last thing I want. You kids are the new shoots that the olive tree sends out before dying. If you graft those shoots onto a young tree, they'll be the most productive. The branches are young, but the sap is old. Do you understand?"

"I think so," I said, though I did not fully grasp what he meant.

"What I mean is that you're carrying my blood in your veins, the blood of all your ancestors, rough peasants from Castilla la Nueva.

It doesn't matter where you live or what you do because that blood will be passed on to your children. We can't break the chain. If even one link is missing, the whole thing's no good."

I nodded even though he couldn't see me.

"So take care of your sisters. I don't know what'll happen to us adults, but I don't think they'll dare touch you children, though in a civil war one can never know. Hatred grows like a weed, and it's not easy to destroy."

We were halfway through our journey when we saw a light moving ahead on the road.

"It's a surveillance point. Let me do the talking," Grandpa said with the composure of age.

Three legionnaires stopped us, and my grandfather pulled on the mule's reins.

"Where are you going in the middle of the night?" the corporal asked. "Can't you tell it's about to snow? The reds are just a couple miles up the road."

"Blasted reds!" my grandfather growled.

"Yes, they're like ticks," the corporal said.

"I'm taking the kids to their mother. They came to visit last Sunday, but it's time for them to be getting back to school." His voice was calm, as if he did this every week.

"School? We're on the front lines here. You'd better head back home."

"If I go back to the farm, my wife will have my head."

"So you prefer death by reds than at your wife's hand?" the corporal joked.

"I've got a few chorizos in the back I was going to take to my daughter, but I could leave you one or two. I'm sure the night shift gets long."

"That's an understatement. We haven't eaten all day! This war will be won by the ones who don't die of hunger first." The corporal walked around and took two chorizos out of the back of the wagon, holding them high like a trophy. He turned back to my grandfather and said, "You've got two little angels back there. Be careful. You'll hear a lot of gunshots along this road."

"Thank you. I'll be very careful," Grandpa said, flicking the reins gently.

"If you come across any other guards, tell them Corporal Marchena has let you pass. They won't bother you after that."

As we moved through the control point, my grandfather nodded his thanks and the corporal called out, "Godspeed!"

We reached Rivas by early morning. There were soldiers from the International Brigades along the outskirts, some from Italy but most from the United States. After a quick search of the wagon, they let us pass. We stopped at one of the town's wineries, and Grandpa served us some slices of sausage as we waited for our mother.

Just as the sun appeared on the horizon, we heard the sound of a car motor. Looking up, we saw a green Renault convertible. A soldier and an officer we didn't recognize at first were in the front, and a woman sat in the back.

My sisters ran up to the car. Our mother got out and hugged the girls as if she never wanted to let go. I walked slowly, feeling a heavy weight lift off me. Perhaps I could be a kid again, dwelling in my own imaginary world.

The officer stood in front of me, and when he took off his hat, I recognized my father. He smiled and swooped me up in a hug, and I let myself cry. It was all I could do after the terrible months and all the fear we'd felt. Finally, I could go home.

The girls let Mom go so she could come to me. She kissed me over and over until I started to laugh, the first time I'd laughed in a very long time.

"Look at my big boy," she said, her huge eyes and beautiful smile lighting up. I understood then that a boy never stops being a young child to his mother.

"Mom!" I said, the joy of the entire world held in that one syllable. I'd heard people say that when grown men are dying, the only one they call for is their mother, as if returning to the womb they left in the beginning.

"I'll never let you go away again!" she promised that winter morning.

But before summer, we would flee the war once more. No one ever manages to fully escape war. War stays forever in the hearts of those who have looked it straight in the eye and walked away unscathed.

We piled into the car full of joy. My sisters rattled nonstop about everything that had happened since we'd last seen our parents, and Dad stroked my hair and sang a song that spread out across the plains of Castilla la Nueva like snow covering fields destined for blood.

Chapter 9

# The Road to France

Madrid
May 19, 1937

Within months war had taken deep root, and we all had given up hope that it would end soon. The bombings decreased somewhat, in part thanks to the Soviet planes, and after the failure of the Battle of Jarama, the fascists turned away from Madrid to concentrate on the northern front. Food supplies kept arriving from Valencia, the only route still open, but they grew scarcer and lower in quality with each passing day. Some British Quakers in the city ran soup kitchens, which offered us a reduced diet of beans, black bread, and watery soup. I was hungry all the time, from the moment I woke up until I went to sleep at night. I even dreamed about food. My sisters mopped up the very last drop of their soup and scarfed down potato peels.

We hardly dared to imagine anymore the world that was promised to us every day on the huge signs around the city or on the radio. We kept going to school, though the children attended infrequently because of air raids or our parents' fear that rumors about Madrid's imminent invasion were true. The dream that one day the children of workers could be treated with dignity and become whatever we wanted in life was turning into a nightmare. Party infighting and the little power that the communist party had begun to gain left no room for doubt that, even if we managed to win the war, we had already lost peace.

Despite the grim signs of the time and the extreme needs, we were happy to be back with our parents. We felt like we could endure anything as long as we were together. Because of my parents, their hope for the future, and their faith in us, I did dare to dream a little. Smiling, I always told them, "I have a dream, which is to keep dreaming. I want to dream of justice, liberty, and peace."

And they always answered the same way: "Being a dreamer is better than being a cynic."

One morning in May, my mother surprised us with some news that would do away with all my dreams in one fell swoop. "While you were asleep," she said, "I packed your suitcases. It's been very hard to make this decision, but we think it's best for everyone."

My sisters and I looked at her in surprise. She held our clothes in her arms, along with some extra warm items. That year spring was late in coming, and it was still quite cold.

"But, Mom, where are we going?" Isabel asked. She had just woken up and already started to cry.

"The war is going very poorly, and we don't know how long it will last. So it's better for you three to leave. A lot of families are sending their children to France or Russia, but with the way things are going in Europe, we think it's better for you to go to Mexico."

She worked to make her voice sound calm and chipper, but her eyes said something else.

"Mexico? Where's that?" Ana asked.

"In the Americas, dummy," Isabel answered.

"But then that means it's really far," Ana said, wiping her eyes.

My mother hugged them both and held her arms out for me to join.

"It won't be for long. If things get much worse here, your father and I will try to join you. And if we win the war, we'll bring you back home."

"Mom, what will we do in Mexico?" I asked.

"The president, Lázaro Cárdenas, and his wife, Amalia, are preparing a place for you. There's a committee in charge of helping refugee children from the Republic. We have to get you to Valencia before the others leave."

"The others? Other kids are going too?" I asked in dismay. For a moment I had thought my sisters and I were going to live at the president's house.

"Yes. I don't know how many, but more than two hundred. I don't know, maybe even five hundred."

My sisters looked at each other, frightened, surely wondering where so many children could possibly go.

"Come on now; let's get you dressed. Your father is waiting for us in a car, and our friend will drive us to Valencia. It's a dangerous journey, but we will get through it." She wiped tears from her eyes.

"Are you coming with us?" Ana asked.

"Your father can't, but I'll go with you to Valencia. The rest of the journey you'll have comrades and supervisors looking after you. I'm sure you'll enjoy it. You'll get to ride on a big boat—like an adventure."

Ana let herself get a little excited. "We've never seen the ocean," she said.

Isabel held out. "A boat? What happens if we get seasick or if we sink?"

"Come, come! We don't have time for all this. I'm sure everything will be fine. As soon as you get there, you must write to me. We'll stay in touch, and you'll be taken care of there. They speak Spanish there, and they're revolutionaries like we are."

Her words didn't cheer us up much, but we had no option but to obey.

Mom prepared breakfast, and as my sisters ate, she pulled me aside. "I need you to take care of them. You took such good care of them when you were at your grandparents', but it's going to be harder this time. You have a long trip ahead of you, and Mexico is a foreign country."

"I'll look out for them," I answered, not taking my eyes off my sisters sitting around the table. "Please don't worry."

At age twelve, Isabel had the hints of being a woman, but she was shy and easily frightened. Ana, on the other hand, was restless and mischievous, but too little to understand what was happening around us.

We took our time carrying the suitcases to the car, trying to prolong the inevitable. As we moved down the stairs, I studied the peeling walls, the splintered wood floor, and the dust that covered everything. To me our home was the most beautiful place in the world, and I still recall it with a stab of nostalgia. The place we were born and were once happy always remains magic and irreplaceable in our minds. I knew it was normal to feel this way. Even so, the more a boy becomes an adult, the more he understands that the world is difficult and complex, a dangerous place where survival isn't simple. But feeling let down by the world can't be everything. Hope must remain infinite. It doesn't help to throw oneself over the cliff of desperation. After all, existence always finds a way forward.

Outside my father was talking with another militiaman. Both were smoking and looking up at the windows as if they expected us to fall out of the sky at any moment.

Dad hurried us when we got to the car. "Let's go, kids! The roads get more dangerous at night."

First he kissed my sisters and spoke with each for a few minutes. He seemed calm; perhaps the war had toughened up his sensitive spots some. The only way to survive the suffering was to form a shield and not let anything through, though this also produced terrible discomfort and a kind of anesthesia and meaninglessness that seemed to invade all the adults.

"Son, take care of your sisters. Don't forget that if you don't have something worth dying for, your life's not worth living. Your only homeland is your family now; they're your most important responsibility. Will you give me your word of honor that you'll defend them with your life if you must?"

"Of course, Dad. No harm will come to them."

"I know you're afraid. It's a long journey, full of danger, but don't forget that we have to build a dam of courage to hold back the floods of fear. The world is an inhospitable place, and you'll be foreigners in Mexico. But it's safer than here in Madrid."

We hugged, and I could feel his tears on my cheeks. I had never seen him cry before, but that morning our impending separation shook him to the core.

As my sisters climbed into the back of the car, my father and mother kissed goodbye. Hugging her, Dad said, "I hope we're doing the right thing."

"The right thing is to keep them safe. Fascism might be defeated in Spain, but it'll take the upper hand in Europe. We've got to get them away from here," she answered. She could afford to be calmer, knowing she still had some time left with us.

"You must hurry. The boat is leaving in just a few hours for Barcelona, and then you'll take a train from the França Station. The organizers won't wait for anyone."

"We'll get there in time," she answered, settling between the girls.

I sat up front. I'd never sat in the passenger's seat before, and for a few seconds the excitement of something new overpowered the pain of what was happening.

As the car pulled away, I looked at my dad in the rearview mirror. I could see him waving the whole time until he was nothing more than a speck of dust behind us. Then the street where we'd grown up and which had been our whole universe disappeared as well. We made our way slowly along the streets with cobblestones uprooted by bombs, headed toward Atocha Station. The car turned right, and just over a half hour later we were in the outskirts of the city, traveling through olive, pine, and oak groves where there were no longer any livestock. We passed through three control points before fully leaving Madrid behind. The trip was unbearable to me. It wasn't the same as going to live with my grandparents or leaving town to spend a day in the country. I knew I'd never return to my beloved city because, even if fate allowed me to come back and even if the same old buildings and beautiful stone streets were still intact, I'd never be the same person again.

"You all right, young man?" the driver asked. Until then, I hadn't paid him any attention. He was much younger than my father but was old enough to have been around the block a few times.

"I think so."

"I'd love to skip off to Mexico and leave all this behind. War, hunger, and death aren't exactly what we were promised. They say they're building a better world, but I can promise you one thing: War isn't the best brush for painting a future of peace. Before the fascist coup, I worked in a bookbinding factory, which is how I know your dad. I didn't make much, but I could go dancing on the weekends, enjoy a good meal at a restaurant, and take a pretty girl out for a stroll along Alcalá Street. It wasn't much, but it sure was enough." He whistled to make his point.

I looked at him with curiosity. My father, too, appreciated a simple, unpretentious life, but he also understood that it was a trick of the oppressors who never wanted those below them to aspire for what the powerful worked so hard to preserve.

Slightly peeved, I answered, "Life was no bed of roses before. The capital had us all on our knees, and we had no hope for change. My dad always says that if we bend over, someone will always clobber us. If we bend over, we'll never be able to stand up again. And if they win, there'll be no future for anybody." I was annoyed because most people were starting to lose the war in their hearts.

The driver kept his eyes looking straight ahead, seemingly miffed by my impudence. "You don't know what you're talking about yet. Most people just want a quiet life and a future in peace. This war isn't going to bring either of those things."

In my heart I knew he was right, but if the Republic disappeared while we children were far away, we wouldn't have a home to return to. In a way, by trampling on my hope, that driver was throwing me down a terrible pit, into absolute nothingness from which I could never escape.

꘎

My mother was shocked when the organizers told her the children had left the day before on a boat headed to Barcelona and that the next day they'd be on a train headed for France. We were in a strange city with very little money, and now we faced the impossibility of getting to Barcelona before the rest of the children departed. For my sisters and me it was great news, but we tried not to act happy. We didn't want Mom to feel bad. She was convinced that the war was worsening and that the best thing was to evacuate us from Spain as soon as possible. My mother was a very persistent woman, so she managed to convince a fisherman to take us in his boat to Barcelona. The man warned us it would take at least a day to travel the 180-plus miles to Barcelona. Mom thought it would be safer than driving, even though the fascists would also bomb ships that tried to travel between the cities.

The captain of the fishing boat perked up when my mother offered him her wedding ring, some earrings, and a solid gold choker Grandpa had given her when he took us to Rivas a few months before.

"We'll travel through the night, and I bet I can get you there first thing in the morning," he said, flashing a dark, gap-toothed smile.

As soon as we got on board the ship, we realized it was a bad idea. It was the first time we'd ever seen the ocean, and after the initial awe and wonder, we were terrified to find ourselves surrounded by water and buffeted by the waves. Isabel clung to Mom the entire trip, while Ana stuck to me like glue. I studied her eyes as blue as the water and her bright blonde hair, wondering how I would ever be able to protect her on the other side of the world. At least Isabel was twelve and could take care of herself a bit.

"Why don't we go back home?" Ana whispered to me. Typically she was a brave, determined child, but the terror in her eyes was plain as day as the boat rose and fell like a carousel.

"We can't. Mom has decided that we're to go to Mexico."

"But it's so far away. Isabel told me we have to cross an ocean even bigger than this one. I'll die!" she exclaimed, whimpering. I held her close to me, and she eventually fell asleep.

The captain let us try to sleep in the cabin, but the blankets were hardly enough to warm us, and the wet chill that blew in from every crack kept us awake. A few times I had to run to the deck to vomit, and I felt as though my stomach would never get used to that infernal up and down. Finally, my body gave in to a restless, nightmarish sleep.

The next morning, we could glimpse Barcelona through a dense fog. We got off the boat so dizzy that the solid ground swam beneath our feet. We asked some sailors where the Franca Train Station was, where the expedition was set to leave. We took a trolley and were at the station by ten o'clock in the morning, our clothes reeking of fish. We ran down the platforms with empty stomachs and the sensation of falling toward a fatal and tragic end. Then, despite all our efforts, we learned that the train had left an hour before.

We went to the offices of the Central Committee for Refugee Assistance of Catalonia. A policeman let us into the building after my mother explained what had happened. In the waiting room, a young woman told us to go up to the second floor. There we found a large room full of people. A secretary took our names and asked us to wait. My mother explained the urgency of our situation, but dozens of other people had fled the most dangerous regions and were also begging for help.

We sat down on the floor beside a woman with five children. They had come from Zaragoza. She was crying and hugging the youngest child to her, who was so skinny his face looked sunken in. The baby was all skin and bones. He stared at us with his wide, inexpressive eyes, with no energy even to smile. My mother tried to comfort the woman and offered to hold the child so the mother could sleep awhile.

"No, I'd rather hold him," she answered in a thin voice. Her exhaustion was palpable.

Four or five hours went by, and the room slowly started to empty.

We had eaten nothing in over twenty-four hours, and my sisters were getting desperate. Mom pulled a few small pieces of bread out of her purse and distributed them. The children next to us on the floor watched with wide eyes but said nothing. Isabel broke her bread into three pieces and gave it to them. They gobbled it up without blinking, offering a smile for the first time since we'd seen them. Ana did the same and so did I, despite the hunger gnawing at me. Mom smiled at us with pride. Giving out of excess can be considered generosity, but willingly sharing from meager stores is something else altogether: it's handing over the most valuable thing we possess, our love for others.

The mother holding her baby now had tears of gratitude in her eyes. The baby started to whimper louder, and she gave him her breast to nurse. The child tried to suckle, but the woman was so thin, and nothing came out. The child's moan broke our hearts.

An hour later the four of us were called back to an office, exhausted and hoping to get out of there as soon as possible.

A thin man with a sharp nose and round glasses was seated behind a large desk strewn with papers. His hair was combed back, revealing a pale, bony forehead. He gestured for us to sit down and asked my mother to explain the situation.

Afterward, he said, "Mrs. Alcalde, I can't do much for you. The train has left for France and will be arriving by now. From there, they'll take a bus to Bordeaux. The boat is supposed to leave at the end of the month, though I can't say for sure the exact date. I'd encourage you to go back to Madrid. Things are not looking good here, and we can't be responsible for you."

"We've come all this way, and we're not going back home. The situation in Madrid is very concerning, especially for the little ones—"

"Have you seen the children in the waiting room? Well, this is just one aid agency. Our orphanages are overflowing, we have schools stuffed to the brim with cots, thousands are coming to the city every day . . ." the man explained, losing patience.

"I don't want to bother you. I'm only asking you to help us find some transportation to France. I'll figure it out from there."

"Have you lost your mind? Bordeaux is over three hundred miles from Perpignan. The French authorities are detaining nearly everyone who crosses the border. Most of them are sent back to Spain, and the rest are taken to internment camps."

My mother looked at us for a long moment, weighing the options. Finally, she lifted her gaze and, with a serious nod, told the man, "I think it's my responsibility. We're living in times when we have to try the impossible. The only thing I'm asking is for help crossing the border."

The man frowned. I expected him to send us away, but he took a sheet of paper and wrote on it for a moment. Then he looked up and said, "There's a convoy headed for Perpignan tonight. In the city there's a committee of the Catalonian government that helps refugees. With this letter, they'll give you some money and bus tickets to Bordeaux."

My mother jumped up and embraced the man, who shrank back in annoyance. My sisters and I remained unmoved, not understanding why our mom was so happy.

We left the office with our heads down, carrying our small, lightweight luggage. Before leaving, my mom went up to the mother from Zaragoza. She stroked the baby's head, then looked up with a start. She motioned for us to distract the woman's other children, then bent down and whispered, "I'm sorry. The child is . . ."

The woman shook her head and started to weep. She pressed the child so tightly to her that, had he been alive, she would've suffocated him.

"There, there," my mother said, stroking her face, but the mother wouldn't release her grip on the child. "He won't suffer anymore," she choked out.

The woman finally loosened her hold and let an office worker take the baby. She gave him one last look, kissed his forehead, and released him forever.

# Chapter 10

# Bordeaux

Barcelona
May 20, 1937

We were to take the train right before midnight. Despite the late hour, the station was packed. Soldiers and policemen kept the crowd from getting on the first train of the day that left for France. Showing authorization was required for even approaching the platform, and few people had it. Most refugees came to the border on foot or in trucks traveling to neighboring countries in search of fruit, vegetables, or anything that could nourish a country on the brink of starvation. We slipped our way through the crowd and got into a short line. Despite the pushing and shoving, we made it to where the soldiers were. Mom held out the letter from the immigration officer, and the soldier counted us and let us through. Things on the other side of the rope weren't much easier. Shipping agents ran every which way carrying packages, boxes, and equipment. A few well-dressed people got into first-class cars, seemingly going on vacation instead of into uncertain exile. Right then I understood that social classes hold steady even amid misfortune and that suffering is always harsher for those who have nothing.

My mother stopped a young man, and he pointed out the mail car to her. It was apparently the only place they could make room for us. And we weren't the only ones. Around fifty people sat and waited among the huge sacks or smoked at the entrance of the half-open cargo door. We found a free spot and huddled up together like chicks in a nest, Mom spreading her arms over us.

An hour later, the train began to move. The soft, melancholy *clickety-clack* of the wagons lulled us to sleep and helped us forget the hunger and fear for a moment. I didn't wake 'til eight in the morning when people began to move about the wagon, many desperate to use a bathroom. I shimmied up to a small window and looked out. The fresh air woke me up, and I briefly forgot where I was in the joy of traveling. I was still young enough that anything could turn into an adventure. I felt a tug on my coat and turned. My little sister's dirty face was smiling up at me. She lifted her arms, and I picked her up and put her beside me. Together, we stared out the window at the gray sky. We had no way of knowing that, a few yards back, those clouds had stopped belonging to our country. We were now in a foreign land. Up to that point we hadn't really known what it felt like to be a foreigner, but we would never be able to forget the feeling.

The train stopped in Perpignan. We disembarked in order, then formed a long line, and the gendarmes registered us all on a list. Those granted free passage went to the right—everyone else moved to the left. The reality was that most people were in the group that would wind up in a holding center and, once again, those who were clean and well-dressed breezed through the control point without a pause.

We approached the desk. I noticed my mother was shaking as my sisters clung to her from both sides.

"Please tell me your full name, the names of your children, and the reason for your visit to France, ma'am," said the man at the desk in very correct Spanish. Mom relaxed a bit when she heard him speaking our language.

After giving our names, she said, "We're going to Bordeaux. In a few days the children will board a ship sailing to Mexico, and we must get there before it sets sail." She placed our papers on the well-worn desk.

The gendarme was young, but he had a full, dark mustache that made him look older. First he looked at us. Ana hid behind me, and Isabel smiled shyly. "You're going to leave your children? And what will you do after that?" he asked, regaining the harsh look he had at first.

"I'll go back to my country."

"To Spain? No one goes back to Spain on purpose," the man said, incredulous.

"My husband is in Madrid, and I can assure you I'll return to him. The war may be terrible, but it's even worse to betray the person you love most in the world."

The gendarme stamped our letter, then looked up. "You've got three months' permission. If the police detain you after that period, you'll be deported to Spain. Understood?"

"Yes," my mother said, hardly daring to look at him.

We walked down a hallway and out to the street. We were dazed by the sight of a walled city, the streets overflowing with flowers and the bakeries bursting with so many breads, cakes, and pastries that we thought we had arrived in paradise. Yet, once again, it was only an illusion.

❧

A man named Francisco Ortega waited for Spaniards who passed customs control, then dispersed them in different means of transportation. When we reached him, he looked taken aback, not having been expecting us. My mother showed him the Barcelona agent's letter, and he read it carefully despite having been in such a hurry moments before. Francisco stared hard at us, as if we were there to make life difficult for him, then told us to stand off to the side. When he finished with the rest of those who had recently arrived and the various vehicles had gone their separate ways, he motioned for us to follow him. We got into an old Renault and went across town under a heavy rainfall that slowed traffic considerably. In French, Francisco cursed several drivers who cut him off or butted ahead of him on the road. We eventually got out of the city and arrived at an old mansion, which from afar looked like a haunted house. The unkempt yard and bare trees spooked me and my sisters. Francisco stopped the car at the front door, and we ran to the portico to escape the rain. Francisco then opened the door with a huge gold key, and we followed him into a dark, cold vestibule.

"You'll spend the night here," he said. "Tomorrow there's a car heading to Toulouse, but from there you'll have to travel by train. We don't take people far west because fascist Spanish agents are operating on the border. It wouldn't be the first time they grabbed someone and sent them to Navarre. You follow me?"

My mother did not know what he was talking about any more than we children did. I had presumed that, once we were on the French side of the border, we'd be safe. But apparently our enemy's reach was longer and more dangerous than we had imagined.

He took us to a cold, damp room on the top floor. He was about to shut us in for the night when my mother approached him. "Please," she said, "my children haven't eaten anything since we left Madrid."

Francisco made a face but told us to leave our suitcases and come downstairs with him. We followed in silence through the dark house and entered what seemed to be a large living room. He turned on the light, and the white tiles flashed so brightly that it blinded us for a moment. Francisco went to a cupboard and took out a thin sausage, some bread, some chocolates, and milk. We stared at the bounty in shock. It had been months since we'd had most of those foods. My mother seared us with a look to keep us from touching anything until we had been given permission.

"Sit down and eat. Forgive my lack of courtesy. It may be hard to believe, but my job isn't easy. We have very few means, and more and more people arrive every day. The consulate is overwhelmed, and so are all the agencies. The French barely cooperate with us, and I fear that within a few months complete chaos will overtake us."

My mother smiled at him. She had us sit down, then handed out small portions. We ate with greed, Isabel almost choking at one point.

"Poor things," Francisco said, watching us devour the meal.

"Spain is a disaster. I don't know who will win the war, but soon there won't be much left to govern," my mother said.

Francisco nodded and drank a glass of milk. "To be honest, if I were you, I'd get on that boat to Mexico with your kids and never come back."

My mother nodded as well but said, "I can't do that. My husband is in Madrid. If things get much worse, we'll try to escape too."

"I'm sorry to tell you this, ma'am, but if Madrid surrenders or is surrounded by the rebel troops, you won't be able to go anywhere. Haven't you heard what the fascists do with their prisoners? In the cities they overtake, the executions go on for days. They say that in

Badajoz the blood ran down the streets. Write to your husband and beg him to get out of the city and join you in Mexico."

"But if we all leave, who will fight the war?"

Francisco took another sip of milk and grimaced as if it were sour, but I understood it was the taste of defeat that bothered him. It was emanating from all around, and as our country disappeared, little by little, we were being robbed of the home we loved.

☙❧

The next morning, a car was waiting for us at the door. After eating and sleeping in a warmish bed, bathing, and changing clothes, we were feeling much better. Francisco said farewell to us at the door, and I noticed a tenderness in his face. Perhaps for the first time in a long time he had let down the emotional guard that enabled him to keep forging ahead despite it all.

The driver was a young man from Lleida named Andrés. He had come to France a few months ago and had gotten to know the highways and byways to get around the surveillance guards along the border. Every now and then he went back home and helped struggling souls who had made it to the Pyrenees but didn't know how to cross to the other side. His smile and strong accent were very funny to us. He was only eighteen, if that, and seemed quite content to drive to Toulouse, eager for the chance to venture away from the border and let loose, forgetting all that he was leaving behind.

"Thank you so much for taking us," my mother said from the backseat where she sat between my sisters.

"We've all got to lend a hand in times like these. I never dreamed I'd be driving a car, much less in France!" He laughed like a little kid enjoying an adventure.

"How far is Bordeaux from Toulouse?"

"Well, ma'am, I think we've got a good three hundred miles or so ahead of us, depending on the route. But don't worry. Francisco told me to get you all straight to Bordeaux and then bring you back. We'll get there tonight, after about twelve hours. The backroads aren't in great shape, and this piece of metal's not the fastest horse in the barn."

The motor of the old Citroën car growled and threatened to stall at any moment, but it held steady through cities and towns, over bridges and mountains, all the while getting us closer to Bordeaux and taking us farther from our beloved country. My sisters played games with Mom in the back, and I passed the time studying the scenery and talking every now and then with Andrés.

"Boy," he told me, "you're luckier than you can even imagine. I'd love to go to the Americas. My dad says that, after Spain, the fascists are going to take over all of Europe, so there'll be nothing left for us here. Were it me, I'd get on that boat in a heartbeat and never look back."

"But I don't want to leave my parents," I said, embarrassed even as the words left my mouth. I didn't want to seem like a child, but that's what I was.

"I get it. You're from Madrid, right? In my valley there's nothing, just mountains and rivers. My dad told me not to come back, to go look for a better future. It hasn't gone so bad up to now. Spain is already becoming a distant memory for me. Sometimes I go back to help people out, but I'm not sure I'll keep doing that. It gets more and more dangerous each time."

We got to the outskirts of the city during the night. During the last stretch, we passed by endless vineyards and idyllic towns with shiny churches and painted homes. I felt as though we had entered a different world.

Following the wide Garonne River into the city, we drove through a beautiful plaza and were amazed at the straight avenues, the carefully crafted buildings, and the well-dressed people who strolled along the streets without a care. It was a warm night. The reflections from windows and streetlights shone on the roads still wet from the hoses of the street-cleaners. The aromas of pastries, bread, and meat permeated everything, as if the city were from a fairy tale, all of it ready to be gobbled up.

Andrés stopped the car at a small hotel with red awnings and little balconies, and we thought surely he had made a mistake. We ran up the stairs and entered a fancy waiting room of finely crafted wood. A woman in a plaid suit who had her hair pulled back in a bun welcomed us with a smile. Andrés gave her a letter in French, and the woman took a key from a little box and handed it to Andrés, pointing to the stairs.

"Where will you sleep?" my mom asked Andrés.

"Don't worry about me. I'll stay in the car. I'm used to sleeping any old place. Francisco wanted me to wait for you, so tomorrow, after we leave the children with their guardians, we'll head back to Perpignan, if that's all right."

For the first time I saw my mother's face grow dark. The moment of saying goodbye was growing closer and closer. The next morning, our paths would separate, and we'd have to leave for Mexico within a few days.

We went up to the room in silence. My mother helped Ana get ready for bed, tucked us all in, then went to the bathroom. She was there a long time. I was just drifting off to sleep when I heard the sound of her crying. I went to the door and opened it a crack. She was sitting on the floor, her head hung low. When she heard the creak of the door, she looked up and held out her arms to me. She held me in silence for a long time until I, too, began to weep. The tension of the trip, the uncertainty of the future, the fear of our impending separation—it all crashed down at once. The feelings were jammed up in my heart, and I felt like I was drowning.

"Don't worry, Marco. I'd go to hell to find you if I had to."

"I know," I gasped between sobs.

"Sometimes mothers have to make the greatest sacrifice of all for love. I feel as if I'm being ripped apart inside, but at the same time I know this is the right thing to do. You'll be all right. I hope this war will be over soon. If it lasts too long, I can promise you I'll die from grief!"

There were no more words to say. Her arms cradled me for the last time, and I felt in my heart I would never again be embraced like that no matter how long I managed to live. I was alone in the world, and that sense of unease would follow me forever.

Part 2

# Exile Bound

# Chapter 11

# Separation

Bordeaux
May 23, 1937

At that point I still did not know it takes a lifetime to learn how to really live. I was about to turn fourteen, and I was pretty sure I had learned everything there was to learn. I was unaware of how my parents had given me practically everything up to that point, and not just clothing and food but security and the peace of a happy home. That morning my sisters and I had to say goodbye to my mother and had no idea if we would ever see her again.

I was the last one to wake. I didn't want morning to come; I didn't want to see my mother walk away again. Finally, she came over to my bed. "Marco," she said, kissing my forehead, "it's time to get up."

I stretched and turned a bit longer, and she hugged me. I remembered all the mornings of the world, the hundreds of times she had woken me up with kisses and snuggles. I knew I would miss that.

"Can't I sleep a little longer?" I asked.

"No, we have to go to the hotel where the other children are staying. I don't want you to miss the boat after coming all this way," she said with a little smile, though her face could not help but reflect the anguish roiling within her.

"We could stay in France. I bet you'd find work easily enough. They have everything here—"

"We've gone over this a thousand times. You're getting on that boat to Mexico," she said, her eyebrows raised in sternness. I hadn't meant to, but I was making this bitter pill even harder for her to swallow.

I took a long shower, then studied myself in the mirror. My blond hair was getting long and disheveled, and pockets of gray hung beneath my blue eyes. I got dressed listlessly, and when I came out of the bathroom, my mother and sisters were waiting for me at the door. We went downstairs for breakfast, and I ate until my stomach hurt. It had been so long since I'd been able to eat as much as I wanted that it felt like I was in a dream.

"Girls," my mother began, "I want you to obey your brother. He's the head of the family now. Don't leave his side even for a minute. Don't trust strangers. And please, be very prudent. You're going to live in a foreign country, so you must be respectful toward what you encounter. I'll send a letter as soon as I know where they'll place you. I hope this war won't last more than a year."

We looked at her in silence. Ana guzzled her glass of milk, and Isabel hung her head to hide her tears.

"Don't cry, darling," Mom continued. "The trip will be like a long vacation, a true adventure. In a few years, you can tell your friends all about it, and you'll miss living there."

Mom was trying to cheer us up, but it was hopeless. We tried to mask our sadness so she wouldn't feel worse. Then we gathered our suitcases and went toward the waiting room. It was a beautiful day, and the sun lit up the downtown streets. It seemed to me that I'd never seen anywhere as beautiful as Bordeaux. Andrés got out of the car he had parked by the front door and helped us get in. He drove to a nearby hotel, and we got out in silence. We walked in a line and stood waiting at the front desk. There, my mother asked for someone from the Ibero-American Committee for Aid to the Spanish Peoples.

The man at the front desk called for one of the bellhops, and soon a middle-aged man came out and greeted my mother politely, stroking Ana's hair. Ana gave him a stern look, not wanting to be treated like a little girl.

"My name is Genaro Muñoz. How may I help you, ma'am?"

While my mother explained the long journey we'd made to Bordeaux, I noticed the first few of the Spaniard children that we would be traveling with. Half a dozen young kids, no older than six or seven, were playing marbles off in a corner. Beside them, three girls played with rag dolls while a teacher watched them from a short distance away.

"Don't worry," the man said. He took out a list and looked for our names. Once he confirmed that everything was in order, he assigned us to a room. At first he wanted to separate me and my sisters, but at my mother's insistence he placed us all in the same place.

"When does the ship sail?" Mom asked.

"Well, it's scheduled for May 26, but that could always change. We're entirely dependent on the ship's captain and any unforeseen events."

We all went up to the room. It was large, with more than ten beds. Though it was clean and tidy, it was nothing like the hotel we'd stayed in the night before. Mom helped us settle our suitcases, then we followed her back downstairs to the hotel waiting room. We walked down the front steps and found Andrés already in the car, the motor idling.

Mom stopped beside the vehicle, and we all four had knots in our stomachs. The first one to cry was Isabel, clinging to my mother and sobbing. Then Ana threw herself onto them both with tears flooding her dark eyes. Finally, I joined the group embrace. I swallowed back my tears in an effort to cheer them up.

"God in heaven!" Mom exclaimed, blind with tears.

Ana wailed, "Don't leave us!"

"It's going to be okay," Mom choked out. "I'll bring you back. Every day I'll dream about you and about bringing you back home."

"Don't leave!" Isabel cried, refusing to let go of our mother's hands.

We were so sad that nothing in the world could have consoled us. My mother lifted her head. Her eyes were nestled into wrinkles, and she narrowed her gaze to steel herself from our anguish. "Remember me, and don't cry. Please, don't ever forget who your mother is."

"We'll never forget you! And soon we'll be back together," Isabel said, smothering Mom's cheeks with kisses.

My mother's words were engraved in my memory. I would never forget her until I was back in her arms. I was so scared that, when I saw her get into the car and wave, I tried to lock that moment away in my brain forever. I didn't want the memory to disappear into some corner of my heart. I was terrified. Fear is the worst feeling in the world. It rules like a tyrant, takes advantage of us, and turns us into wretched beings.

My sisters hugged me, their island in the middle of a stormy ocean. I thought about how we always love whatever's close at hand, but if our hearts are full of love, then what's far away can also be near to us, regardless of the physical distance. Our mother would always be our mother; nothing and no one could change this truth.

"I'll remember you," I said as the car drove out of sight. Then I took my sisters back inside the hotel. Together we started the greatest adventure of our lives.

# Chapter 12

# The Hunt for Red Children

Bordeaux
May 24, 1937

The next morning I woke up feeling untethered, as if I were floating in the air. I had not before understood how my mother was the rock upon which our life as a family was built. She had taught us nearly everything we knew and about everything that actually mattered. Our attachments, expressions of love, and meanings of life in the present we owed to her. For me, the only son, my father was the model for the future, the person I wanted to emulate and be like when I grew up. And now they were both out of reach. I opened my eyes with the fear that comes from loneliness. I now belonged to the battalion of desperate souls, all the world's orphans, exiles, and dead.

I looked at the bed beside me where my sisters were still asleep. The other children in the room were quiet. I went to the bathroom and took a shower. By the time I returned, most kids were making their beds, and my sisters had already gotten dressed and combed their hair.

"Let's go eat breakfast," I said, willing a calmness I didn't feel into a smile. It's impossible to ignore the pain of an open wound, and loneliness is one of the deepest gashes in the soul.

There were already over fifty children sitting around the tables when we got to the dining room, where women were serving toast, several flavors of jam, cheese, and milk. We gobbled our portions down, our stomachs still bearing the hunger from Spain.

One of the monitors called for silence and then gave instructions about the rest of our stay. "We'll be leaving in a couple days, and we need to behave well while we're here in the city. The good people of Bordeaux have been so kind and generous with us. Let's not give them a reason to believe Spaniard children are rude and misbehaving. Even though you are all very young, you represent Spain and her Republic. The eyes of thousands of people are watching you. You're a privileged group. Hundreds of people are dying every day in our beloved country, and most cannot enjoy the delicacies we have eaten this morning. The Mexican government is our host; they are paying for all of this. Therefore, we want the reports they receive about you to be excellent. Then people all over the world can sing the praises of Spaniard children."

The short speech from Ms. Laura Serra—we were just starting to learn the names of our new guardians and teachers—made a big impression on us. There were five other groups of boys and girls in different parts of the city, all coming from different places in Spain:

Basque Country, Catalonia, Valencia, Andalusia, Asturias, and several parts of Castile. Some spoke only their native languages, and when we were all talking at the same time, it sounded like a miniature Tower of Babel. Most of the children were very young, but we were with the group of older children. The age limit for traveling to Mexico was roughly between five and twelve years old, but those limits had not been strictly enforced. We saw kids as young as four and as old as seventeen.

Ms. Serra again called for silence. Behind her thick glasses, her small, dark eyes seemed to catch everything. "Don't go far from the hotel, don't walk alone, don't go off with adults. The youngest children must always be with an adult. You can accept food and other things from the French, but be careful if they speak to you in Spanish. We are aware of fascists in the area who are trying to take children and send them back to Spain."

As soon as Ms. Serra announced we could go outside, everyone forgot her instructions and ran to the door. Yet my sisters and I stayed seated. We didn't know the city at all and had hardly spoken a word to any of the other children.

A hefty boy came up to our table and held out his hand. "What's your name?" he asked. "Are you three new? I thought we were all here by now."

"Our mom dropped us off yesterday," I said, shaking his hand.

"Oh, sorry. It's horrible to be separated from your parents, at least according to some."

His words puzzled me. I couldn't believe that some of the children wouldn't care about losing their parents, but there were still many things I didn't know about life.

"If you want, I can show you around the city."

The three of us exchanged a glance and happily went out with our new friend.

"I'm Manuel," he said. "I'm from Granada. I don't know how I ended up here, but I guess I got lucky. As for my parents, well . . . I don't know what's happening with them. The fascists took my dad a few months ago. He was in the socialist party. My mom took me to Valencia and left me with my dad's sister. Then she boarded a merchant ship headed for South America. I have a feeling I'll never see her again."

"I'm sorry," I said as we went out to the street.

"We were never really very close. I figure someone has to bring you into the world, but for that person to love you—that's a different story."

We walked along narrow alleys. Our hotel was in the northern part of the city, a neighborhood called Chartrons. When we got to the river, we were surprised to see how wide it was. Huge boats traveled up and down like it was an ocean. On the dock, shipping agents loaded crates of wine and other merchandise into a boat. After poking around a little, we walked along the river for about half an hour. We went by several parks and gardens and then came to the Bourse Plaza right on the riverfront.

"It looks like Puerta del Sol back home," Isabel said. She had not let go of Ana's hand since we'd left the hotel.

"But it's bigger and prettier," Ana said, wriggling out of Isabel's grip and taking off at a run. Isabel called out and ran after her, and it turned into playful chase. Manuel and I watched from not far away.

"So how did you three get here?" Manuel asked.

I told him everything that had happened in Valencia, the trip to Barcelona, and our trek across France. My mother had left me a little bit of money, so we went up to a food stall and bought four pieces of candy. Though I didn't understand how to count out the change, the lady at the stall was very kind and gave back all the extra.

We went down one street and came upon the cathedral. People

were milling about enjoying the pleasant temperature, and for the first time in a long time we could look up at the sky and not be afraid of fascist airplanes flying overhead.

"How was your trip here?" I asked Manuel after calling for my sisters to come and get their candy.

"Rough. We left Valencia on a big boat. Not far out from the dock, a fascist boat started following us. We thought it was going to attack, but thanks to the captain's skill, we managed to leave it behind. Most of us got horribly seasick, and some kids were really bad off, but people perked back up once we made it to Barcelona. We spent a couple nights in the Regina Hotel. Before supper, the people from the National Delegation of Evacuated Children gave us all a blue cardboard suitcase with clothes and shoes. They put nametags on us in case we got lost, so the police would know where to send us, and we got to enjoy the city."

Ana and Isabel came over and sat on a sunny bench to eat their candy. Manuel and I wandered toward a big fountain.

"Then a couple days later, we all boarded a train at the Franca Station. We walked there in formation, like a little army. People stopped to stare at us, some shouting and applauding and cheering the Republic. Women were crying because I guess we looked pretty helpless, all in a line with our matching blue suitcases. Old ladies stepped forward to hug and kiss us. It felt like we were pretty important. But our guardians weren't real happy. Rumor was, the fascists were going to bomb the train. I didn't believe it, though. They're horrible brutes, but even they know it's not good press to kill a big group of kids."

"True enough," I said. I glanced over to make sure my sisters were still on their bench.

"The worst part was at the station. There were so many parents there, especially those from Catalonia. When they saw us, the crying and screaming began. Some mothers broke through the police barrier to give their kids one last kiss. They were all carrying on, howling and swearing they'd see them again soon. The kids were crying and trying to reach their parents. The guardians couldn't pry the kids away from their mothers, who had changed their minds and wanted to take the kids back home. What a scene." Manuel shook his head.

I thought about my mom from the day before and made a herculean effort not to cry. I glanced toward the bench again, and a chill ran up my spine when I saw it was empty. I remembered Ms. Serra's warning and started running around the plaza in front of the cathedral. Manuel helped me look for my sisters, but we couldn't find them anywhere. They couldn't have just disappeared. We kept calling their names and looking in all the shops and stalls. Had something happened to them? My heart was racing. How could I have already lost them? We found a group of other Spaniard kids who helped us look for them, too, but it was no use. There was no sign of them anywhere.

## Chapter 13

# Just a Minute Ago

Bordeaux

May 24, 1937

I was distraught. I hadn't known that anguish had physical symptoms, but my chest constricted and made it hard to breathe. Manuel told me sit on a bench to calm down, but the pain just got worse, not better. An older woman saw how upset I was and came up to us. We couldn't understand her French, but she called a gendarme over.

"I speak some Spanish," the policeman said. "My grandmother was from Spain."

Manuel and I looked at each other hopefully. But, after a few questions, the gendarme had a grave look on his face. "We've had several cases of Spaniard children disappearing. It seems the Spanish rebels kidnap them and take them back across the border."

It was hard to believe the wickedness of our enemy went so far.

"How long has it been since you've seen them?" he asked.

"About fifteen minutes," I answered.

The gendarme raised his voice for everyone around to hear him. "Someone must have seen something." The adults in the shops and stalls who had ignored us before now started talking, pointing in the direction my sisters had gone. We walked down alleyways to a central market, which smelled like rotten vegetables and fish. At the gendarme's questions, a shopkeeper pointed to an old, three-story building. From the outside it looked like a medieval house, with a balcony barely held up by strips of wood and rafters weakly supporting the cracked exterior. The door was unlocked. We went in, and the gendarme knocked at the first door he came to. No one answered. The same thing happened at every door until we reached the top floor.

We heard a creak of wood from behind the door, footsteps that halted, and the sound of the peephole being opened. Bolts were unlocked, and before us appeared a very old woman with gray hair, round glasses, and a look of complete surprise on her face.

"Excuse the interruption, ma'am, but we're looking for two Spaniard girls."

The old woman appeared surprised, but she smiled sweetly and assured the policeman that she had been home all day and hadn't seen anyone. The gendarme turned to us with a resigned shrug. The old woman started to close the door, but I heard something that resembled the muffled cry of a child.

"Ana!" I yelled.

"Marco!" came a voice from the back of the house.

I shoved the door, and the woman fell backward. The gendarme jumped over her, and we tore down the hall to one of the rooms at the back, but the door was locked.

"Where are the keys?" the gendarme demanded. The old woman

just shook her head. The policeman took a few steps back and kicked the door. The old wood splintered. I pushed through and my sisters lunged at me, and we all fell into a pile.

"I'm so sorry!" Ana wailed, hiding her face in my lap. Isabel clung to us both, and it took us a while to stand again.

The old woman, however, sprang up with more agility than anyone would have expected and started screaming at us in Spanish. "You're a bunch of communist brats! I could've sent you back home and you'd at least have the chance to change your ways, but you're hopeless! You belong to an accursed race!"

Manuel was beside the woman. "You're insane!" he spat.

"Insane? There are patriots risking everything to save Spain. Those disgusting reds—"

The gendarme went up to her and spoke calmly. "What you've done is very serious. These children are here at the invitation of the French government, on their way to Mexico. They have suffered enough and don't need people like you doing them any more harm."

"Communist lackeys!" The woman was nearly spitting in the gendarme's face. "Their hour has come. It won't be long before decent people recover this continent from the red hordes. The Popular Front is a disgrace for France and will lead us into another war or to anarchy."

The gendarme wrote down the woman's information, then the five of us made our way out of the house. The woman started yelling at us from the doorway of the top floor in a mix of Spanish and French, her voice echoing off the landings as we descended. Ana and Isabel trembled as the gendarme opened the front door. He walked us back to the cathedral and paid for a taxi to take us back to our hotel.

"I'm so sorry for everything. I'll make sure that woman receives her due," he said before shutting the door.

"Thank you for helping us, sir." My voice came out as a strangled croak.

The gendarme took off his hat and saluted us as the taxi headed for the road that went along the river. Within minutes we were back at the hotel. We let out a collective sigh of relief to find ourselves in a safe place, and we sat down on the steps of the entryway. Before I could even ask what had happened, Isabel started talking.

"We had no idea that lady was a witch. We were sitting on the bench, and she passed by with lots of bags. She stopped in front of us and started talking in French, but we couldn't understand her. When she heard us talking, she switched to Spanish. She told us she was from Spain but had lived for a long time in France, that she was retired and lived alone. She asked us for help carrying her bags and said she didn't live far. We felt bad for her and started walking with her, taking some of her bags. We thought we'd be right back, which is why we didn't say anything to you, Marco. She was so sweet and asked us where we were headed and if our parents were nearby. She was surprised we were traveling so far away from Spain. So we explained all about the war and that it was for our safety."

Ana filled in the rest. "We went through the front gate and took the bags to her house. She told us she had some candy she'd give us and asked us to wait in a room. Before we realized it, she had locked us in. I was so scared."

I stood up in front of my sisters. "I'm really, really sorry, but you've got to learn we can't trust anybody."

"She was just an old woman, and we only wanted to help her," Isabel explained.

"But she was an old fascist woman," I answered. "You're my responsibility now, and you can't go away from me under any circumstance. What would've happened if we hadn't found you? I can barely even think about that."

Manuel put a hand on my shoulder. "It's all right."

I tried to calm down. One of the other kids came out to tell us it was time to eat. As we headed toward the dining room, my mother's words resounded in my ears. I was responsible for my sisters. We had lost everything: our family, our home, our country, and our poor childhood. We couldn't afford to be naïve. Innocence was too dangerous right then.

# Chapter 14

# Forbidden Suffering

Bordeaux
May 26, 1937

After the incident with the old woman, we didn't venture outside the hotel. Rumors swirled about rebels kidnapping Spaniard children and sending them back to the peninsula. I hardly slept the night Ana and Isabel had been kidnapped. I spent the next day reading the few books I had brought and playing with Ana, who was getting more anxious as the time approached for boarding the *Mexique*.

The morning of May 26 was warm. Our guardians asked us to pack our blue suitcases and get everything ready to board the ship. We had a light breakfast, as the adults didn't want us to spend the whole trip with sick stomachs. Most of the children had never been on a boat before, and we weren't used to the motion of the waves.

We went back to our room to get our suitcases and ID tags, then made a big pile of luggage near the front door. We would walk in formation to the train station so that no one got lost. From there we would go to the port and before sundown be on our way to Mexico. We were all swinging between excited and scared. Our departure was imminent and, in a way, we just wanted it to be over.

Ana and Isabel chatted with some of the girls they had befriended while Manuel and I joked around, studying the other kids and making bets about who would make the whole voyage without barfing. Just then one of the older boys walked by me and shoved me into the pile of luggage. I jumped up in a rage and grabbed his arm. "Hey, who do you think you are?" I yelled.

The boy looked down at me from his towering height like I was a germ. He stuck his face right in mine. "You got a problem, Madrid?" He spit a little as he spoke, though it was hard to tell if it was intentional.

I knew this boy's name was Luis and that he was from Barcelona. "You pushed me. Be more careful next time," I said.

"And what are you gonna do if I don't?" he taunted.

Manuel grabbed my arm to hold me back, but it was too late. I wasn't in the habit of losing my cool, though it wasn't the first time I'd been in a fight. When I fought, I was usually sticking up for people weaker than myself.

The giant boy grabbed me by the front of my shirt, lifted me up like a feather, and threw me back down on the suitcases. Several kids scrambled out of the way to avoid any crossfire. I got up awkwardly, and Luis took the opportunity to kick me in the stomach. I doubled over in pain, and that's when Don Alfonso, one of the Spaniard guardians, showed up. Luis became calm and quiet. I had heard other kids talk about Don Alfonso, and though I'd only run into him a couple of times, I didn't want to make him angry.

"Quiet!" he barked. "Just now as we're leaving, you two little know-it-alls want to ruin everything with a fistfight! I swear I'll leave you here on dry ground. I won't have bullies in my group. Besides, you two are above the age limit. I don't care who your parents are. I'll leave you here in France or you can walk back to Spain."

He picked me up by the shirt and seared me with his cold, impenetrable blue eyes. "Is that clear, little Madrid? You kids from the capital are all so cocky," he boomed in fury.

He put me down and then looked to Luis. "And you—this is your second warning. There won't be a third."

Luis hung his head and, after apologizing, went out to the street. Don Alfonso turned his piercing gaze back to me. "I don't like you, boy. Those arrogant eyes worry me, your prideful look, the hardness in your face. I won't let you jeopardize this journey. We're guests of a foreign government, and we represent the Spanish Republic, if that even means anything anymore. Now, get out of my sight!"

My sisters had watched everything from the back of the waiting room, and they ran toward me as soon as I left the luggage area.

"Are you okay?" Isabel asked.

I gingerly touched my stomach. It was still very sore from the impact of Luis's foot. "Yeah," I said. "It hurts a little, but it'll go away soon."

After another hour of waiting, the teachers and guardians instructed us to take our luggage and line up in front of the hotel. We got into two long lines in age order. My sisters didn't want to leave my side, but they had to stay with the girls in front. That didn't worry me since I could see them from my place in line.

Genaro, the man who had first welcomed us when we got to the hotel, signaled for us to start walking, and we started off down the street. There were not many cars out, and the few we came across stopped to let us pass. People stared at us with a mixture of compassion and relief. Humans are always happy when misfortune passes by their door and knocks at the neighbor's house instead. In many ways, the French saw us as a reflection of themselves. Tensions between Germany and France were already rising, and though they weren't at war yet, most people knew it was inevitable.

We rounded a corner and met up with another group of children. Within five minutes, we were nearly five-hundred strong. The French smiled and waved as we marched past. Some reached out to hand us candy or pastries. My companions stuffed their pockets with rolls and sweets or ate them right then and there, as if their lives depended on it.

When we got to the station, a retinue of French workers bade us an official farewell by singing the workers' anthem "The International" and waving little Republican flags. We held our fists high as a final goodbye.

We walked into the station amidst happy cheers and tears of sadness. The younger children were calling for their mothers, and the older ones held out as well as we could, though we would've rather cried along with the younger children. Police officers checked our papers before we were allowed onto the platform. Then we were divided among several train cars and, half an hour later, were on our way to the port.

The train left the station slowly, as if wanting to delay us. I sat next to Manuel, and a boy named Guillermo sat on his other side. I'd only spoken to him once or twice. He had the look of a rich kid. Not everyone on the ship was from the working class. Some high-ranking government officials had sent their kids with us to keep them safe.

Guillermo said, "Have you guys heard about the German submarine?" We looked at him uneasily. We hadn't heard anything about any submarine.

"No. What do you mean?" Manuel asked, intrigued.

"There's a rumor that the fascists know about the ship that's taking us to Mexico. Supposedly they want to sink it," Guillermo said. Fear made his voice tremble.

"That's ridiculous," I answered. "They're not going to sink a ship full of kids."

"Are you sure? They've killed tons of kids in Barcelona with bombs. I don't think it matters much to them," Guillermo said. He seemed convinced that a fascist attack would occur as soon as we got out to sea.

Manuel smiled. "Well, you just don't know."

"I was thinking about sneaking away on the port and going back home. My parents would be happy to see me again," said Guillermo.

"Are you crazy? The Francoists would snatch you up, and then you'd really never see your parents again. The war is a disaster, and the fascists are advancing with each passing day. My parents don't have much hope for the Republic, which is why they wanted to get us out of the country. It's not just because of the dangers," I explained.

"I know," said Guillermo, "but it's better to stay in Spain. What are we going to do in Mexico?" He was on the verge of tears. He must've been around eleven years old, and though he was skinny, he still had a boyish face.

"It's okay," I said, putting a hand on his shoulder. "Think about this journey like an adventure. We're going to the Caribbean, to the land of pirates. Imagine all the excitement we're going to feel. I'm sure that when we come back in a few months you'll be able to tell your parents all about it." I fed him the lines I'd been told to cheer him up.

He didn't buy it, but he did calm down on the way to the port. When we arrived, a new crowd was waiting for us at the foot of the boat. Our teachers and guardians had us line up, and we boarded the ship in order while the crowd cheered and waved, as if their own children were heading off to exile. As we walked up the gangway, some of the younger kids stopped short, crying like mad. The caretakers and teachers tried to move them along, but the little ones, holding their tiny suitcases, looked so pitiful that we all ended up crying. The first-class passengers had at first seemed annoyed at the presence of so many children, but when they saw us all crying, they threw chocolates at us and called out in French, "Long live the Spaniards!"

We were all scared by the time we stepped onto the deck. My sisters broke from their line and ran toward me. I tried to comfort them as they hung on to me, but a sizable lump sat in my own throat. The caretakers called for us to go to our cabins, and I had to leave my sisters again. Their horrified faces were burned into my mind, a memory to torture me in misfortune. We walked along the narrow passageways of the boat to the cabins, and we were not to leave those cabins until the boat weighed anchor. After being shut in for several hours, we were allowed back up on deck. It was such a relief to be under the open sky again. It was already nighttime, and the light breeze had a calming effect on me. I searched out my sisters, and with Manuel we went up to the second-class deck.

We stood at the rails and watched as the boat slowly moved away from the harbor. We heard a whistling and saw white smoke rise from the enormous chimneys that towered above us. Our eyes dried the farther we ventured into the dark ocean, which seemed like a reflection of night itself. The lights of the coast disappeared like shooting stars, and the breeze carried the smells of the sea. Fewer kids were crying now, though perhaps more from exhaustion than from anything else. Our hearts remained there in Old Europe while our little bodies headed for the New World—one long journey toward the adventure of our young lives.

Chapter 15

# In Bed

Atlantic Ocean
May 26, 1937

We had been told that traveling by boat wouldn't be simple, but none of us expected to spend the first several days in bed without a moment free of seasickness. It was chaos from the start. Manuel and I managed to get assigned to the same cabin, but boys and girls were separated from each other, so siblings and close friends couldn't be together. Some had known one another from their hometowns, others had become friends during the journey, but our guardians couldn't make everyone happy. At one point, I argued with one of the teachers who made my sisters leave our cabin and took them back to the girls' quarters. No matter how much I explained that my mother had ordered me to take care of them, I couldn't convince her. She said that for decency's sake the girls and boys had to travel separately. The Mexican caretakers were much more conservative than the few Spaniards who traveled with us. We didn't understand that until later, though. For them, religion wasn't something bad like it was for us. We had known the Catholic Church to be on the side of the powerful, having baptized the civil war as a crusade against communism. Priests, nuns, and religion were our enemies, together with the military and the bourgeoisie. That was the world we'd come from and where we'd grown up. We knew nothing else.

The first night on the *Mexique* was awful. Children screamed and cried out for their mothers all night long. The caretakers eventually just left them alone since they refused to be comforted. The guardians didn't even intervene when the older kids, fed up with the noise, threatened to hurt the little ones if they didn't quiet down. I was so dizzy I couldn't care much about what was happening around me. For me, seasickness was a new sensation.

I hadn't been able to eat anything. The mere thought of food made me want to vomit. Most of the kids seemed to feel the same way, except for some of the Basques who'd grown up on the sea.

By morning, I was terribly dizzy on an empty stomach. A little kid beside me named Fermín, only six or seven years old, was traveling alone. He had wet his pants and spat up all over himself. He looked at me with his big green eyes, and I couldn't help but think about my sisters and how they would feel if they were making this trip by themselves.

"Come with me," I said, trying to control the impulse to gag.

I took him to the bathroom and helped him clean up. He thanked me with a big smile. He was calm and withdrawn, and I wondered whose idea it had been to send him so far from home. The longer the war went on, the less sensitive we all became, perhaps intuiting that only the strongest would survive.

I went to the area where the youngest boys were staying, and it was complete chaos. There were no caretakers in sight. Finally, I found Genaro, who came up to me with a smile.

"I want you to gather all the boys together. Tell them to bring any money their parents or the French have given them. You understand? Your friend can help you," he said, pointing to Manuel.

We went through the hallways, evidence of the seasickness everywhere we stepped. The dirty, abandoned children smiled when they saw us, as if we might bring some relief. Manuel and I finally rounded most of them up, except for the ones too ill to get out of bed. We crammed nearly two hundred boys into the meeting room and waited for the teacher to give us instructions.

"Well, boys, this trip will be long and difficult. Some of your parents have given you money for Mexico, but neither pesetas nor francs are worth anything in Mexico. Please give me your money and I'll exchange it when we get there. I don't want you to get robbed or for the money to get lost."

The boys went forward in a line. Some only had a few cents, others just one peseta. Genaro put all the money together in a box and locked it, though he hadn't collected much in total. "Very well, please remember, boys, how much money you gave me so I can return it to you in Mexico."

Genaro left the room followed by the older boys. The younger ones stayed there, quiet, dirty, and hungry. They weren't sure what to do or where they were supposed to go. I couldn't believe the adults weren't doing anything about it.

"We can't just leave them like this," I told Manuel. "I'm going to look for something to eat."

I left the big room and raced up and down the hallways. Why wasn't anyone in charge? I asked several boys, and they told me most of the teachers and monitors were in first class enjoying the trip. I found my way to one of the kitchens, and an Argentine kitchen helper gave me some bread and meat for the boys. On my way back, I ran into a couple I had seen a few times, Mr. and Mrs. Méndez.

"The boys are all hungry and filthy. You've got to do something," I begged them.

They followed me to the room and stopped short when they saw the children. They sent us to get diapers, clean clothes, and food. We were supposed to find a teacher named Loreto, the one in charge of the supplies the children would need on the voyage. Mrs. Méndez told me the Mexican government had provided enough money for the trip, so we should not lack for anything.

I found Mrs. Loreto seasick in her cabin, but she got up and took me to the storage room where everything was kept. We brought food and clean clothes for the boys, and a little while later everyone was clean and happily playing on the second and third decks.

Mrs. Loreto and the Méndezes looked worn out, but they invited me and Manuel to have a snack up on the first-class deck. Manuel and I had not yet been past the rope that separated first and second, but as soon as we did, we understood the enormous difference between the two. We sat at a table with a view of the sea and were served orange juice that tasted like nectar of the gods.

"This trip is a complete disaster," Mrs. Loreto said.

"Some of the Spaniards who've come along have done it just to escape Spain and live the high life. They're a bunch of cowards and traitors, leaving the children in that state!" Mr. Méndez said with a scowl. He seemed to be the oldest of the teachers.

"We can't count on them, dear. We should organize things ourselves," his wife answered.

I left my glass on the metal table and looked out at the ocean, feeling relaxed for the first time. Manuel smiled at me from the other side of the table.

"Surely it will be better in Mexico," Mrs. Loreto continued. "President Cárdenas is seeing to things himself."

"Why are they taking us to Mexico?" I dared to ask.

"Well, the Ibero-American Committee for Aid to the Spanish Peoples wanted to get as many children away from the conflict as possible. Many youngsters have gone to Holland, Belgium, Russia, England, and France, but it's safer to take you to the Americas. Things in Europe are going to get very ugly," Mr. Méndez explained.

"I see." Even so, I would've preferred another country in Europe so I didn't have to go so far away from my parents.

"They wanted to host five hundred in Mexico, but given the haste and the fact that several parents backed out at the last minute, there are about 460 of you. President Cárdenas's wife was insistent that he get you all out of Spain as soon as possible. They say that Amalia Solórzano is a champion advocate for children," Mrs. Méndez said.

"Carmela Gil de Vázquez and Matilde Rodríguez Cabo de Múgica are also on that committee," her husband added.

"Where are we going to stay?" I asked.

"They haven't given us many details," Mrs. Loreto answered. "I imagine they've prepared boardinghouses. What they have assured us is that they'll keep you all together."

"Will they divide us up again, boys and girls?" I didn't want my sisters to be alone. I couldn't protect them without being near them.

"I'm afraid so. Mexicans are very conservative and won't allow boys and girls to be mixed."

We finished our refreshments and took a walk around the first-class deck. Some passengers looked at us with an evident mixture of curiosity and disdain. Our clothes were in poor condition, though we didn't care. We were still young enough not to understand all that class differences entailed or worry much about what others might be thinking. When we got tired of wandering about, we went back to our deck.

Walking along one of the side passages near the lifeboats, we heard shouting. We looked all around, but no one else was visible in that part of the boat. We kept walking and heard the shouting again. We got close to one of the lifeboats and confirmed that the voices were coming from inside. It was covered with canvas, but Manuel lifted one side, and we discovered a sailor on top of one of the girls from our group. The girl with blonde braids was kicking and shrieking. She couldn't have been more than thirteen or fourteen years old.

"What are you doing to her?" I shouted at the sailor and climbed inside the boat.

The sailor turned and glared at us, growling, "This is none of your business!"

Manuel joined me and started kicking the man. The sailor got up with his pants half unbuttoned and shoved me. I felt a sharp pain in my side. Then the sailor jumped out of the boat and ran off. The girl's eyes were full of tears. She straightened her clothes, and we helped her down from the boat.

"Are you all right?" we kept asking.

She nodded, and we took her back to the rest of the girls. She couldn't stop crying. Isabel came over to us while Ana was playing with some friends.

"What's happened?" Isabel asked when she saw the girl crying.

"Well, somebody tried to hurt her. The girls better not walk around alone on the deck."

Isabel went to the girl and gently asked, "What's your name?"

"Carmen," the girl choked out.

"Here, come with me," said Isabel, who put her arm around Carmen's waist.

Another girl came up too. I had noticed her before, but we hadn't spoken.

"Thank you," she said. "I'm Mercedes. It's nice to know at least someone's looking out for us."

I blushed, smiled, and then turned to leave. As we returned to the boys' area, I started feeling sick again.

"You okay?" Manuel asked.

My side hurt so badly. I reached under my shirt to touch the spot, and my fingers were dotted with blood when I pulled them out. I felt woozy at the sight. Manuel supported me all the way back to our cabin, and after I fell into my bed, I lost consciousness. Three days later, I awoke.

# Chapter 16

# Havana

Atlantic Ocean
May 30, 1937

I remember very little, but Isabel and Manuel told me that I had been delirious and sweating with a high fever. They had given me lemon water and tried to lower the fever with damp cloths. None of the adults had helped them. Apparently our lives were not very valuable. On the third day, I woke up with fierce hunger and thirst, and my body was terribly sore. I was pale and had rings around my eyes that made me look like a ghost. They brought me milk and biscuits so I could regain my strength slowly. I wanted to get out of bed and get up on deck because I needed fresh air on my face to convince me I was still alive. Supported by my sister and my friend, I struggled up the stairs. When we got on deck, I gasped with greed to take as much of the aroma of sea and freedom into my lungs as possible. I sat on a bench and enjoyed the warm, blue sky. The climate grew more and more temperate the closer we got to the equator.

"They've told us we'll be in Cuba in just a few days. There's a layover there to restock supplies. From there we'll sail to Mexico," Manuel said, trying to lift my spirits.

The rise and fall of the boat now affected me even more than before. I forced a smile. "Despite all the awful things we've gone through, this trip really is an adventure."

"We're going to the land of pirates! Ahoy!" Manuel jumped up and sliced the air with an imaginary sword, then drove his pretend enemy overboard.

I smiled again and asked, "How's the girl?"

"You mean Carmen?" Isabel asked. I nodded, and she pursed her lips in exasperation. "Nobody's even tried to find the sailor who attacked her."

"Did you tell Genaro?"

"The only thing he cares about is money," Isabel said. She stood and walked to the railing.

"What's eating her?" I asked Manuel. Before this trip, my sister was always happy and upbeat.

"She's scared. None of the girls dare go around by themselves. We have to go with them, or they have to stick together to even walk around. She's been a nervous wreck with you being so sick. Your fever just wouldn't break, and she was scared you'd, you know . . . She couldn't bear to think what life would be like if it was just her and Ana. Think about it. She's lost her mom and dad, and now you and Ana are all she's got."

Up to that point I'd been too preoccupied with how I felt to think too much about what my sisters might be feeling. Part of me thought they were too young to really understand our circumstances. Clearly,

I was wrong. Isabel would soon be a young woman, and Ana was more mature than she seemed.

"And there's something else."

I looked quickly at Manuel. How could things have changed so fast in the few days I'd been sick? "What is it?" I demanded.

"We've gotten to know a French sailor named Marcel. He told us the captain thinks a hurricane might be headed our way."

"A hurricane? What the devil is that?" I asked, more intrigued than worried.

"It's a kind of storm. Some boats can't survive a hurricane and wind up at the bottom of the ocean. Apparently hurricanes are common in the Caribbean Sea. Most travel inland and destroy everything in their path, but it looks like this one is headed toward us. That's why the wind is so strong. Look," he said, pointing to the sky.

Though the sun was shining, in the distance we could see foreboding dark-gray clouds.

"Marcel told us the boat doesn't have enough life vests or lifeboats for everyone. If the *Mexique* goes nose up, we'll go down with it."

His words caused a different kind of tremor in me than what I'd experienced the past few days. I could barely swim. Like most of the kids traveling with us, I'd never experienced a storm at sea. Goosebumps spread over my whole body.

"When will it reach us?" I asked.

"Tonight maybe, but it's hard to say. If the hurricane doesn't hit us full force, we may have a chance. But if we're right in the middle of its path, the boat won't hold up." Manuel was matter-of-fact in his delivery of this devastating news.

I struggled to get up and lurched toward Isabel. I put my arm around her shoulder and whispered in her ear, "I'm fine now. Don't worry, nothing on earth can pull us apart. We'll get back to Spain, and we'll find our parents. The war can't last forever."

"Did Manuel tell you about the hurricane?" she asked. I could hear the fear collecting in her throat.

"Yes. But up to now we've managed to beat all the odds, and we'll get through this as well. We'll look for life vests, and we'll be ready when the storm arrives."

The three of us searched for life jackets in the lifeboats but came up empty-handed. Then we looked along the stern but had no luck. We were headed back to the cabins when we ran into one of the teachers.

"What are you doing on deck?" Doña María Jesús asked. "A big storm is coming. You'd better head back to your cabins."

"We don't have life jackets," I said.

"You won't need them. The storm won't last long."

Yet her words failed to comfort me. She must have read it in my face because she asked us to follow her. She took us to a locked room and searched among the boxes and stacks of things stored there. We were surprised to see food, clothing, and other things that should've belonged to our group. She found two life jackets and handed them to us. "These are the last two. Guard them with your lives."

Manuel and I went back to our cabin and gathered up a few things, then went to join Ana and the other girls. I didn't want to be away from my sisters at a time like this.

An hour later, the boat began to toss. At first it just felt like being on a Ferris wheel, but little by little, the ship started moving with violence. We tried to hold ourselves steady by grabbing on to the beds and tables that were attached to the floor, but even so we ended up falling all over one another. Ana began to scream. I put my arms around her and tried to calm her, but she was a nervous wreck, shaking and crying uncontrollably.

"Calm down. It's going to be okay," I kept saying.

We could hear screams in the hallway and the banging of things hitting the metal walls. The waves were beating against the ship, and it seemed everything would crack open at any moment.

Half an hour later, the ocean's force grew. Most of the boys with us had thrown up, and several were bruised from objects that had fallen and hit them. Ana broke out of my arms and ran toward the hallway. Right then, the lights went out, and I had to follow her by feeling my way along the walls.

"Ana, please, come back!" I yelled, hoping she would return. Yet panic had overpowered her, and she had fled to the deck, not realizing it was the most dangerous place for her to go.

By the time I caught up to her, she was already at the door that led to the deck. I tried to grab her, but she slipped away. As soon as I got outside, the salty water that was strangely warm hit me square in the face. When I opened my eyes again, I wished I hadn't. The sky was black as midnight, and the rain was falling in impenetrable sheets. It was like walking through endless curtains that wouldn't let me see more than an inch ahead. The deck was nearly flooded, and the boat moved so violently I crouched down to crawl along the floor. One strong lurch threw me against the railing and pinned me there while I watched with terror as the waves devoured everything. I managed to pry myself away and grab hold of a wall. From there, I could hear screams above the roar of the storm. Ana stood at the deck railing, her hands clutching the rusty metal rails and screaming. If a wave broke on that side, it would swallow her like that whale in the Bible that swallowed someone. I tried to reach for her, but each time the boat turned and threw me backward again. Finally I lunged toward the railing and grabbed it. I made my way toward her, hand over hand. Ana sobbed, and her body shook as her fingers slowly lost their grip on the rail. I grabbed her by the wrists just as she let go. She looked at me in sheer panic and shut her mouth, paralyzed with fear.

A wave hit us hard, and the force of it drew us seaward, wedging me between two bars of the railing. Ana was dangling in my hands over the storming abyss below, and I didn't know how long I could hold her. I yanked with all my strength but couldn't pull her up. She was slipping, and no matter how hard I gripped her, it seemed her wrists were greased with oil.

"Calm down!" I yelled. She gathered her strength and tried to climb up, but she couldn't. She looked down and started flailing, which threw me further off balance and made me slip out farther over the railing.

"Stop moving!" I yelled.

I could see another wave coming, and I shut my eyes tight. I knew it was next to impossible for me to keep my grip on her after that wall of water hit the boat.

It rushed at me like a punch in the face. I tried to hold on to Ana, but she slipped out and, a second later, I was holding nothing but air. I kept telling myself it couldn't be.

"Hang on!" I heard someone yell from behind me. I looked to the side and saw one of the teachers holding my sister. He managed to drag her up and back onto the deck, then grabbed my shirt and yanked me free. We moved backward before another wave crashed against the boat, then grabbed hold of something jutting out from the wall. We ran toward the door, and the teacher slammed it shut once we were inside.

"What on earth were you doing out there? You nearly got yourselves killed!" the man said. He had dark skin and a black mustache, and he was completely drenched. I recognized him as one of the Mexicans traveling with our group, but I hadn't spoken with him before.

"I'm sorry. My sister—"

"Don't bother, kid. The important thing is I got you. Now get back to your cabin."

We thanked him over and over, then returned to the cabin, soaked and shivering. The lights were back on, and Isabel nearly attacked us when we came through the door. The three of us were a sopping, tangled mess of arms and tears while Manuel looked on, grinning. The storm raged for two more hours. It turned out that the captain had managed to avoid the hurricane itself and what we had endured was just a miniscule part of its fury, but it was enough to nearly sink the *Mexique*.

The first few days of June were much less eventful. We calmed down and tried to enjoy the trip. We explored every nook and cranny of the ship, invented a thousand games, and even played tricks on the teachers and other passengers. It wasn't easy to keep nearly five hundred children calm and quiet in a relatively small space for such a long time.

One morning in particular the heat had become unbearable. The day before, we had seen birds flying in the blue sky and guessed we couldn't be far from land. Early in the morning, right after breakfast, they announced that we would dock at the port in Havana. We put on our best clothes for the occasion, eager to walk on solid ground and get out of that huge metal shell.

"How do I look?" I asked Manuel. I had combed back my hair, which had grown out and usually hung over my eyes.

"Well, not bad for a gangster," Manuel snorted.

We heard cries and ran up to the deck. The sea was a glittering shade of turquoise, and we leaned our heads against the banister, mesmerized by the sublime beauty.

"So this is the first thing Columbus saw when he got here," Manuel mused.

"I've never seen anything so pretty," Ana said. She seemed much older now than she did just weeks ago in Madrid.

The blare of boats sounded. Several smaller vessels pulled up alongside us. Fishermen and crew members waved and shouted, "Long live the Spaniard children! Viva the Republic!"

We waved back with excitement. Our boat approached the harbor, and from our distance we could take in the whole bay and Cuba's beautiful capital city. It looked like a pretty silver cup with its yellows and grays. The lighthouse and a stone fortress were the first things we could see, then we made out church spires and the buildings of Old Havana.

When the boat docked, a crowd was waiting for us. They waved flags of the Republic and sang some of the songs that had become famous during the war. We lined up in formation to disembark, the teachers and monitors exiting first, anxious to step on solid ground. Then the captain, dressed in brilliant white, approached Don Genaro. "I'm so sorry, but you can't get off here. We're not authorized. Only a few passengers, the crew members, and those for whom Havana is their final destination can disembark."

"But the children . . ."

The captain shrugged. "I'm sorry."

We broke our lines. People kept cheering us from the dock, but several police cars drove up and pushed the crowd back, forming a wider security zone.

We sat on the floor of the deck right up against the railing, our legs swinging over the edge.

"Well, I sure hope the same thing doesn't happen in Mexico," Manuel said.

I was staring sadly at the beautiful city in the middle of the beautiful Caribbean Sea. I sighed and answered, "My dad told me there's a dictator in Cuba . . . Batista maybe? Anyway, he's probably not real thrilled at the idea of a big crowd cheering on a bunch of red children. For him we're the enemy."

We spent hours up on deck just looking at the city. Eventually we had lunch and then went back to the deck in the afternoon to watch as we departed the port. The captain and other crew members were arguing with some of the Mexican delegation, so we moved close enough to hear what they were saying.

"We've got to go," the captain said.

"But we cannot leave Ernesto Madero here," a member of the Mexican delegation said.

"He knew what time we were leaving, and we can't delay any longer. We've got to be in Veracruz tomorrow. The Mexican authorities will be waiting for us. Plus, the other passengers need to get to their destinations on time."

"I understand, Captain, but we can't just leave one of our own behind."

We crept away and huddled up in a group. Most of the Spaniard children knew Madero. He was the one who'd saved me and Ana in the storm.

"I'm sorry," the captain said with a shrug, lifting his hand to give the order to cast off.

We had been spreading the word among the children, and they all piled out onto the deck. We started chanting, "We want Madero! We want Madero!"

The crowd still gathered on the dock started echoing our chant. Then one of the children spied Madero among the policemen. For some reason they weren't allowing him back on the boat.

"Look, there he is!" the boy yelled, pointing to him.

We all started to point, and a few members of the Mexican

delegation went to talk with the police. The children grew quiet, waiting. Below, the policemen refused to let Madero board. Finally the captain intervened, and Madero was allowed up.

We all cheered with joy and sang victory songs while the young man made his way to the deck.

"What happened, Ernesto?" one of his colleagues asked.

"I couldn't find the password for boarding, and the police wouldn't let me on," he answered, still visibly upset.

The gangways were removed, and the ship slowly retreated from the port. The crowd waved goodbye while we shouted to them and sang at the top of our lungs. The thrill of their welcome made us feel like protagonists of our own destiny. Most times we were just puppets in the hands of chance and fate, lost and insignificant in the world. Yet for a few hours that day outside of Havana we mattered to some people. At the very least, our journey would throw into relief the suffering of Spaniard children and the terrible reality of the war we'd left behind.

Chapter 17

# Veracruz

Veracruz
June 7, 1937

The last day on the *Mexique* was exciting. We were so anxious about getting to Mexico we could hardly sleep. How would they greet us? Would they be as welcoming as the Cubans on the dock? Manuel lay awake on the pallet next to mine, staring up at the dark ceiling of our cabin and sweating. The other boys were asleep or at least seemed to be, based on the sounds of their breathing.

"You awake?" Manuel asked.

"Yeah." It came out like a nervous little squeak.

The arrival at Havana had made me realize how far away we were from our families. An ocean, two weeks of travel, and a war separated us. There was no way for us children to have any news of them. Not knowing anything about how my parents were almost felt as if they had ceased to exist. In Mexico our new life would be so different from our life in Spain that our memories would slowly fade away like dreams after a long night of sleep.

"There's not much farther to go. I'm dying to reach solid ground, but I actually thought the voyage would be a lot worse," Manuel said.

"Worse? The ship nearly sank!"

Manuel burst out laughing, and I couldn't help but cheer up.

"We can't get separated, you and me. I don't know what they've got planned for us, but let's stay together," he said.

"That's what I'm hoping for, friend. Sometimes you feel like the brother I never had. You know I adore Isabel and Ana, but a brother is different. Girls like other kinds of stuff. They're just different."

"I don't have any brothers or sisters, and it's hard for me—though I can't remember if I told you I did have a little sister. She was just a few months old, born at the beginning of the war. Some nights I was the one to take care of her because my parents were working in a weapons factory. One night the air raid alarms went off, and I got scared. I ran down to the basement that was our neighborhood's shelter, and five minutes later I realized I'd left my sister in the house. I tried to go get her, but they wouldn't let me out of the shelter. We could already hear the planes flying over the roofs and the whistling of the bombs. I curled up in a corner crying and praying nothing would happen to her. The hour in the shelter lasted forever. I dashed out of there as soon as it was clear. Smoke burned my eyes and everything smelled burned. I ran up the stairs two by two, and when I opened the door to our house . . ."

"What happened?" I whispered after a moment. Manuel had started to cry, reliving the horrible night. He turned to me, and though I couldn't see his face in the darkness, I heard his sobs and gasping breath.

"Half the house was gone. The electricity was out, of course, but the fires from the bombing gave enough light for me to see the gaping hole where a wall used to be. I went up to the hole and amid the debris could make out pieces of her crib. It was me, my fault. I killed her." He barely got the last few words out.

I got up from my pallet and sat beside him, putting my hand on his shoulder. His body shook with the effort to stop crying.

"You didn't drop that bomb. You tried to get her, but it was just too late."

"But how could I forget her? Lucía, that was her name. She was so cute. I'll never forget her."

I stretched out beside him and tried to relax, staring up in the dark toward the ceiling, hoping sleep would take us into its magical world where grief and sadness make no logical sense. I was thinking about friendship, about the indestructible ties of love between two people who until a certain time had been complete strangers, but who, somehow, on the solitary path of life, found another soul with whom to share the journey. Soon both Manuel and I were asleep.

❧

The excited cries of the other boys woke us. The promised land was in sight. We got dressed as fast as we could and ran up to the deck. We elbowed our way through to a spot at the railing and stared out at the infinite sea. At first, we could only barely make out a thin line sketched by the wind on the horizon. Little by little it grew to become a lovely brushstroke of intense green, then a thick slash of sand and jungle. While Mexico grew on the horizon, we felt slightly less orphaned in the world since there was a place for us there. We didn't know then that the kind, welcoming people would open their arms to us, not only the government or the president. The whole nation would open themselves to protect us and give us a new home.

An hour later, we were washed, dressed, and ready for the welcome party. This would be the end of the voyage. We had put on our best clothes and gone up to the deck with our caretakers, and we could see around fifty vessels of all shapes and sizes coming toward us by oar, by sail, or by motor. Most had wooden hulls, but others were a resplendent white metal. From these other boats, people cheered and greeted us in musical accents, almost as if singing. Their toasted brown skin made their bright smiles stand out even more as the wind ruffled their straw hats.

"Viva the Republic! Long live the Spaniard children!" they called.

It was thrilling to hear. This welcome was even bigger and more spectacular than in Havana. The throng at the port of Veracruz was so big that some were pushed into the water by the press of the crowd. Instead of getting angry, they just swam toward us, waving and calling out their good wishes.

"Children, line up!" Don Genaro called out.

We got into our two long lines. The youngest children went first, then the older ones, and then the teachers. The ship maneuvered into mooring position, and the sailors laid out the gangway. This time the children were the first passengers to disembark, carrying our blue suitcases and wiping our tears from all the excitement. We felt like ambassadors, but not necessarily from our country, because homeland for us was the warmth of our mother and the embrace of our father. We heard "The International" and instinctively raised our left fists and sang along with joy.

People crowded around us as soon as we got off the boat. Most were poor farmworkers or fishermen dressed in their finest garb. They handed out fruit and candy, and tearful women hugged and kissed us as if we were their long-lost children. Kind words showered down on us.

"May the Virgin of Guadalupe guard you, my child."

"Don't be afraid, you're home now."

"Viva the motherland!"

We made our way down the carpet of flowers covering the streets, drying our eyes and enjoying the flavors of the fruits our kindred had given us. They were so different, yet so similar to Spaniards. They were simple folk who had only affection to offer, which is exactly what we needed. We ate up their hugs and kisses, the food that nourishes children into adulthood far more than any king's banquet.

Farther ahead of me in line, my sisters seemed to be pleased with the attention. Mexican girls were putting flowers in the hair of the girls from Spain and draping flower garlands around their necks. Some were even giving away their rag dolls and the food they had with them for the day.

"Look at all of this!" Manuel said. I smiled at him, momentarily forgetting we were foreigners and that, when the euphoria of a welcome passes and monotony installs itself in the soul, loneliness returns in a rage to remind you of all you've lost.

We went through the tunnel of human affection and reached the train station, where nurses waited inside the train cars. We all got in and continued waving to the crowd, some of whom got close enough to the windows to keep giving us things. Off to one side, a group of men strummed guitars and sang happy songs as the train lurched forward.

I'll never forget that day or the love gushing out of generous hearts that gave even what they couldn't afford to make a few lost children happy. For me, Mexico isn't a landscape, nor is it a way of understanding the world. Mexico is the thousands of faces from that morning in Veracruz: the features all swimming together of children, women, men, and the elderly, the mass of long-suffering people who haven't forgotten that the greatest gift people can give is their love. That day I lost my identity but gained something I hadn't expected: another nation to call home.

# Chapter 18

# Mexico City

## Mexico City
### June 8, 1937

The first time I laid eyes on Mexico City it was through tears. For most of the trip since we'd left France, I had managed to hold back my crying, as had the rest of the older boys. But when we got off the train at Colonia Station, I couldn't take it anymore. Just a few days before we had been shaking under the bombing of Madrid, Barcelona, or Bilbao—children of war and suffering. Now, in the midst of that great city, we were little heroes, the unweaned cubs of the Republic—a wounded lioness defending herself from foes. We left the station crowded with people who had come to greet us and walked down streets packed with Mexicans hoping to see the little Spaniards. We were a battalion of miserable, needy children of poverty. We had left behind everything we had, which amounted to little materially but a great deal emotionally—mothers' kisses, grandparents' hugs, and fathers' hands on our shoulders when they returned home from work.

We were taken to the Sons of the Army School in San Julia. I never took my eyes off my sisters, who walked with their heads held high, proud to be the cause of so much fuss, though I could see them wiping tears away as well.

As we prepared to enter the schoolyard where President Cárdenas, his wife, and other officials were waiting for us, we heard an airplane overhead. Most of the Spaniard children crouched to the ground in fear. The younger ones screamed and cried, while we older kids ran to protect our younger siblings. The airplane was only dropping little colored pieces of paper to celebrate our arrival, but for us it was far from festive. The onlooking crowd grew upset seeing how the planes affected us. Yet soon they understood that this was no game for us, that it wasn't just a welcome party or a nice outing. We had managed to escape the war, but we still carried the war inside us. It tormented our young souls from within, and we were too young to understand that war's shadow would follow us forever.

The Francoists had achieved much more than pitting brother against brother. More than anything else, they had robbed us of our future and our inner peace. Our memories could be summed up by hunger, fear, and hatred. We would have to find a way to rid ourselves of them in order to survive.

Once we calmed down, we lined up again. President Cárdenas was a big man with bright eyes and a commanding presence. He greeted each of us with a joke, a hug, or a handshake.

"What's your name?" he asked, shaking my hand when it was my turn. I was so nervous I hesitated a moment before answering.

"Marco Alcalde, at your service. Viva the Republic!"

"Very good, boy. You're one of the oldest, so take care of these little ones for me. They've got to be strong and happy 'til they go home. The war will be over soon. Those fascists are complete cowards."

"Thank you, Mr. President," I said, in disbelief that he actually spoke with me.

"Call me Lázaro, like Jesus's friend. The one he raised from the dead." He ruffled my blond hair before moving on to the next child. He spoke to every one of us, giving candy to some or a hug to others, especially the ones who were crying. After that greeting, we knew we had a father in Mexico.

We were seated at large tables with Mexican children according to our ages. The president and his wife presided over the event and spent their time calling Spaniard children over to them to talk to them or give them gifts.

Manuel and I sat together, with two Mexican boys facing us. When they told us they were named Gaspar and Baltasar, we chuckled and asked what their names meant.

"We're brothers. Gaspar and Baltasar are two of the wise men." Seeing our puzzled expressions, Gaspar, the older of the two, asked, "You don't know who the wise men are?" He looked so much like his brother, with huge, dark eyes.

"No, we've never heard of them," Manuel said.

"They're the three kings who went to see Jesus and took him gifts when he was born. If you don't know who the wise men are, then who brings you gifts at Christmastime in Spain?" Gaspar asked, confused.

"Our parents. In my family, no king would dare bring us anything. We're Republicans," I explained, thinking that solved the matter.

Baltasar was not satisfied with my explanation. "I never knew there were kids who didn't know who the wise men are."

After the meal we were allowed to play for a while, and we learned that the Mexican children would be going with us to a place called

Morelia. We had no idea where that was and, even if they'd told us, we wouldn't have understood. Mexico was a completely foreign country to us.

Ana came up and asked me to help her find a bathroom. We walked through endless hallways until we found one, and I waited for her outside. When she came out, her eyes looked weary and sad.

"What's going on?" I asked, giving her a kiss on the cheek.

"Nothing . . . just that every time I feel a little happy, I also feel guilty. I can't feel happy while Mom and Dad are in so much danger. They're still in Spain, and the war around them is dangerous," she said.

"They know how to take care of themselves, and I'm sure we'll get news from them soon. Mom told me the government promised they could write us letters. Think of this like a really long vacation. The war will end soon, and then we'll go back. Promise me that you'll think of them often so as not to forget them. You're still small, and at your age, memories fade away. I'll help you always keep them present."

At that, Ana started crying again. "How could I forget them? They're the people I love most in this world!"

I put my hand on her shoulder, and we went back out to the schoolyard, where servants were clearing the tables. Manuel and I went up to the rooftop patio and looked out at the beautiful sunset over Mexico City. There was a slight chill in the air, and the rose-colored sky reminded us of Spain.

"Did you think Mexico would be this pretty?" he asked.

"To be honest, I hadn't thought much about what it would be like. I'd still rather be in Madrid, even if they drop bombs on me all day long. People don't want to leave their homeland. There's something that connects us to where we're from, and when we leave it behind, it rips out part of our heart. I'm always thinking of places like Cibeles Plaza, El Retiro Park, Casa de Campo, and Gran Vía. After all, they say Madrid is heaven . . ." I trailed off.

"I've never been to Madrid," Manuel said.

"When all of this is over, you should come visit me. I'll show you all around."

Manuel smiled at me, intuiting that such a day was a long way off. The world had gone mad. People were killing one another and dying for their ideals without a clue that the only worthwhile ideology is the one that makes all people brothers and sisters.

The next day we'd board a train for Morelia. Who knew how far it would be, but we'd already come halfway across the world to get there.

Part 3

# Morelia

Chapter 19

# A Provincial Town

Morelia
June 10, 1937

The next day, we went back to Colonia Station and boarded a very long train. We would spend the night in sleeping cars since we wouldn't get to Morelia 'til the next day. Manuel and I were once again placed with Gaspar and Baltasar. As we pulled out of Mexico City, we were surprised to see the landscape was much drier, yet still mysterious and different from what we knew at home.

Baltasar, the younger brother, asked us, "You want to go to the steam engine?" We nodded in response and started making our way through our train car, which was one of the last in the line. The monitors, teachers, and some nurses were in the caboose, though from time to time they made rounds to see if everything was all right. Most of the time we kids got to do pretty much whatever we wanted. We got to a freight car and then to the coal car, which was right next to the train's engine. There, a man stood with his back to us. His clothes were black with soot. He turned when he heard our noises.

"What are you doing here, boys? Passengers aren't allowed up here."

"Gil, leave the kids alone," said another man, who appeared to be the engineer. Gil was the fireman who fed the flames for the boiler.

We went up to the engine, and the engineer smiled at us. He pulled the train's whistle and showed us the controls. "We're not going fast. They've asked me to go slow and careful with you kids. You're like porcelain dolls for us," he explained. We learned his name was Gilberto Arellano and, together with Gil Hobart, they were volunteering their services to support the children from Spain.

"So what's Spain like?" Gilberto asked. His question took us off guard. Truth was, we didn't know. Manuel and I had hardly seen anything outside our respective cities, plus the route through France.

"Well, it's really different from here, but at the same time there's a lot that's the same. People are more serious, but everybody does get happier on holidays. The buildings are really old; it feels like the Romans must have built them forever ago. The poor people are really poor, and the rich people are really rich," I struggled to say. I wasn't very pleased with my description, but at that time I hadn't yet learned that the idea of a country is much greater than the sum of its characteristics. At its core, a nation is an idea, a way of living that's not easy to explain.

"That's the same way everywhere, kid. We've got a pretty good president right now, but the Spaniards left us a rotten heritage: poverty, inequality, hunger. Someday things will change. People have to live as brothers and sisters. That's why we offered to drive this route for you all. Our skin or eye color might be a little different, but the same red blood runs through our veins."

We spent a couple hours there in the engine car, and Gilberto and Gil shared their lunch with us. Then we headed back to our wagon. Though it wasn't late, we were all tired. The past few days had been so emotionally exhausting, we felt as if we'd been chopping wood or shoveling coal nonstop. The roller-coaster ride of experiences we'd been on for too long now had worn us down.

By the time we woke up, we were already close to Morelia. The train station was much more modest than the one in Mexico City, but it seemed the whole town turned out to greet us. The endless sea of humanity welcomed us with the same enthusiasm as the other crowds we'd come across in the Americas. Perhaps that's why the place made such a deep impression on us: the contrast between what the crowd's enthusiasm led us to expect—a palace or some spectacular dwelling full of luxurious furniture and comfortable rooms—and the much harsher reality of Morelia.

The governor, Gildardo Magaña, gave a welcome speech before we marched up the main avenue amid cheering and confetti. The streets felt oddly familiar to us. Some of the kids from Andalusia were excited because apparently the place looked a lot like Seville, with little villas and pretty tiled patios. We later learned the city was originally named Valladolid after a city in Spain, but the name had been changed to honor a local distinguished citizen who was crucial in winning Mexico's independence.

The city's leaders led us to two large buildings labeled The Spain–Mexico Industrial School. A spacious yard separated the buildings, which had served as a convent for nuns before the government refurbished it for us. The crowds stayed at the gate, and we children lined up in front of the director. From the outside, the buildings looked ominous, like prison cell blocks.

"Dear children—our Spaniard and Mexican boys and girls: My name is Lamberto Moreno, and this is the Spain–Mexico School. Our beloved country has opened its arms to you with true Mexican hospitality, even to those who, it must be acknowledged, represent the cruel oppression of colonialism. We Mexicans endured the severity of the Spanish empire, but despite this tortured past, we align ourselves as brothers with your Republic and its cause for freedom. We Mexicans have always earned what we have with hard work and tenacity. No one ever gave us anything for free and, therefore, no one will give you anything for free here either. You'll earn your bread with the sweat of your brow. We won't tolerate indolence, laziness, or miscreant behavior. You must set an example for Morelia and for your Mexican classmates. A guest must know how to behave when in someone else's home, and this is not your home. The girls will now go to that building and the boys to this one. You'll go in military orderliness. Disobedience will be punished. Think of this place as military quarters and of yourselves as young soldiers. Now, off to your barracks! You've each been assigned a bed, articles for personal cleanliness, and food. You'll have free time until lunch and will then help clean the rooms before supper. Classes will officially begin tomorrow."

Several of the children began to complain, especially the older boys. Manuel and I tried to stay out of it, but the director's words grew more and more insulting: "You colonists are a bunch of ingrates! If I could I'd slice open my veins and expunge every drop of Spanish blood in my body. You're an abominable race."

The older boys started throwing anything they could find at the director and the teachers. The younger ones began to scream, and it was total chaos. I was terrified of what a man like that—one who nursed such an obvious hatred for Spaniards—would do to us. Lamberto Moreno had truly shocked us. Everywhere else we'd been, the Mexican people's deep love had been palpable through their warm embraces, cheers, and gifts. But this man was to be our leader, and he was treating us like prisoners.

The older boys kept throwing things at the teachers, especially the boys from San Sebastián in Basque Country. They would turn out to be a bunch of thugs who tried to impose their own rules on the school and rarely showed up for classes or workshops. They would only make appearances at mealtime. And at that point the director, Moreno, just fixed a schedule to the doorway and made himself scarce.

Still, we had no option but to obey, and boys began to drift toward our building. I waved goodbye to Ana and Isabel, distraught at having to leave them but helpless to do anything about it. The littlest kids were the worst off after the director's brusque introduction to our new residence. They began begging and crying to go back home.

Walking into our building felt like walking through the remains of a shipwreck. The walls were damp and peeling, the floors scratched and dirty, and the remains of rats lingered everywhere we looked. From the looks of things, we'd all be covered in fleas and bedbugs in no time.

The second floor held long rooms with beds. At least the beds and the blankets looked new. Manuel and I picked out two along the aisle. We were leery of some of the boys we'd be sharing the dorm with, especially the ones who wasted no time in establishing themselves as bullies. Some of them I'd hardly seen since the boat ride, but they did their best to make our stay in Morelia unbearable.

We all went downstairs on time for dinner. Despite the fights between boys and the exasperation of the teachers and the director, we could all agree that food was sacred. Manuel and I sat at a table as close to my sisters as we could and waited impatiently for whatever had been prepared for us.

A few women came out of the kitchen and asked if we liked tortillas. We all answered a hearty affirmative. We hadn't had our customary potato and onion Spanish tortilla since before the war, as potatoes and eggs were difficult to come by. The smiling women returned from the kitchen and put little baskets on the table, as well as bowls of beans, salsas, beef strips, and other things we'd never seen. When we opened the baskets and saw what looked like stacks of thin, round pieces of paper, we were puzzled. They were dry and tasteless.

"Excuse me," I asked one of the ladies serving us. "What are these?"

"They're tortillas," she answered, looking at me in disbelief. She must have assumed I was playing a joke.

"Tortillas? But where are the eggs and the potatoes?" I asked, turning the thing over in my hand. The grumbling all around the tables turned into a chant: "We want Spanish tortilla!"

One of the cooks frowned. "Well, we don't have anything like that."

Someone threw one of the flimsy things they called tortillas up in the air, and it landed on another kid's face. Then we all started throwing them up and seeing how far they would go, spinning in the air. Our monitors were helpless to stop the chaos. "Stop it, Spaniards!" one of them yelled.

Eventually we noticed that the Mexican kids with us, who were clearly from poor families and had probably never seen so much food at once, were quietly piling things onto the little round discs and shoving them down their throats. Some of us were hungry enough to follow their lead.

Several of my classmates went to bed that night without having touched their supper. That didn't stop them from wreaking havoc and throwing or breaking whatever they could find. After the euphoria of our arrival and the effusive welcome from the politicians and the Mexican people, we went to bed with the disquieting sense that things were not all right. It would not take us long to figure out that, in the end, we had been abandoned to fate.

Chapter 20

# The Incident

Morelia
June 18, 1937

That first night at the Spain–Mexico School was terrible. We could hear bats circling in the high ceilings and rats scurrying over the floors and under our beds. Some of the older kids were rough with the younger or weaker ones, but I made it to the next day unscathed. It wasn't too cold, and we were so exhausted that sleep vanquished us without a fight despite our being in a new, eerie place.

We eventually got used to the military routines of the school. The six o'clock bugle call announced it was time to wake. We dressed and marched in military formation down the lane to the girls' building, where the dining hall was located. Then we went to class, where they called roll. Some of the kids skipped classes, but they were never punished. The teachers and monitors turned a blind eye to the offenses of some of the older boys.

We had recess midmorning and then more classes before lunch. Not even the bullies skipped lunch, which annoyed the rest of us, especially the Mexican kids, who didn't have the cheek that most of us had developed as a survival tactic during the war.

All day long we navigated our lives in an effort to evade the bullies, whether by avoiding the spots where they typically hung out or traveling in groups to better defend ourselves. They would steal from and rough up anyone they could catch off guard. The director was indifferent to the point of seeming to enjoy the harm inflicted by the troublemakers.

Thankfully, the assistant director turned out to be a kind person we could trust. Miguel Escalona Godínez was a former army major who treated us with respect and affection. We all called him Major Godínez.

After lunch we went to the workshops in our building, and after a light dinner at six o'clock we had free time until nine.

At first, we were hesitant to leave the school grounds, afraid of what we might find outside. But as the days went by, we grew more confident and started venturing out to explore the town. People received us warmly, though the first conflicts were not long in coming.

Morelia's citizens were not used to children like us. The folk songs we belted out were sprinkled with colorful language, and some of the rascals and troublemakers would steal anything they could get away with. But the worst was yet to come.

That afternoon we went out like we'd been doing the last few days, and we headed down the main street, greeting people. Most of the townsfolk were generous and would give us coins or fruit as we passed by, which we would often exchange for food to make up for the meager, unappetizing fare at school. Adolescents never seem to get full, and we were always hungry.

Manuel and I were walking by one of the churches when a group of the most troublesome Spaniard boys started singing obscene ditties to one of the priests on his way into the church. Offended, the man turned and rebuked the kids. "Is this how you were raised? Have you no shame?"

"Don't start with our parents, old geezer," said the one we called Mr. Handsome because of how much time he spent in front of the mirror. He was one of the worst in our group.

"They should send you all back to your country. You're a bunch of rotten apples!" The priest slipped inside the building, and Mr. Handsome launched a rock that hit the door just as the priest shut it tight.

"You son of a—" Mr. Handsome started, but I interrupted him, shocked at his audacity.

"What are you doing?" I demanded.

"Stay out of this, Madrid," he jeered.

Manuel grabbed me by the arm and dragged me back. The boys all began picking up rocks and lobbing them at the church's stained-glass windows, swearing and laughing like maniacs. For them, the Catholic Church was the enemy, and they could not understand the religiosity of the Mexicans.

The windows shattered under the onslaught, the fragments scattering over the street in a rain of colors. Inside the church building, praying women began to scream.

Mr. Handsome ran toward the building, flung open the door, and together with his cronies started throwing rocks at the wooden statues. Once satisfied with their mess, they ran out and toward another church building, calling to another group of Spaniard boys to join them.

"Let's get back to the school," Manuel said, pulling on my sleeve.

"But we have to tell the police!" I was worried. If we were accused of destroying churches a few days after arriving in the town, I didn't know how long Mexico would put up with us. I had gotten my hands on a newspaper a couple days earlier and had read about how things were going in Spain. The fascists kept advancing, and from all indications, the war would last another year or two.

"But they'll blame us for what's happened," Manuel said.

I had made up my mind to go find the police when we saw the rabble-rousers headed straight toward us with dozens of angry Mexicans on their heels. We didn't think twice. We ran back to the school as fast as we could and slammed and bolted the gate shut as soon as all the Spaniards were inside. From our cover inside the main building, we could hear the wooden gate creaking and Morelia's townsfolk shouting for the vandals to come out.

Major Godínez found us hiding in our room and asked what had happened. I ran through the situation, and he went out to speak to his countrymen. First, he asked them to calm down, and then he opened the gate. We crouched down behind the windows so they wouldn't see us.

One of the Mexicans said, "These Spaniard children are little devils!"

"They're just children," Major Godínez said, "and things are different in Spain. Over there, the church is against the Republic, just like it was here during the revolution. This won't happen again." His pudgy, friendly demeanor didn't quite divert the rage of the angry parishioners of the vandalized churches.

While Major Godínez tried to calm down the crowd, one of the teachers called the police to come protect the school. Soon the police had cordoned off the buildings and asked the crowd to disperse.

People trickled away, but for several days we weren't allowed to leave the school grounds, and police were stationed on guard.

❧

Life in Morelia eventually fell into a routine. Things had calmed down after the incident with the vandalized church, though the bullies still had free rein at school. Manuel and I had joined forces with some Asturian boys in an effort to protect some of the Mexican students, especially Gaspar and Baltasar, who had become our good friends.

One morning a few weeks after the church incident we heard screams coming from the yard outside. It was the voice of Saturnino, one of the guards in charge of opening and shutting the gate.

Manuel turned to me. "Did you hear that?"

We dashed down the stairs and out to the yard. Saturnino was bent over next to the gate, and a child's body lay beside him. We ran to him and found little Paquito, who was motionless.

We looked at his blackened body. Some of his hair was missing, and his face was contorted in frozen pain.

"What happened?" we asked Saturnino.

"I don't know," he answered in a daze. Then we heard voices on the other side of the gate.

"Open the gate!" we insisted. Saturnino hesitated for a moment, then unlatched the lock and pulled back the wooden doors. Four trembling girls stared at us for a moment, then threw themselves into our arms, sobbing.

"What happened?" we asked.

"We don't know," said Paquito's younger sister. "Yesterday we went to the movies, and we got back a little late. We knocked at the gate, but nobody answered. We were scared, so we beat and kicked at the gate, but the guard told us the gate was shut and he couldn't open it after hours. Paquito started climbing the wall to jump over so he could open it up himself. We saw him get to the top and jump, but then we heard a scream and saw a big spark." She dissolved into tears. Paquito was her only sibling, and now she was truly alone in the world. Her friends hugged her while dozens of kids ran out of the building and gathered around the corpse.

Lamberto Moreno, the director, showed up half dressed. When he saw the boy's scorched body, he started screaming like a madman. "Bloody Spaniards! Curse my luck! Get away from here, all of you! Back to your dorms!"

We headed back inside with our heads hung low. As I sank down onto my bunk, I was grateful my sisters hadn't been there to see the body.

"Why did they bring us here anyway?" Manuel demanded, fuming.

"To kill us," one of the Asturians snapped.

I wanted to cheer them up, to assure them it would all work out, but nobody had the energy for that. I was also wondering what we were doing on the other side of the world where nobody cared enough to take care of us. In Spain, despite the war and the hunger, at least our parents loved us and would never have allowed something like what happened to Paquito to occur.

That day lasted forever, and nobody got much sleep that night. Early the next morning would be the burial. Four of Paquito's friends carried his white coffin down the streets of Morelia while the rest of us followed in silence. The little kids cried openly, but we older ones swallowed back our tears in fury and fear.

The funeral was short and sterile, and we clamped our mouths shut in a pact of silent suffering. For the first time since our journey had begun, we realized that something had linked us all together in a bond that could never be broken. We belonged to the army of the defenseless, the poor Children of Morelia. Yet we were eager for justice. We knew who was guilty of Paquito's death: the director and his henchmen who from the very start had treated us with indifference or outright contempt.

When the unemotional funeral was over, the gravediggers lowered the body of our classmate into the grave. With each shovelful, the sound of dirt hitting the newly hewn wood concentrated our indignation. One of the older boys couldn't hold it in anymore and started yelling at Moreno. He grabbed a rock and threw it at the director, though he missed. Moreno stared at him, then took off running toward the church. The rest of the teachers followed their leader even as more and more children picked up rocks to throw. The adults shut themselves inside the church before the onslaught, but we pushed our way inside the church and gave free rein to our pent-up fury, destroying everything we could touch. I couldn't think straight. I had never given my rage such complete control over my body. It slowly worked its way out in that frenetic, uncontrolled mob.

Moreno managed to escape and headed back toward the school. We followed and cornered him along with several other caretakers and cooks who had done nothing but disparage us for the past weeks. One of the adults, Cabanillas, screamed from the other side of the door they were hiding behind that we lowlifes had gotten what we deserved.

The police showed up to rescue the director and his assistants, who filed out of the school with security. That was the only good thing to come from the sad death of our classmate. We had begun 1937 in Spain with our families, but we now found ourselves in a foreign country, under the care of malicious, lazy people who had stolen the money the Mexican government had set aside for our upkeep.

I went and found my sisters in one of the rooms in the girls' building. They looked as sad as the day we said goodbye to Mom in Bordeaux. I embraced them both, hoping that at least the warmth of my body could help pull them out of this terrible day's gloom. Isabel's eyes begged for help, and that night I swore we'd go back to Spain. I wanted to die in our land, next to the people we loved most in the world. It didn't matter how long it took us or how awful the journey might be. Nothing could keep us apart from our parents. We would overcome every obstacle along the way because we were fueled by the greatest strength a human being can experience: the invincible power of love.

# Chapter 21

# The Story of a Journey

Morelia

January 6, 1938

In the months after our arrival, some children went to live with family members who were already living in Mexico. Others went to live with extended family in Mexico or were sent to Mexico City because they were too old for the program.

The winter days got cooler. Though the temperature in that region of the country nearly always hovered around 68 degrees, some mornings were chilly. Christmas was coming, and we were all feeling glum. We hadn't heard from our parents, and the prospect of celebrating Christmas in a faraway place seemed dismal. Even though we didn't celebrate like the Catholics, we still were used to spending time with our families and enjoying a special meal.

Christmas came and went without much ado. Then twelve days later, the magic night when mythical beings bring presents to girls and boys was one of the saddest nights in Morelia. In Spain, most of us hadn't celebrated the arrival of the magi—also known as the three wise men, or the three kings. In many places in Spain, the event was no longer commemorated, and the people of Madrid substituted three magic queens for the kings, as a joke on Christianity.

Manuel, some of my friends, and I had gathered some items together to surprise the younger kids, including my sisters. We'd hidden our loot in one of the workshops, and when everyone else went to sleep, we retrieved our gifts and left them beside the little boys' shoes. Then some of the older girls did the same for the younger girls. After setting out all the presents, we went to our bunks.

"What are you thinking about?" Manuel asked me.

"I don't know. This just isn't at all what I'd imagined. Things are going from bad to worse."

"I heard they're bringing us a new director."

I sighed. "I hope so too, but don't count on it being any better."

We slept so deeply that we didn't wake up 'til we heard the little kids screaming. We thought they were screaming with delight, so we ran toward their room, but soon we could tell they were not screaming for joy. Manuel and I looked at each other in disbelief. What had happened? We figured the older boys had been messing with us again. The little kids carried on with their tears. As Manuel and I went toward them, one little boy named Miguel ran up and threw himself into my arms.

"What's going on?" I asked.

"Our shoes!" he moaned, pointing.

We stepped toward the shoes and were repulsed by the stench. They boys' shoes were filled with feces. Someone had spent the night stealing their presents and leaving behind a mess.

"This is the last straw!" I roared.

"What are you going to do?" Manuel sounded worried.

I dashed back to our dorm. Five of the big bullies were roaring with laughter at the cries of the poor children. I stood to my full height in front of the ringleader and stared into his face from a distance of mere inches.

"What's eating your lunch, Madrid? Did the wise men forget to leave you a present? I thought the reds didn't believe that garbage."

"You monsters! How could you do that to those little kids after everything they've been through? What kind of savage beasts are you?" I raged.

"The kind that'll rip your guts out if you don't get off our backs. At least we can have a bit of fun. Those little snots have to learn what life is really like since Mommy and Daddy aren't here to spoil them anymore."

I balled my hands up and lunged at the ringleader's neck. We fell to the ground, and he easily pinned me, raining his fists down on my face. Manuel shoved him back and tackled him, while the Asturians and the two Mexican brothers went after the rest. As I struggled to my feet, I smiled through my blackening eye. The jerks got what was coming to them for once.

Eventually we heard the approaching footsteps of adults. We must have really been making a ruckus for them to care enough to investigate.

After they separated us, my friends and I went outside, pleased at finally having stood up to the bullies. At least they would know from then on that they couldn't get away with cruelty without tasting a bit of their own medicine.

# Chapter 22

# Costly Change

Morelia
January 10, 1938

A few days after the magi incident, the school's new director arrived. We didn't have much to lose. After the horrible experience with Moreno, we assumed anyone could do better. But, to our surprise, our circumstances worsened. The new director showed up incognito a few days after Three Kings Day and interviewed some children under the guise of being a newspaper reporter. He was trying to discover what really happened at the school. The next day he revealed his actual identity, to the consternation of the students who'd talked about the cruelty and mistreatment by the previous director.

His name was Reyes Pérez, and he was relentless. From the start, he wanted to impose military-style discipline in both buildings. I've never liked military discipline or people barking commands at me. Things would've worked much better in the school if they'd thought about solidarity and basic principles for getting along. Instead, they focused on authority.

Reyes Pérez showed up in a uniform, high black boots, and a khaki combat jacket. He didn't have a soldier's build, but he made up for it with his demeanor.

"Boys and girls from the Motherland," he began, "your first six months in Mexico have been difficult, but things are about to change. The first thing I can promise is that you'll be able to write your parents. I'm aware that up to now they've not been able to contact you, but I'll ask for just a little more of your patience. Tomorrow we'll gather up the letters you want to write, and we hope that within two months you'll receive an answer. The food, cleanliness, and upkeep of our campus will improve. We plan to disinfect everything, get organized, and help you become useful men and women. When you return to Spain, you'll take back to your great nation the knowledge you acquire here to help the Republic put itself back together after the war."

His words cheered us. Despite what adults often think, adolescents appreciate discipline and clear rules and boundaries on their lives. Children raised in anarchy become insecure, fickle, unhappy adults. What we didn't yet understand was that we would pay for these school improvements through suffering.

"To maintain order and discipline, and to be able to work better together," Reyes Pérez continued, "we'll adopt a hierarchy. I've chosen the most capable students from among you, those who demonstrate leadership qualities. They will receive a higher rank, and the rest of the students will obey them as if I myself were giving the commands. Do you understand?"

We nodded and answered in unison, "Yes, sir!"

Then the director named the students who would be our leaders, and he pinned badges on them so we would recognize their new roles. I was dismayed to see that most of the students named were the wretched bullies I'd had run-ins with on several occasions: Mr. Handsome, Luis, and others who were even worse. Such were the ones the new director handpicked to impart order. Most of the children in the "shock troops," as Reyes Pérez called them, were the ones who threatened the other students, harassed the girls, skipped class, and stole things in town. Among the teachers, Reyes Pérez selected a group of communists as hardline as himself.

The last student's name to be called for the shock troops was my own, which dumbfounded me. Perhaps he had heard rumors of my fight with the bullies on Three Kings Day.

Contrary to our initial hopes, the changes instituted at school only made things worse. It's true that food and hygiene improved and that our schedule ran like clockwork, but these came at a price. The school became an environment of terror because the bullies could and did do anything they wanted. I was a brake on their train, but when I wasn't around, they had their way with the others.

That afternoon of Reyes Pérez's initial speech, we got busy writing letters to our families. I went to look for Isabel and Ana, and we sat under a tree to write.

At first, we didn't know what to say. So many things had happened, and we didn't know what to tell them and what to leave out. We didn't want them to worry even more than they likely already did.

"What are you saying?" Ana asked me. She'd only jotted down a couple lines.

"Want me to read it out loud?" I asked. They nodded, so I leaned over the yellow paper and studied my fine, nearly perfect script.

Dear Mom and Dad,

I hope you're both healthy and safe. We haven't had news of you in six months, and we really hope you're all right. We don't know what is happening in Spain. We don't get much outside news here.

The trip to Mexico was pretty calm. Though it isn't easy crossing the sea in a boat, we got to Cuba without any major catastrophes, and the people there welcomed us enthusiastically and affectionately. From there we went on to the port of Veracruz.

The Mexicans received us with open arms. They gave us everything they had, especially their kindness. The people and the climate on this side of the world are very warm. They're always smiling and happy, and they like to sing and celebrate, though they take more care with their language than we do.

The thing we liked most when we got to Mexico was the fruit. It's like ours but tastes so much better. Mexican food is pretty spicy, and it's really different from what we eat in Spain. We don't care for it much, but we're getting used to it.

We live in Morelia, which is a small inland city. It's a calm little town. The people are kind and treat us well, though we've had a few run-ins with the Catholics. They don't like our revolutionary songs and can't understand why we don't go to Mass.

Here at the school, boys and girls are in separate groups, and some Mexican kids from poor families attend the school too. Every day we have classes, and in the afternoon we have workshops to learn a trade. Dad, I'm in the printing workshop, so I can help you at the printing press when we get back to Spain. Isabel and Ana are in the sewing workshop, so you might receive some sewn presents when we see you next!

We miss you terribly, and we love you so much. It's really sad that we needed an ocean between us to figure out that you two are what's most important in our life. You brought us into the world, and your love and affection have made us full human beings. There's so much we miss, but what we really long for are your hugs and kisses.

I'd give anything to see you again, to sit at your feet and listen to the family stories you always like to tell. I remember your smiles, and—I don't know why—but I picture you dancing at Verbena de la Paloma. Dad always gets that happy look on his face when words can't express how content he is. And you, Mom, are smiling in a way that could calm the worst hurricane—something we know a little about now, but that's another story!

The hardest part about being separated is knowing that each day away from you is a day lost. We hope to be with you again. That will be the happiest day of our lives. We miss you so much.

> Sending you big kisses and
> long hugs,
> Your son who loves you forever,
> Marco Alcalde

When I looked up, Isabel was cradling Ana in her lap, and their tear-filled eyes reminded me of the blue skies of Madrid. I missed my country. But what I really missed was my mother calling us to breakfast before school, my father's smoker's cough, our family suppers, my grandmother's cooking, the flowers my mother would put in a vase in the living room in springtime, the cold, the heat, and the streets of my home city.

"Come on," I encouraged them. "Let's finish your letters too."

Isabel got to writing, and I helped Ana with her message. Then we sealed the letters in their envelopes, and I walked back to my building. Later that day I took them to the director's office and left them on the table. I was about to leave when I heard a voice behind me.

"Marco. Your name is Marco, right?"

"Yes, sir, Director."

"I hope you are honorably fulfilling the duties entrusted to you. I've been watching you, and I see you have natural leadership gifts. That's a good thing, but don't stray from the path. I'll have my eye on you. I'm the only one you need to obey, so if you don't question my authority, everything will be fine. The war in Spain seems to be at a standstill. You won't be going home anytime soon, so just follow the rules and enjoy your stay in Mexico as best you can."

"Yes, sir, Director."

Reyes Pérez wasn't a bad man, but he had a different way of understanding the world than I did. For him, life needed to be controlled down to the smallest detail. People had to obey and not ask questions. The world he believed in was a military barracks, one in which everything had a time and place. He dreamed of a golden prison to show the world what he could do with his undisciplined, rebellious Spaniards. He never comprehended our pain, never tried to see what life was like from our perspective—so he never really understood us. I came to understand that this man had a mission: return the children left in his care back to Spain, no matter what happened in the meantime.

Chapter 23

# Family

Morelia
March 20, 1938

O ne free afternoon, my friends and I went walking around the town with my sisters. We needed to escape school for a bit, get out of the environment of increasing pressure. We'd never felt at home on campus, but since Reyes Pérez arrived, the military order he'd imposed felt unbearable.

Every time we would wander around town, we would run into a kind, older couple who greeted us warmly. Their names were Octavio and Soledad Ponce.

"Hello, children. How are you today?" Mr. Ponce asked us when we saw them.

Manuel greeted them in return. He had adapted better than I had to life in Mexico, and it was evident even in the slightly Mexican accent he had acquired. I was grateful this country had received me, but I was counting down the days to get out and return to my family. I never doubted I'd be going back home. It was different for Manuel.

"We've got some treats for you," Mrs. Ponce said, beckoning us back to their house. It was small and sparse, but they always had something for the children from the school.

"How are your parents?" Mr. Ponce asked Gaspar and Baltasar.

"Doing well, thank the Lord. We're hoping to get to see them this summer," Gaspar answered. Unless they were orphans, the Mexican students went home for holidays and often received letters.

We all sat around their small round table, and Mr. Ponce poured lemonade. "Surely these dear little ladies will want something to drink?"

Isabel and Ana glanced at me for approval before drinking. They didn't want to seem rude, but sweets and lemonade were an outrageous delicacy compared to what we were used to eating at school. When I nodded, they drank gratefully.

Our clothes were in bad shape and no longer fit. Since we'd arrived, we'd only been given a shirt and a pair of pants. Our shoes were worn-out, and our feet got wet when it rained.

"Why don't they buy clothes for you?" Mrs. Ponce asked. "I'm sure President Cárdenas is unaware of all this."

"Out of sight, out of mind," I answered. "I'm sure the president trusts the people in charge of our care, but the money intended for the school is winding up in someone's pocket, not to mention the proceeds from everything we make in workshop."

"No good, no good," Mrs. Ponce muttered with a tsk.

"Do you know how the war's going in Spain?" I asked Mr. Ponce. He was our best source of news, informed by what he heard on the radio or in the cantina.

"The Francoists are advancing through Aragon."

"Aragon?!" I exclaimed. If they took over Aragon, Catalonia would be next to fall.

"Is that bad?" Ana asked. She was growing like a weed, and as the days went by, she seemed to remember less and less of our parents.

"Yes, the Republic is constantly losing ground," Isabel explained in a huff, furious at having to stay longer in Mexico.

We finished eating our snack and then said goodbye to our kind hosts.

"I'll have something else for you in a few days," Mrs. Ponce said. "You're too skinny, the whole lot of you."

We hugged her, and she held us tight, trying to press love into us amid our desert of affection. Simple touch was one of the things we missed the most. I tried to be affectionate with Isabel and Ana, but we hardly saw one another during the day. Mealtimes and the occasional free afternoon were our only chances to be together. My sisters were still close, which was fortunate, but I felt more and more left behind.

One thing I noticed about Morelia was that people kept their distance from one another. Sometimes when we played soccer and someone scored a goal, we would hug in celebration—but otherwise, the Spaniard students would go weeks without any physical touch. This lack only aggravated our loneliness and sadness.

Orphanhood is the worst kind of separation. Parents use hugs and expressions of affection to make their children feel as if they belong somewhere. Knowing you're loved helps you feel like you matter. But in Morelia, we went without such family connection—and friendships with classmates could not replace it.

After our snack with the Ponces, we dragged our feet all the way back to school, having no reason to hurry back. But then we saw a commotion in front of the boys' building and ran toward it. A man was shouting out names and delivering letters to our classmates.

"Letters from Spain!" Ana shrieked, jumping up and down.

We threw ourselves into the crowd and waited with desperation for our names to be called. When kids received letters, they would go off by themselves to read them in private. As we waited, the group slowly dwindled.

Minutes later, Manuel's name was called. My friend ran up to the mailman, grabbed the letter, and pressed it against his chest in excitement.

"Lucky duck!" I said, truly happy for him, but discouraged that neither my sisters nor I had been called.

Finally, the mailman announced, "Marco, Isabel, and Ana Alcalde!"

Ana took the letter, and we huddled up near the stairs.

"Who should open it?" Ana asked, holding the precious envelope out.

"You do it, go ahead," Isabel snapped, clearly trying to hold back tears.

Ana opened the envelope carefully, took out several sheets of paper folded up together, and started reading aloud. She stumbled over the words so much that eventually Isabel snatched the papers and started to read.

Madrid
February 15, 1938

Dear children,

Receiving your letters has restored the joy I lost that sad day in Bordeaux. Since then I haven't laughed, enjoyed life, or even had one peaceful day. When a mother goes away from her children, a hot iron jabs into her stomach and turns her inside out, and her heart nearly stops.

We're still living in our same building. Thankfully it's managed to escape the bombs. I'm not going to lie to you: Things in Madrid are a little worse each day. That's why, in my heart, I really believe it's better for you three to be in Mexico. I will never be able to thank those people enough for receiving you. It's quite a challenge to find anything to eat here, and the winter is just merciless. We can't heat our homes, and we head out at dawn every day for the shelters.

Many have fled the city. Franco's troops are eager to destroy the capital, but for some reason we can't understand, they aren't attacking yet.

I've begged your father to let us go to Valencia, but he doesn't want to abandon his comrades. He's not at the Prado Museum anymore. Now he's a guard at one of the political prisons. He comes home with atrocious stories every day, but at least he's trying to do good in the midst of so much evil and horror.

I'm so relieved you made it to Mexico safely. It must be so pretty there, though I bet you miss things here at home as well. Especially our food—our green beans and potato tortillas—but I assure you that the food in Mexico is better! We have not seen fresh vegetables or tortillas in such a long time. The best we can hope for is a bit of rice, lentils full of weevils, and old potatoes.

The war isn't going well, but it must end someday. Then we'll all be together again.

Now I truly do know that happiness is being together, no matter what we've got or what we do. Happiness is about seeing each other's faces, being able to hug and kiss each other. For me, that's the only real source of joy and peace.

I love the three of you with all my heart. This separation feels like it's killing me, but I know it's better for you to be away from the war and the hunger. I don't know what'll be left of Spain after the war, but my heart trembles at all the suffering and pain.

Your father sends oodles of hugs and kisses. You should've seen his face as he pored over your letters! He was like a boy with a new toy on Christmas. Those eyes of his that have seen so much pain were overflowing with hope again.

It grieves me that you three have had to learn at such a young age how cruel the world is. Sometimes parents don't know if our job is to prepare our kids to face the world or to protect them from it. I guess at the core it's both at once, but right now I feel like I cannot do either.

Little Ana, my princess, I love you beyond words. I know you're growing up to be a beautiful young lady. I can't cradle you in my arms anymore, but you'll always have a place under my wings. I love you, my child.

My Isabelita, the sweet child who's becoming a woman. There are so many things I wish I could explain to you before you have to discover them on your own. Becoming a woman means moving on from the child you used to be and grieving the golden-haired little beauty with braids you once were, always smiling and happy. Growing up involves heartache, but when you become a woman, you'll know that we have a gift men can't even fathom, a tenderness that makes us invincible, an unconditional love for those who come from within us. A mother's soul is divided up into different bodies, and a mother's sons and daughters forever remain her babies. Teach your sister the things I haven't been able to show you. I love you, my darling.

My dear son, what can I say to you? You're the son every mother dreams of. You're good, attentive, helpful, and obedient. You possess a huge, noble heart, and you'll always be my boy. You're the one who inaugurated me into the club of motherhood and helped me understand that nothing is greater in this world than the gift of life. Live worthy of the legacy your father and I have left you. Be honorable and good, even though you're surrounded by evil and greed in this world. Take care of your sisters and give them the love that I can't. Teach them how nothing is more valuable than family. I love you, my little prince. Don't let life change you. You have the power to change things and to cherish hope. I love you with all my strength.

You will never stop being my children!

We'll see you soon.

Your loving parents,

Francisco and Amparo

The letter had a strange effect on us. While it encouraged us to forge ahead, it also made us feel lonely, vulnerable, and sad. The ground fell out from under us. Knowing we were so well-loved restored our individuality, our unique identity, which had grown blurry amid the multitude of disinherited children and cold, distant caretakers. Feeling lonely showed us that, without our family, we were little more than cut flowers whose beauty and fragrance fades.

We cried and hugged one another, feeling our mother's warmth in our embraces despite the distance. Manuel came over, disoriented, staring blankly into an inscrutable abyss at his feet. I understood then that his letter held bad news, and I stood to put my arms around him.

# Chapter 24

# The Punishment

Morelia
May 4, 1938

Manuel changed completely after that first batch of letters. He told me the letter he received was from his aunt, the one who'd taken care of him after his mother abandoned him. The aunt said she'd had word that Manuel's father, who had been captured by the fascists in Granada, was dead. Manuel had been expecting to learn of his father's execution, but he hadn't expected what came next: his beloved grandparents, his father's parents, had also been killed by the fascists when a jealous neighbor accused them of being communists. Manuel had been hoping to live with them if he ever returned to Spain. And his aunt, who had taken him in before, had resorted to a brothel and would no longer be able to care for him. Manuel was all alone in the world, and in a way, he never recovered.

A few days later, he started avoiding me and spending time with the worst students at school. He began stealing from the little ones, getting in trouble with the teachers, and skipping class. I felt the person who'd been my best friend since the start of that difficult journey had ceased to exist. I took refuge in my sisters, but things weren't the same. Friendship is one of the few things we choose in life, and it can get us through the worst of times. And it seemed my best friend had left me for good.

The arrival of spring didn't improve things much at school. The director maintained his ironfisted discipline and sent some kids to live with people in town. Even though he was a communist, he had placed some of the older girls at a convent in Morelia, and he continued to rely on the bullies to impose his reign of terror among the students.

We had almost been in Mexico a full year. It had dragged on endlessly for me and felt much longer than twelve months.

One day in May, it was my turn to oversee the kitchen and the pantry. Some thefts had occurred, and the director was furious. I wasn't all that surprised because we were still not being fed enough, and the food quality was poor.

While I made my rounds that afternoon, I heard a noise. I flipped on the light and went down the hallway between the kitchen and the pantry. Once there, I could hear voices. I got close and saw three boys holding cans and some sausages.

"Can I ask what you're doing?" I questioned.

"Stay out of this, Madrid. You didn't see a thing, you hear?" Luis threatened.

"If anything's missing from the pantry, they'll blame me. So drop everything right now!" I ordered. The director took such care of them, but these bullies took any chance available to do as they pleased.

The three boys surrounded me, and one threw a punch. I defended myself as best I could, but it was impossible once all three boys teamed together. Luis prodded the other two on while he went back to putting food in their sack. They threw me to the ground, kicking my stomach and kidneys. I screamed in desperation, afraid they really would kill me. Out of the corner of my eye, I spotted Manuel. He'd been keeping guard outside.

"With all this noise someone's going to hear us!" he scolded as he walked in. "What the . . . ?" He stopped short when he saw me on the floor.

"Your little friend stuck his nose where it doesn't belong," said Luis.

"Leave him be. He's worth more than all of you combined," Manuel spat out.

Then the bullies jumped him and started pounding him too. When they heard footsteps, the bullies ran off, leaving me and Manuel alone and in pain on the floor. One of the teachers looked in, and after seeing us there, ran to fetch the director. Reyes Pérez showed up soon with his cold stare and military garb.

"What's going on here?" he barked, not even asking how I was.

I struggled to my feet and sat on a box. "A couple of boys were stealing food and—"

"Was Manuel here among them? Lately he's been causing problems, and you know what happens with problems."

"No, he helped me. He defended me from the bullies. It was Luis and his gang," I said, annoyed.

The director never listened. He always thought he knew everything that went on in the school, though he didn't know the half of it.

"Luis? That's a lie. You're just trying to protect your friend here, but you've run out of chances for that. Manuel, I'll be sending you to the capital with the rest of the students who refuse to be disciplined. I treat you like my own children, and look how you repay me," he said, jerking Manuel's shirt to pull him to his feet.

"I didn't do anything!" Manuel said in self-defense.

"But before we send you to Mexico City, we'll give you what you deserve," the director said. He ordered Manuel to lean against some of the boxes in the pantry, then grabbed a wooden rod that was propped against the wall. Reyes Pérez told the other teacher to hold Manuel still and, with all his might, he buffeted Manuel's back with the rod.

Manuel started to scream. I tried to grab Reyes Pérez's hands, but he shoved me so hard I fell sprawling on the ground. "You little bastard! You dare to interfere? I'll deal with you next."

Reyes Pérez beat Manuel until he fell unconscious. He told the teacher to carry Manuel to the nurse, then he turned to me. "I thought you were smarter than this. Now you'll pay for trying to stop me. I don't tolerate disrespect." He grabbed me by the neck of my shirt, dragged me down the hallway to the deepest part of the basement, opened a metal door, and pushed me inside. "You'll be in here until you learn to follow the rules and respect your director," he said, slamming the door.

Thick darkness enveloped me. As his footsteps receded down the hallway, the silence made me tremble in terror. After a while I heard the quiet pitter-patter of rats and sensed their eyes on me, so I curled up and held on to my legs for comfort. I hummed a song and tried to manipulate my own fears, but it's never easy to laugh off what truly terrifies us. I thought about my parents, about happy days of being at home. I imagined walking along Alcalá Street holding my dad's hand in one hand and ice cream in the other. I took a deep breath and hoped the nightmare would be over as soon as possible.

# Chapter 25

# The President's Visit

Morelia
June 15, 1938

I was allowed to return to the boys' building after two days in solitary confinement. Along with two other classmates, Manuel had been sent to Mexico City, and I never saw him again. My sisters were worried sick when they didn't see me for two days. No one had told them I'd been punished for trying to stop the director from beating my friend. Afterward I tried to carry on with as normal a life as possible, knowing I had to endure school for my parents' sake. Soon it would all be over, and we'd go back to being a family.

Summer was near, along with the anniversary of our arrival to Mexico. We heard that President Cárdenas, whom we hadn't heard from in a long time, planned to visit, but we didn't know if he was alarmed by reports from the school or if he was just coming to commemorate the anniversary. One way or another, we all hoped that if he could see the deplorable state of things, he would help us.

The school's employees and students spent the first part of June working to dress up the foul buildings. We painted, fixed windows and doors, repaired chairs, and cleaned everything in sight. Reyes Pérez wanted everything to be perfect for the president's visit. Even the streets of Morelia were decorated for the momentous event.

The day before the president arrived, I got to spend some time with my sisters. We had hardly spoken at meals lately. Together, we read one of my mother's latest letters. With every correspondence, she grew sadder and more depressed because of the advance of the Francoists, the likely Republican defeat, and our separation, which tormented her to the point of no longer wanting to live.

"We have to get out of here," I said emphatically. It wasn't the first time we'd talked about it, but on this occasion I was more determined than ever. If the war was lost, what did it matter if we went back or stayed in a school thousands of miles from home?

"But Mom doesn't want us to come back," Isabel said. She knew perfectly well that Mom was worried about us but also that it was much worse in Spain.

"But at least we'd be together," I said.

Ana was unsure. On the one hand, she desperately wanted to go back. On the other hand, she was terrified of the war. We could still recall the bombs, the fires, and the maddening hunger.

Isabel cast her gaze downward. "The fascists are capable of giving us up for adoption," she said.

"You know as well as I do they're already doing that here with the older girls—sending them off to convents and whatnot. Do you two want to become nuns?" I was annoyed. I hated it when they contradicted me. I knew they were right, but I couldn't stand Morelia any longer.

"We have to stay, Marco. Let's stop talking about it," Isabel said in a huff.

The next day we would welcome the president. But first, that afternoon, the director's henchmen brought us new clothes and shoes, and we spent hours going over the program and practicing our line formation so that everything would look as perfect as possible. When it was finally dark, we ate a hurried supper and fell into bed exhausted.

The next morning, we awoke at the first light. The capital was almost two hundred miles away, but President Cárdenas had left early to get a good start on the day. We were to meet the president upon his arrival, so we formed our lines and marched toward the train station. The inhabitants of Morelia were dressed in their finest and stood all along the sidewalk to welcome the presidential retinue, which included Cárdenas's wife and one of his children.

We entered the crowded station and waited on the platform, fidgeting all the while. The welcome ceremony broke the prison-like monotony of the school, and it felt a little like Christmas. New clothes and the promise of better food occupied our minds.

The convoy arrived about half an hour late. The younger kids were impatient, and others were very sleepy, but when we saw the president's gleaming train approach, we all revived and began to bang our tambourines. The station reverberated with the noise. People shouted, and children waved Mexican flags. The steam engine pulled up to the platform, and for a few moments smoke blinded us. When the train finally came to a full stop, the police formed a protective barrier and a station employee placed stairs below the door of the main car. When the door opened, we saw President Cárdenas's face. He was smiling happily alongside his wife and son. The president waved to the crowd and stepped down from the train, helping his family step down as well. They walked along the aisle prepared for them as music played and the crowd roared. The president went up to a small podium and addressed the crowd.

"People of Morelia, my friends and countrymen, dear Spaniard children: It's an honor for us to be here on this sunny June day. We would've liked to come earlier, but the responsibilities of my office have prevented me. I've been keeping close tabs on the progress and challenges of the Children of Morelia, as well as the great love the town's inhabitants have shared with them. Two brother peoples united by war, but above all, by solidarity and their love for freedom. Viva Mexico!"

The people answered with a resounding, "Viva Spain!"

Reyes Pérez had chosen one of his faithful lackeys to address the president. Andresito, a shy boy with glasses, stepped in front of Cárdenas and read from a paper in his hands.

"Most excellent Mr. President Cárdenas and Mrs. Solórzano, the Spaniard and Mexican children of the Spain–Mexico School thank you for your visit. We are deeply grateful to the people of Mexico for your solidarity with the Republic of Spain and to the city of Morelia for welcoming us as their own. We hope to be worthy of this honor and unite our nations with the eternal bond of brotherhood among peoples."

Several of my classmates started laughing at the triteness of the speech so obviously prepared by the director. I couldn't hold it in, and one chuckle escaped my mouth. Reyes Pérez glared at me from the corner of his eye, and I froze in fear.

Cárdenas's wife was handed a bouquet of flowers, and the presidential family headed for the car that waited for them at the station door. A procession of police cars followed them, and we children came along behind, playing music and maintaining our marching order.

We soon arrived back at the school, moments after the president's car. The entryway was decorated with flower garlands, and from the outside the buildings looked nearly perfect. It hardly resembled the place we had been living for the past year.

In the large schoolyard, we put on dances and performances. By noon, we were exhausted but happy. We anticipated a good meal waiting for us.

President Cárdenas wanted to eat with the children, so on that day we enjoyed meat and all sorts of delicacies we were rarely, if ever, allowed. Countless children had been sick over the long months because of the quality of the food, and many others because of parasites that ranged freely at the school.

The president's son sat right next to us, and he seemed kind and sincere.

"How do they treat you here?" he asked.

The monitors roved all around, making sure we were on our best behavior and also making sure we kept our mouths shut.

"Well, we have food and a roof over our heads, and we can keep studying," answered one of my friends who didn't want to make any trouble.

I quickly glanced around and noticed no caretakers within earshot, so I decided to tell the truth. "The first director treated us terribly. Some kids have been sent to families in the area, even though they aren't orphans. And some of the girls have been sent to the convent in Morelia or another one in Guadalajara. Plus, they've sent some of the older boys to Mexico City. The food is usually inedible, and our clothing is all worn-out and old. They only gave us these new outfits yesterday because of your visit. This place is more like military barracks than a school."

The boy looked at me with his eyes wide in disbelief. "I'm so sorry," he said. "I'll tell my dad. What's your name?"

I hesitated. If I told him my name and then Reyes Pérez found out, there would be hell to pay. But finally I did say my name, and the boy went to talk with his dad while the party continued.

After the meal, they gave us the day off, and we played and lazed about the school grounds. While I was talking with some friends, a policeman approached and asked me to come with him. I started to tremble, but I saw no way out of it.

The officer took me to a room near the workshops in the boys' building. Inside, the president was sitting in a chair. I hadn't spoken to him since I'd arrived in Mexico, when he greeted each and every one of us from Spain. With hesitation I walked forward and stood before him as if before a general.

"At ease, soldier," he joked, and I tried to relax my rigid body.

"Your excellency, Mr. President," I squeaked out.

"Call me Lázaro."

"Mr. . . . Lázaro, sir, I would like to ask you to help us. We Spaniard children are so grateful for all you've done for us. You and your wife have saved us from the war in Spain. We've been in Mexico for a year, and we've learned a lot. Thanks to your wonderful citizens, we're learning a trade. But it hasn't all been good. I'm sure you already know about the problems with the first director. Things have gotten a little better with the new director, but—"

"That's good to hear . . ."

"But I want you to know that we don't normally eat well like we did today, nor do we wear nice clothes like this."

The president frowned. "Are you sure what you're telling me is true? I've asked to be kept informed, and I've been assured that you children have plenty to eat and are treated very well."

I stood there thinking. I didn't want to contradict the president or get into trouble, nor did I want my sisters to be punished for what I was doing.

"Some of the children have been given up for adoption, several girls have been sent to a convent, and some of the older boys have been sent to the capital. Our government sent us to Mexico to be taken care of, and your country has promised to send us back once the war is over. However, at this rate, you won't have many Spaniard students left at the school by the time the conflict ends."

"My dear Marco, I'm afraid the war is going to last a long time. Things are not going well in Spain, and it's natural that some of you would be better situated in other places. In fact, our initial intention was to place you all in homes, but it wasn't practical. I understand what you're saying. I'll speak to my secretary of education, and we'll look for a solution. I promise. What I can do for you right away, to protect your rights, is to name you all adopted children of Mexico. That way you'll have the same rights as any Mexican."

My jaw dropped. I hadn't expected such a response. The most powerful man in the country was right in front of me, listening to a simple, exiled, working-class foreigner.

"Thank you, Mr. Lázaro, sir," I said, smiling.

"No need to thank me. The Republic of Spain's struggle and our struggle here in Mexico are one and the same. When we're born, our parents give us a country as inheritance. We can settle and accept things as they are or change it. A nation's destiny depends on us. I love this country with all my heart, but Mexico grieves me. To see so many helpless children, so much injustice and inequality . . . It breaks my heart. The Republic has also wanted to change the destiny of her disadvantaged citizens, of the ones who've never counted for much; but powerful forces resist change. I hope the teachers are doing a good job with you all because you are our future. You're the future not only of Mexico but also of the whole world."

The president's words were imprinted with fire in my brain. My father had instilled in me that same desire to change things. Although in the past few months I had settled for surviving, I knew that the only path to happiness was fighting to reach it. I could do it in a self-ish way, designing my own future, or I could strive for change. After that day, I behaved differently in Morelia. I needed to fight for more than survival. My classmates and I needed to remember our dreams.

# Chapter 26

# Summer

Morelia
September 12, 1938

Summer was long and tedious. Many of the Mexican students returned home, but the Spaniards had to stay at school all summer. The only relief from the strict routine and schedule was when the teachers would take us to the nearby hot springs and water park in Cointzio. We were allowed to swim there 'til the park started cleaning the pools in the late afternoon.

One morning we set out early so we could stay at the park all day. My sisters were happy. They loved swimming and, more than anything else, getting away from school for a few hours. In the year plus a few months that we'd been in Mexico, they had undergone striking physical changes. It pained me that our parents were missing out on so much of the girls' childhood.

"It's been a while since we got a letter from Mom," Isabel said, walking beside me.

I still spent my free time with my Mexican and Asturian friends, but no one had taken Manuel's place. I missed him acutely on outings like this one.

"I hope she writes soon," I said. "I'm really worried about the war. I always thought we'd be back in Spain after a year, but soon enough it'll be Christmas and New Year again here in Mexico."

One of my Asturian friends, Felipe, came up and said, "Rumors are flying."

"The Republic is losing ground every day," another boy piped up. "Pretty soon it'll crumble if Prime Minister Negrín doesn't do something to stop it."

"The Republic is attacking in the area of Ebro," I said. I had read about how, in the turning-point battle, the Republicans had reclaimed territory and pushed the fascists back for the first time in a long time.

"Ugh!" Ana grunted. "You boys are always talking about battles. I don't care who wins. I just want to go home." My sweet sister couldn't yet understand how much our return home depended on the outcome of the fighting.

We got to the park and put on our bathing suits. Much to the chagrin of other guests who'd come to enjoy the warm waters in peace, we rushed to the pools and commenced our raucous games.

While my sisters waged a splashing war, I looked around, and my eye caught a dark-haired girl who was there with her parents. She looked to be around my age. From the first glance, I was struck by her beauty. She had black hair and dark eyes, light skin and slightly sunburned cheeks. She wore a fancy new bathing suit and was splashing her feet in the pool next to her dad, who was jumping in and out of the water.

I glanced at her over and over, but she never acknowledged it.

Finally, I gave up and started talking with my friends, trying to think about something else. That's when she did look at me. I caught her furtive eyes and noticed her blushing at being discovered. The rest of the day I was absent from what my body was doing in the pool with my friends. Instead I watched the girl and tried to figure out who she was. I asked Isabel and Ana to try to play with her, hoping they'd become friends. Otherwise, I'd have to come up with a reason of my own to talk with her.

We ate our frugal lunch, and while the mysterious girl's parents napped on chaise longues by the pool, I gathered up my courage to approach her. She was sitting on the side of the pool, dangling her feet in. The sun shimmered on her milky-white skin.

"Hi there. I'd like to introduce myself. I'm Marco Alcalde."

"You're Ana and Isabel's brother," she said with a little smile, as if she'd been expecting me.

"Yes. We're from Spain."

"Your sisters told me. From the Spain–Mexico School."

I shrank a little in embarrassment. I didn't want her, like most of the town's inhabitants, to think I was like the troublemaking Republican kids. For many of the well-to-do townsfolk, even for some of the resident Spaniards, the Children of Morelia were little more than a nuisance.

I nodded. "And we also have Mexican classmates."

The girl smiled at me, and I couldn't help but feel intimidated. I'd never tried to woo a girl before. It was the first time I'd ever felt attracted.

"I suppose you do," she answered, still smiling.

I took a deep breath to steady myself. "So, are you from Morelia?"

"Well, actually from Guadalajara, but my dad was transferred here for work. I've got to start a new school and make new friends, but this isn't the first time."

I hazarded a crucial question: "What's your name?"

"María Soledad de la Cruz."

The girl's father shifted on the chaise longue, and I stepped back, prepared to run the moment he opened his eyes.

"Do you want to take a walk around with me?" I asked nervously. I wanted to get as far away as possible from that large man who might not take it kindly that I was talking to his daughter.

María Soledad got out of the water and put on a white cover-up and flip-flops. She looked toward her mother, who was also dozing peacefully, her chin sunk into the book she had been reading.

We walked in silence beneath the surrounding trees for a few minutes. Eventually I turned to María Soledad and said in earnest, "You're the most beautiful girl I've ever met."

She threw her head back and laughed, saying, "You haven't lived long! I'm sure you'll meet prettier girls than me."

I was dumbstruck, not having expected that response. The Mexican girls I had been around were much shyer than Spaniard girls, but they also seemed much more determined.

"Little Spaniard, take my hand," she said.

I held out my hand and felt an electric shock when she touched me. Her fingers entwined in mine burned into my skin while I seemed to float in the air, hardly touching the ground.

We sat in an out-of-the-way corner and talked for almost an hour. Had we known each other forever? It was such a new and odd sensation, as if we'd been looking for each other our whole lives.

Ana appeared and smiled when she saw me sitting next to her friend. "María Soledad," she said, "your dad's looking for you. You'd better come back with me."

The girl looked at me one last time and, before saying goodbye, gave me a quick kiss on the cheek.

"Where do you live?" I called after her. I was afraid of losing her forever and that our time together would turn out to be just a mirage.

"Don't worry. We can see each other next Sunday at the noon Mass at St. John's."

I felt my heart being wrenched out of my chest with each step she took away from me. I started counting down the seconds until I could see her again.

A few days later, I put on my least dirty clothes, and my sisters and I went to church. The townsfolk raised their eyebrows and stared when they saw us come in, because the Spaniard children hardly ever went to church unless forced. A few of the Basques were religious, though they tried to hide it to avoid trouble with the rest of the students.

We sat in one of the pews at the back. As the service began and the parishioners followed the rituals, we tried fumblingly to copy them. My parents had never taken us to Mass, and the few times I'd stepped into a church had been to consider it more as a monument than as a sacred space.

As the priest recited the prayers and read the text from what I later learned was called the missal, I searched in desperation for a glimpse of María Soledad. Finally, I spotted her toward the front of the large crowd. She turned as if also looking for me, and our eyes met for the briefest of seconds, just long enough to send chills down my neck.

The service didn't last much longer, and afterward, the crowd spilled out onto the plaza outside. Some went to the nearby cantinas, and the children drank something that looked like colored ice as their parents watched from a distance.

María Soledad was walking between two friends. They moved toward the grove of trees and sat down on a bench. When Isabel, Ana, and I approached them, María Soledad waved everyone else away.

"I didn't expect you to actually come," she said. Her sincerity took me aback.

"Why wouldn't I come? I don't care for Mass, but I wanted to see you."

She lowered her head, and I leaned a little closer. "My father is strict, Marco. If he finds out you're courting me, he won't let me leave the house at all. We must be careful. My friends are trustworthy and won't say anything, but we'll only be able to see each other on Sundays after Mass so my father won't suspect anything."

From that day on, I spent every week waiting impatiently for the next Sunday to come. That young love helped me live out the rest of 1938 with something like hope and happiness, despite the fact that news coming from Spain was worse and worse and that my mother's letters came further and further apart. I hadn't yet learned that love was a force strong enough to transform the harshest and most difficult life into the most pleasant existence. I couldn't explain it, but that girl from Guadalajara accomplished what school, parades, and speeches had failed to do: embed Mexico into my heart.

# Chapter 27

# News from Spain

Morelia
April 3, 1939

Bad news tends to spread quicker than good news, and we re-fused to believe one rumor in particular. Students were saying the war in Spain was over, but we were holding out until the news-papers came from the capital. It wouldn't have been the first time false reports had spread. We did know that things were looking dire for the Republic. City after city had fallen into the hands of the rebels, and we knew that, of late, Republican resistance had been weak.

The director called everyone out to the main yard. We glanced at one another nervously. By then, fewer of the original Spaniard students were left at the school. If the rumors were true, we would no longer have a government to defend us. We would become stateless people.

"Students, companions, it is my duty to share news that is grievous to Spain and to the world. After a fratricidal war that has claimed hundreds of thousands of lives, Franco's army has taken control of the final Republican holdout, the port of Alicante. General Franco has declared the war to be over, and we don't know what will happen from here. Some think he'll restore the monarchy, and others believe Franco himself will rule as a dictator. But whatever the final result, the Republic is no more."

A murmur ran through our well-ordered lines, and the younger children started to cry. We all knew how terrible Franco's reprisals were against his enemies—thousands of people executed, tens of thousands imprisoned, not to mention the atrocities committed by Francoist troops amid their march through the land, especially the armies stationed in Africa.

Reyes Pérez continued, "At this point in time, we do not know what the future holds. Nor do we know what will happen to you students. As you know, President Cárdenas, whose term ends this year, has named you adopted children of Mexico, which secures you a degree of legal protection in this country should your home refuse to recognize you. Some of you will want to return to your homes now that the war is over. We will inform you of the procedures to follow. This is a sad day for liberty, but as you sing in one of your most well-known songs, 'Liberty is our most prized possession; we must defend it with faith and courage.' Viva Mexico! Viva Spain!"

We answered in unison through our tears. We felt again the familiar sensation of having lost our homeland, but this time it was for good. How could the children of reds return to a fascist Spain? We didn't know what was in store for our parents, much less how we'd be received upon arrival.

We broke our formation but all remained outside in the yard talking in little groups and trying to make sense of the news.

"What are we going to do?" Isabel asked. Ana, not really understanding our situation, was just happy at the idea of seeing our parents again.

I couldn't speak at first, at a loss of how to form words I couldn't even imagine saying. Anything that occurred to me to say sounded utterly stupid. Fear had paralyzed me.

"For now," I struggled to get out, "I suppose we wait to see how things shake out. Hopefully Mom and Dad will be able to contact us." After waiting so long for the war to end, I never pictured it would look or feel like this.

"We have to go back to Spain," Ana demanded, as if the mere idea of staying any longer in Mexico was intolerable.

"Go back? Spain is ruled by the fascists now," Isabel said.

"But I doubt they'd do anything to a few kids. Even fascists have children. Besides, our parents haven't done anything wrong," Ana insisted.

I shook my head. "For the Francoists, defending the Republic is bad enough for them to lock you up or worse."

Ana crossed her arms and sulked. "I want to go home."

One by one the other students drifted away from the yard, heads held low. The ones who didn't understand the news, though, were upbeat and smiling. I requested permission to leave school for a little while. I wanted to see María Soledad and talk to her about what we'd learned.

She lived close to the school, and I arrived at her house ten minutes later. I expected to find her home right then, when her parents usually went out for an afternoon walk. The maid eyed me up and down with suspicion at first, but I hoped she would agree to let María Soledad know I was there so we could talk for a few minutes through the window that looked out onto the back alley. My desperation must have convinced her, because she turned and went to tell María Soledad where to find me.

A few minutes later, our fingers were entwined through the bars on the window.

"What happened?" she asked, worried.

"The Republic lost the war," I choked out.

"So what will happen now?"

"I don't know. The director has told us to sit and wait. In the meantime, I hope to get in touch with my parents."

She started to cry. She knew this was the declaration that sooner or later we would be separated, though we had known from the very start that our love had little chance of lasting, given our circumstances.

"If I have to leave, I promise I'll come back. I'll never forget you."

"Are you crazy? There's no way you'll come back, and that's as it should be. Spain is your country, and my place is here, with my family."

Sometimes the world is too dark. Suffering and misfortune hang over our heads, eager for the slightest opportunity. We live like classic Greek or Roman heroes, torn between the whims of gods and men; yet we also have a will that can push us to fight against destiny.

"I'll come back," I promised with all the certainty of youth, when I believed life was tame and could be controlled with a light hand—not knowing that sometimes the paths of lovers really do separate forever, leaving incomplete souls to wander through all eternity in search of their other half.

# Chapter 28

# White Rats

Morelia
December 1, 1939

O ne lesson we learn as adults is that, if things are going poorly, they can always get worse. Sometimes misfortunes get bundled together in a short period of time. The year of 1939 was one of the worst of my life. Without knowing it, our existence had gotten tangled up with the rest of humanity, as if we were all one giant living organism, a kind of mystically interconnected being. In September of that same year, Word War II broke out, which would bring unfathomable suffering to humanity. First Europe, and then the rest of the planet, was falling under the turbulent shadow of fascism. Hitler invaded Poland, and his troops could not be stopped. One could only wonder how long France and the rest of the continent would hold out. We'd had no communication from our parents, but from the press we knew that hundreds of thousands of Spaniards had escaped through the Pyrenees to neighboring France. Had our parents managed to escape with the other refugees? That's what we hoped, but it unsettled us that, once there, they hadn't tried to contact us.

We had no way of knowing that the French had locked the poor refugees away in concentration camps on the beach. We students who had lost our country a good while ago were all too familiar with the devastation of losing our homes in order to become strangers somewhere else. Mexico had welcomed us with open arms, but we no longer knew what we were.

The new dictatorship in Spain was not content to kill or imprison the tens of thousands of people inside the country, regardless of age or sex; its tentacles reached much farther than we could've imagined. One morning we learned that several Spaniard organizations in Mexico—most of which we'd never even heard of before and which had certainly never done anything to help the students of the Spain–Mexico School—now wanted to deport us back to Spain without our families' knowledge. Those traitorous rats wanted all the children to go back home, but not because they wanted us to be cared for; rather, they wanted to make us bear all the rage and fury they couldn't unleash on our progenitors.

I knew that returning under those conditions was a trap, though it might be the only chance we would ever get to see our parents again. I seriously doubted the Francoists would allow us to be reunited with them, at least not at first. Only the slightest chance existed that after a while things would calm down and provide us the opportunity to be a family again.

My sisters pressured me to take our application to the director. Rumors swirled that, when Lázaro Cárdenas left office, his successor would close the school. If so, perhaps it would be better to leave now instead of waiting for things to get even worse.

That morning two men and a woman showed up at the school. Apparently, they had come from the capital to make a list of the students to send back to Spain as soon as possible. They represented various organizations of Spanish immigrants. We knew they were fascists like Franco, but they'd kept quiet 'til the end of the war. Many of those worthless patriots were fugitives from Spanish law or had fled the country to escape military duty, which explained their desire to get on the new regime's good side.

They lined up all the students and started to call roll. One by one we approached a table and gave all our personal information. Ana was one of the first to be called, and I was close enough to be able to hear the conversation.

"Your name, miss? And your city of origin?"

"My name is Ana Alcalde, from Madrid," she said, her voice shaky with nerves. Though she was the more determined of my sisters, the committee of scoundrels intimidated her.

"Do you have brothers and sisters here among the students?" asked the woman, who wrote everything down in a notebook.

"Yes, my sister, Isabel, and my brother, Marco."

"Are they older than you?"

"Yes, ma'am."

"Are your parents living?"

That question fell on Ana like the lash of a whip. We wanted to believe they were all right, but it had been months since we'd heard from them.

"I don't know, but I think so."

"Mark them down as orphans," one of the men said.

"But why? My parents aren't dead," Ana said, the pitch of her voice rising in alarm.

"The capital was bombed heavily in the final months of the war. Like I said, mark them as orphans."

Ana turned and started to walk away when the man grabbed her arm. I couldn't stop myself: I broke formation and ran up to get between them.

"Who are you?" the man asked.

I studied his bony face, bald head, and mustache that covered thin lips.

"I ask myself the same thing, you fascist. You may have won the war, but here in Mexico we're free. You're not taking my sister anywhere. We're not orphans. Our parents are alive."

Isabel came up to us. Our Mexican caretakers didn't know whether to intervene. No one had told them how this situation was supposed to go.

The two Spaniards stepped forward, as if signaling that they were the ones in charge now that the Republic's government had disappeared. The woman also stood up and said, "There's no reason to make a scene. The Mexican government will be in charge of turning this red trash over to us. We're just supposed to take note of the children who might still be saved. Their parents and teachers have raised them on atheism and revolution, but we might be able to reeducate most of them."

The men neither spoke nor moved. We three slowly backed away and then hightailed it out of there, not returning to the school 'til dark. At supper, we saw for ourselves that not all the students had been as determined as we were. Many of the boys and girls, especially the youngest ones without older siblings, were no longer there.

# Chapter 29

# Missing

Morelia
December 24, 1939

The Spain–Mexico School never lost its military barracks feel, but as more and more students left, the workshops, classes, and dining hall felt emptier and sadder. The sounds of laughter, games, and songs dwindled away. Some of the Mexican students had also gone back to their homes, and the oldest Spaniard boys had been sent to the capital or had run away to make it on their own, with little hope of ever seeing their parents again.

Christmas Eve seemed like any other day at the school. A few students sang carols, and the cook made a meal that was a little better than our usual fare, but these gestures only deepened the reigning melancholy. That afternoon, my sisters and I were sitting near the campus gate when we saw the mailman. We were surprised to see him working on Christmas Eve and even more surprised when he came up to us.

"Good afternoon. I've come here just for you three. This letter arrived a few days ago, but I've been unable to get out here to bring it. It's from France," he said, taking a brown envelope out of his bag and handing it to Isabel.

Isabel was in shock and didn't know what to do with the letter. Finally, Ana grabbed it, ripped it open, and read aloud.

Dear children,

I imagine you know by now the terrible fate of our country. The rebels won the war, and since their victory, they've relentlessly hunted down everyone they consider an enemy. They don't care if you fought honorably or were part of some bloody cheka; the slightest accusation is enough to seal your fate. People accuse others just to exploit their property and belongings, while the accused, whether guilty or innocent, are dragged off to a military trial and often sentenced to the firing squad.

You three know that your father saved countless people in Madrid. He's never been a criminal, doesn't have a drop of murderer in his blood. Even so, when the Francoists entered Madrid, they took him prisoner. It was shocking to see how so many people who had previously cheered and celebrated the Republic now acted like dyed-in-the-wool fascists. The welcome for the dictator was unbelievable. Tens of thousands of Madrid's citizens turned out to receive him. I went to the victory parade out of curiosity and to help myself accept the reality that we had lost. I didn't go to make the new regime happy. But the inhabitants of Madrid screamed their praises for that bloody general as if he were a god.

A few days ago, the Francoists came for your father. They accused him of being a union man, of belonging to the socialist party—both of which are true—and of killing political prisoners in Madrid. They knew the last part was a lie, but the truth is worthless these days. As soon as they took him, I got dressed and ran to Salamanca to see an acquaintance of your father's. Remember when your dad was serving as a guard in that rich neighborhood? He had saved a wealthy notary from a group of communists who were cleaning out the city's jails by killing hundreds of prisoners. The man received me kindly and was very sad about what happened to your father, but he could make no promises and sent me back home. Then I decided to go see the new city governor. I was afraid they'd put me in jail, too, because it's no secret in Madrid that I'm an artist who strongly defended the Republic. But heaven had something else planned. The new governor knew your father, who had saved his life as well. He promised to fetch your dad out of jail on the condition that we leave the country as soon as possible. He knew Francisco was a renowned union leader and had taken part in the attack on the Montaña Barracks.

I was waiting at the prison gate when they let him out the next morning. Those few days had changed him. He had bruises and cuts all over him, and he looked like a skeleton barely able to walk. The governor had given him a letter that assured us free passage throughout Spain and to exit the country, so we headed for France. After a week of challenges and setbacks, we finally made it to Figueras. They weren't letting Spaniards cross into France anymore. Francoist authorities were arresting anyone who tried to cross illegally, and people were landing in prisons in Girona or Barcelona. We were allowed through because of the letter, but as soon as we crossed the border, the French took us to an internment camp in Rivesaltes. The conditions there were bad, but we managed to get beds together and tried to regain our strength. Your father has been very ill, which is why we still haven't been able to leave this place or get in contact with you until now.

We don't know what's going to happen. The Nazis are invading everywhere in Europe, and we don't think France will hold out for long.

Please, do not leave Mexico. Spain is not safe. Please wait until you hear from us again, very soon.

Ana, I'm sure you're so big now. You're such a bright, determined girl. You'll accomplish great things when this world shakes off its lunacy and returns to normal. I love you with all my heart and miss you terribly.

Dear Isabel, you must be nearly a woman by this point. We would have so much in common now! We could be picking out pretty dresses that highlight your figure, but instead we're separated. But we'll be together again soon. Take care of your little sister and make sure she learns everything I taught you, like how women are worth just as much as men and that nobody has the right to our lives. I love you, my girl.

Dear Marco, the apple of my eye. You're already a man, and I know you'll be as good a man as your father: generous and brave, but aware that the most precious treasure we have is our family. Don't forget it. Your sisters are two jewels that you must protect until we're together again.

I love you three with all my heart.

Your father sends his love.

Francisco and Amparo

We were breathless after reading it. Mom's news had opened a deep, painful wound in me, but it hit Ana the hardest. She ran off away from the school grounds. It took Isabel a second to react, but then she ran after her. I sat there staring at the pages, not reading any of the words, just examining my mother's tiny print. That ink had come from a pen that she had held a few months before in France. The paper and the precious strokes from her hand were the only tangible indications that they were alive and that we'd be with them soon.

Isabel's return jerked me out of my stupor. "I can't find Ana," she said, her face tight with pain.

"What?" I asked, still half dazed.

"I can't find our sister anywhere. I'm worried about her. It'll be dark soon."

I looked around stupidly, at a loss. "Do you think she would've gone to see María Soledad?" I asked. Despite the age gap, they had become good friends. Almost every Sunday Ana went with me to Mass and stood guard while María Soledad and I talked.

"It's pretty late, but she might have." Isabel sounded doubtful.

"Stay here. You shouldn't go out at night. There are too many rebels who would love to catch you and deport you to Spain. I'll be back soon."

I set out, a nervous wreck who felt like he might be sick. I'd heard of children going missing and how passive the police and other authorities had been about it. The government seemed eager to be rid of us as soon as possible.

I ran all over town looking for Ana but saw no sign of her in the empty streets. It was Christmas Eve, and most people were home with their families. It didn't take me long to reach María Soledad's house. I tried calling for her softly from below her balcony, but she didn't hear me. The window was closed. I took a chance and climbed up the wall of the house, which was easy enough with the jutting rocks and thick flower vines. I pulled myself up onto the balcony outside María Soledad's room and tapped at the window. She was shocked to see me and cracked the window open.

"Have you gone mad? God only knows what my father will do if he finds you here!"

"We can't find Ana. Have you seen her? We're desperate."

"Someone knocked at the door about half an hour ago, but I didn't see who it was. My dad did go out, which is odd, because we're about to eat."

"Where did he go?" I asked, scared.

She shook her head nervously. "I have no idea."

I knew her father was capable of anything. He despised the Spaniard children and thought we were beasts that needed to be tamed.

"Help me think," I said. "Where could he be? He might be the only one who knows where Ana is."

"He's friends with a Spaniard named Tomás who's got a shop on the main street, where he sells vegetables and other goods."

Before she even finished talking I jumped down from the balcony, nearly cracking my skull open. I had a terrible feeling about the situation. I raced down the empty street and swore I wouldn't go back to the school until I'd found my missing sister—one of the jewels I'd vowed to protect.

Chapter 30

# Kidnapped

Morelia
December 24, 1939

Time is relative. Sometimes it seems to stretch out through inter-
minable hours, but then again it shrinks to make weeks and
months fly by. As I ran toward the house of the Spanish shopkeeper,
time stood still. It no longer existed. I halted in front and watched as
María Soledad's father came out of the store, where the lights were
still on, and headed up the street. I thought about jumping out and
speaking to him, but then decided that would be a bad idea.

The light at the store window went out. I had expected to see a
stairway at the back leading to the home above, but I saw a second
door beside the front door of the store and assumed there was a second way to get from the house above to the store below. Therefore, I

was pretty sure there would be another entrance at the back through the alley as well. I crossed the street with my hands in my pockets, as if I were just meandering about the empty town. I went down the alley and guessed which door might be the back door to the store. Then I looked up. There was a tall fence, which meant the gate didn't lead directly to the house but to a small yard. I made sure no one was following me, took a running leap, and managed to get my hands to the top of the wall. I pulled myself up and jumped over. I was just standing up when I heard a growl behind me. A mastiff was staring at me, his teeth gleaming in the darkness. I'd faced plenty of street dogs in Madrid, and my dad had always told me the most important response was to stay calm.

"There, there, boy. I'm not going to hurt you," I said in a sing-song voice.

The dog started to bark. If he kept it up, the shopkeeper would soon come out and discover me, so I pulled out the small knife I always carried. Weapons were forbidden at school, but I had found it one day lying on the roadside and carried it around since then. The dog jumped toward me, but before his teeth closed around my neck or arm, I struck out with the knife. He let out a pained snarl as it ripped through him, then he fell to the ground, whimpering. It broke my heart to see him there in pain. I'd never imagined killing a living being. My dad was radical in that sense as well. He believed that all animals have a dignity to respect and that we should only kill them to cover our basic needs. That day I learned that doing away with the life of any creature is always unnatural.

I hid the dog's body in the shadows and studied the patio carefully. There were empty wooden crates, a few sacks of potatoes, and some bags of garbage. At the back, two or three steps led up to a door set between two windows. I hid as I heard one of the windows open. Likely alarmed by the dog's barking, the storekeeper poked his head out and called the dog. Then the window closed, and it was quiet again.

I went up to the door and tried to open it, but it was locked. Then I climbed up a pipe connected to the gutters on the roof and slowly inched my way to the height of the window and looked in. I saw a woman, a heavyset man, and two small children in a well-lit room. They were sitting around a table about to eat. I swung over to the other window, which was dark. I pushed, but it was also locked, so I got down and searched among the junk around the patio. A metal bar I found would serve to force the door open. There was a soft splintering sound, and it creaked lightly as it opened. I stepped slowly into the hallway, which smelled of coffee grounds and corn, and soon I was in the store. I saw nothing but food and jugs of wine.

Behind the counter were some steps. I was about to go down to the basement to look around when I heard a sound behind me and then a flash of light. The storekeeper had heard the noise and come over to the store with a shotgun in his hand. The light blinded me for a moment, and I instinctively lifted my hands to my eyes and waited for him to speak.

"What on earth are you doing? You're one of those thieves from the school. Spain shipped our country its worst." Spittle flew from his mouth as he spoke. I looked at him sternly, without fear, weighing my options.

"I've come looking for my sister. Where have you put her?"

The man was quiet, as if he didn't know what I was talking about. "Your sister? What the devil have I got to do with your sister?" he demanded.

"She left school this afternoon, and I know someone brought her here not long ago. What are you planning on doing with her? I'll call the police."

The man burst out laughing, and I couldn't stave off the chill that ran up my spine. "What makes you think you'll get out of here alive? The police won't ask any questions. You're not the first one to break into my store looking to steal. You red scum are a plague. Fortunately, our caudillo in Spain has put an end to your kind!" He was furious, but I stayed completely still, not wanting to give him more reason to pull the trigger.

"I just want to take my sister back with me. I'll take her away, and you'll never hear from me or see her again."

The man raised the shotgun, and I dove to the side. I heard the blast hit the sack of goods that had been directly in front of me. The shopkeeper shot again but missed as I scrambled away. I knew that kind of weapon only had two shots, so I got up and ran toward him. He went sprawling on his back with the force of my shove, and I jumped on top of him and pressed the gun against his neck.

"You monster! Now are you going to tell me where my little sister is?"

The man's face grew red, and I let up on the pressure to let him talk—but instead he started screaming. I slammed the gun down hard again, and he struggled to get it away from his neck. He was strong and working hard to free himself, so I hit him hard in the head. His blood oozed from above one eye.

I heard footsteps behind me. I turned and saw a woman running at me with a knife in her hand, and I rolled away right before she could stab me. The man jumped up, then sat hard on my chest, making it nearly impossible to breathe. "Well," he growled, "I think it's high time we finish this stupid boy off."

"I don't want any problems," the woman said. "Sell him off to a landowner. He'd bring a good price."

"No foreman could break him. This red plague has rebellion in their blood. The girls are a different story, though."

The man studied me with his bulging eyes. I could see he was trying to overcome his desire to strangle me to death. Instead, he took the shotgun and smashed it into my face. Everything turned blurry. Then he hit me again, and I lost consciousness. As my mind started to shut down, I kept hearing my mother's words: *Take care of your sisters. Don't let anything bad happen to them.*

# Chapter 31

# Fleeing

## Morelia
### December 25, 1939

I woke up in a damp basement smelling of rotten fruit. It was very dark, and the pain in my head was all I was aware of for a while. Eventually I tried to study the room around me, but I could see next to nothing in the dark. I tried to move, but my body was one huge throbbing ache, and it felt like I had broken a rib. My hands were tied behind me. I tugged on them and heard something metallic. I felt it in the darkness and determined it was a pipe of some sort. I tried yanking harder, but to no avail. Then I tried and failed to loosen the rope.

"You can't get out of it," a voice from across the room said. It was a female, a girl.

"Who's there?" I asked in anguish. I was terrified about what might have happened to my sister.

"Well, my name is Lisa, but that doesn't matter much. A man locked me in a car yesterday, or maybe the day before . . . I've lost track of time. Then he brought me here. The Spaniard has come down a couple times to give me food and water, but that's all I know."

"Are you alone?"

"No, you're here."

"I mean if there's anyone else. Did they bring another girl here?" There was an uncomfortable silence, but I could hear her breathing.

"There was a big hullabaloo yesterday. I heard some shots, and I was hoping the policeman would come, though he's so corrupt that if the Spaniard gave him something to eat he'd probably just look the other way."

"Last night was Christmas Eve, so people probably just thought it was fireworks." I sighed.

"Then that means I've been here two days, at least. My mom sent me out to buy something for Christmas dinner. My parents are poor farmworkers. People like that Spaniard want kids like us that nobody will bother to look for if we suddenly disappear."

"Did you hear a girl's voice at any point?"

"Yes, I heard her. They brought her down and put her where you are, but when they brought you, she disappeared."

The words of this strange girl depressed me even more. Where would they have taken Ana? I'd heard rumors about child slavery, but I'd never imagined it could happen to us.

I started working desperately to free my hands. After what was surely a few hours, the ropes had started to loosen a bit. If I could get one hand out, I could free myself and get out of there. Every moment that passed was precious. If they took Ana to another city, it would be nearly impossible to find her.

"What's your name?" the girl asked. "Are you one of the Spaniard kids?"

"Yes, I'm from the Spain–Mexico School," I grunted.

"Welcome to Mexico," she said sarcastically.

I wanted to curl up and die, but I kept working on the ropes until I got one hand free. Then I untied the other hand and crept cautiously through the rancid basement. I didn't want to make a single noise that would alert the shopkeeper.

"You got out? Please, untie me!" she begged.

"If you keep quiet and calm, I'll come back. I promise."

"Just untie me now. I'll get out on my own."

I hesitated. If she weren't extremely cautious, the girl might make a noise that alerted the shopkeeper. But I felt my way toward her and untied her hands.

"Now follow me and don't do anything—*anything*—until I tell you," I said severely.

We felt along the wall until we found the door. I turned the knob slowly, but it was locked.

"Did you think he was going to leave it open?" she said. "We can wait 'til he comes back. He should be back soon to bring food."

"But I don't have time to wait. I need to find my sister as soon as possible."

"I'm afraid she'll be a long way from here by now, on the estate of some great landowner—"

"Shut up," I hissed. I knew the girl was right, but I still had to try. That scumbag shopkeeper would tell me what he'd done with Ana, and I'd scrutinize every square inch of the country if I had to.

We sat down to wait until we heard noise, then went back to our spots and got ready. The man opened the door, and the light from the stairs lessened the darkness of the basement. The shopkeeper's enormous body stood out against the backlit doorway. He approached and glared at me with disdain.

"I should let you die of hunger, but you're worth more money than one might think." He dropped a tray of food on the ground and started to feed me spoonfuls of a disgusting paste. Lisa seized the moment to run out of the open door.

"What the—" The man roared and threw the tray down to follow her. But he had hardly taken two steps before I jumped at his neck.

"You pig!" I yelled, knocking him facedown and sitting on his back. The man's nose split and started gushing blood at the sudden impact. "Now you're going to tell me where my sister is!" I screamed in desperation.

His wife appeared in the doorway and jumped toward me, but Lisa reached her first, bringing a cast-iron skillet down on her head and sending her unconscious to the ground.

"Penelope!" the man screamed.

"Where is my sister?" I demanded, smashing his face into the dirt floor with every syllable.

"Go to hell!" he managed to splutter. I throttled him against the floor over and over and then asked again, but he refused to speak.

"I swear I'll burn this store down with all of you inside if you don't tell me!" I was desperate for the truth.

The man was barely conscious, but my threats got through to him. "They took her to a convent."

"What convent?" I demanded, furious.

"Poor Clares. It's in Cuitzeo, up north by the lakes. The nuns need servants, and some of them later become novitiates. They won't hurt her." He was gasping for breath.

I got up, kicked him hard in the ribs, then left the basement. Lisa was stuffing things from the store into a handkerchief, then tied it into a knot and threw it over her back. "I think I've earned it," she said with a bitter smile.

It was just before noon when we left the store, but the streets were nearly empty, as people had been up all night for Christmas Eve.

"Where's your sister?" the girl asked me as we started to walk up the street.

"They sent her to a convent in Cuitzeo. I think it's north of Morelia."

"That's a six or seven hours' walk from here. You can get there tonight if you don't get lost. If you walk me home, I'll drop this off and take you there."

Chapter 32

# Unexpected Friends

Cuitzeo
December 25, 1939

Lisa's house was very poor, though what shocked me most was that her parents didn't appear too concerned about where she'd been the past few days. Mainly they were just happy to see what she'd brought them. We left the small village north of Morelia and started walking. Little hills crowned with low shrubs and plants surrounded us but did little to break up the monotonous landscape. Every now and then we saw a cultivated field and crossed paths with fieldworkers traveling in decrepit wagons. A few cars passed by, but none stopped despite our attempts to wave them down for a ride.

The whole time we walked, my brain bounced back and forth between anguish over Ana and worry for Isabel, whom I'd left alone at the school on Christmas Eve. I hadn't been able to tell her I was going to Cuitzeo—there hadn't been a moment to lose, plus I didn't want to scare her with the news that Ana had been kidnapped.

"Will you tell me about Spain?" Lisa asked.

She looked younger than she had seemed when we were in the store and walking to her house. She had pulled her black hair back into a ponytail and had changed her clothes. The current outfit was as drab and threadbare as the one she'd worn when she was kidnapped, only cleaner.

"It's like Mexico in some ways. At least, where we are now reminds me a lot of where my grandparents live. Madrid is way bigger than Morelia, but it might be smaller than Mexico City. It's cold in the winter and snows a lot, but spring is beautiful, and in the summer it's hot as hades."

"I wish I could go to Madrid, though I've never gone farther than a day's walk from Morelia. Where could someone like me go? Poor people have really small horizons. We're not allowed to dream."

"Well, that could always change. In my country we were fighting for the poor and the rich to be equal."

I had piqued her curiosity. "So what happened?"

"Well"—I swallowed—"now the rich are the rulers. There was a war, and they won."

"Ah." She nodded. "See what I mean? The rich people always end up taking it all."

I knew she was right, at least in part, but my father always said that resignation is an excuse for the weak. "We'll keep fighting. Look at what happened in Russia. The revolution changed everything." I was trying to cheer myself up with my own words.

"The revolution? My parents said there was one here, too, but I don't think it changed much of anything. The rich people pay men with guns to protect them. They have all the land and the money . . .

and if we don't work for them, we die of hunger. People talk about how we have the right to vote, but I don't much see the point. The world doesn't change just because people put pieces of paper into a little box." She had a tired half-smile on her face.

"I'm not talking about voting," I said. "The only way to get rid of injustice is with weapons. The rich and powerful will never give up their wealth and power voluntarily. We've got to take heaven by storm."

The sun sank sleepily behind the hills, and the shadows stretched longer and longer. Within an hour it would be fully dark.

"Do you think we'll be there soon?"

"Maybe by sundown, but the hard part will be coming back. It's not safe at night. There are ghosts, wild animals, and bandits that come out at night looking to hunt."

I wasn't afraid of the dark or of a lonely, dusty walk, but if I was coming back with my sister, I'd have to protect her somehow. I'd lost my knife when I stabbed the dog, and now I was unarmed.

"Maybe we should slip into the convent but not do anything 'til morning," I suggested.

She shook her head. "Mmm, those nuns are really sharp. I don't think we'd be able to get in without them noticing. It's like a fortress, but there are places to spend the night in the town. Don't worry, I brought some burritos for supper."

It was dark by the time we got to the town, and the only light in the stone-paved streets came from the reflection of the moon off the white, run-down façades of the houses. We came to a plaza, and Lisa pointed out the convent. A tall wall surrounded it, and it really did look more like a fortress than a religious establishment.

We sat on a bench and ate in silence. It would be my first time to sleep on the streets, though my companion seemed used to the practice.

"Is it safe to stay here?" I asked, doubtful.

"Nope," she answered with a smile I couldn't understand yet.

In my country we had known plenty of dangers, and we had just endured a war that killed thousands of people—but in Mexico, the law of the jungle was the law of the land. Surviving one day at a time was enough adventure for Lisa. She didn't need to think about what might happen in the future.

After our light supper, she looked for a spot to hide in the bushes, and we crawled inside.

"Does this bother you?" she asked, leaning her head on my arm.

"No," I lied, jittery. I'd never had a girl that close to me before except for María Soledad.

"It's a little chilly," she said, snuggling up next to me.

"Good night," I said, falling asleep within moments.

When I woke the next morning, Lisa was gone. I shook off the sleepiness and wriggled out of the bushes, seeing no sign of the girl. I was about to head to the convent by myself when she showed up with two sombreros in one hand and a few tamales in the other. We sat and ate on a bench, famished.

"I got the sombreros to fool the nuns. It's easier going in the gate than climbing that high wall. We can pretend to be farmhands coming to tend the lawn and the garden. I heard there's a group entering at nine, and I already talked the foreman into letting us work with them."

I was taken aback and impressed. "That's a really good plan."

"You probably think I'm a stupid country girl, but I have a lot of ideas rolling around in here." She knocked on her head. "I know how to read and write. I went to school 'til I was eleven."

"How old are you?" I asked.

"Fourteen, I think. Truth is, we never celebrate birthdays." She was short for her age, but I had no reason to doubt her.

"Why are you doing all this to help me?"

She shrugged and smiled at me again with her big white teeth. "I spend all day looking for something to bring home for my family to eat. At least for today I get to have a little fun with a Spaniard gentleman."

We fell in with the crew of workers. Right at nine o'clock, the doors to the convent were opened, and we were handed tools. Half the workers went to the garden and the other half to the patios and grounds.

"I think they're cloistered," Lisa said.

"What does that mean?" I asked.

"They never leave the convent or talk to anybody from the outside. If they see us, they'll surely hide. And they won't talk to us."

I was dumbstruck. "Well then how are we going to find my sister?"

"I'll look for her," Lisa said, pulling off her hat and a poncho she'd used to hide her clothes. "They won't be suspicious of a girl."

I stayed in one of the courtyards pulling weeds, the sombrero covering up my blond hair. After so long in Mexico, my skin had tanned and my hands were tough from all the hours in the workshop. None of the other workers ever spoke to me or even seemed to take much notice of me.

After an hour, I was beyond nervous. Lisa surely should've been back by then. I propped my sickle up against a wall and slipped inside the main building. I looked in several rooms but didn't see a soul. Finally, I found what appeared to be the kitchen. Some young women were startled at the sight of me and ran out. I had to hurry before they sounded the alarm.

I ran through more rooms until I came to a closed door. I stepped back a bit and threw my shoulder into it. I succeeded in knocking it loose and went through to a dim room. Beyond it, I followed a hallway until I came to a stairway going down. I crept down by feel and found myself before another door. This one was unlocked, so I turned the knob and walked in, discovering two nuns holding Lisa down.

"What are you doing?" I cried, startling the nuns. One turned toward me, and I saw she was holding a whip of some sort. She struck out at me, but I caught her hand and jerked the whip away. The other nun stood paralyzed.

"Let her go!" I demanded. The nun immediately let Lisa go, and she ran to me, screaming.

"Where's the girl they brought yesterday?" I asked, whip still raised. They pointed toward a room behind me. I opened the door and found Ana, curled up and weeping in a corner.

I grabbed her hand and we ran, Lisa right behind us. We wound our way to the convent door and burst through, not slowing our pace until we were as far away as our burning legs would take us.

We started walking back to Morelia right away, fear still coursing through our blood. We made it two hours before Ana collapsed, unable to continue. We sat on the side of the road to rest for a bit. Near us, a car stopped—clean and fancy, despite how dusty the road was. A woman in a suit stepped out and stood in front of us. She spoke in a strange accent, and we stared at her, hypnotized.

"You children look lost. Can I help you?"

I was hesitant. It was a bad idea to trust strangers in Mexico. Noncommittally, I said, "We're headed to Morelia."

A man got down from the car as well. We saw his shiny shoes first and then studied the rest of him. His cold eyes and round face were off-putting.

"Mr. Indalecio," the woman said, "I believe these are some of the Spaniards."

"Get them in the car," he answered.

We backed away. The man, who'd already returned to his seat in the back of the car, rolled down the window and said, "I'm Indalecio Prieto, the representative of the Spanish Republic in exile in Mexico. Please be so kind as to get into the car. I don't want to waste another second in this wasteland."

Chapter 33

# Journey to the Capital

Morelia
August 1, 1940

We stayed in Morelia another six months waiting for news from our parents, but to no avail. No more letters came. After the visit from the Republic's representative, things calmed down a little. Most students enjoyed the day of the visit. Indalecio Prieto and a few other adults handed out chocolates, gave a speech that was supposed to inspire and encourage us, and then drove back to Mexico City. Refugees from Spain were arriving in Mexico in droves, so we kept hoping to see our parents. We knew France had succumbed to the Nazi invasion and that a puppet government was in place in the south while the German army occupied the rest of the country. We knew our parents had been at an internment camp in southern France. But that's all we knew.

President Cárdenas's term would end in November of that year, and we didn't know if his successor would sign an agreement of some sort with Franco, Spain's dictator.

The shopkeeper had left Morelia, perhaps afraid we would alert the authorities to his kidnapping business and to the fact that he'd abducted Ana. María Soledad's father, too, had packed the family up and moved back to Guadalajara. I had only just managed to see her off from afar, her big, black eyes silently telling me goodbye for the last time.

Lisa came to see us sometimes, and Ana and Isabel befriended her too. Ana hadn't wanted to tell us anything about what happened when she was kidnapped, and we didn't pry. Both of my sisters were increasingly anxious the longer we went without news from our parents.

That afternoon in August, we were sitting underneath a tree with Lisa watching cars go by. It was very hot, and I'd bought us some Coke to take the heat off a bit.

I cleared my throat and spoke. "I heard that in Mexico City the exiles have started an organization called the Committee for Aid to Spanish Republicans. Maybe they could help us find our parents. If Mom and Dad make it out of France, they'll go to the capital first."

Ana looked at me with hope in her eyes. She was ten now but remained terrified of walking around by herself after what had happened. The Spain–Mexico School only offered primary education, but the curriculum was lax, and classes tended to stretch out, which meant I had only recently finished primary school. I wouldn't be allowed to stay there much longer. Yet I wasn't about to leave my sisters. Isabel would finish primary school the next year, and I was afraid they'd divide us up, effectively diluting our family and ruining any chance we ever had of returning to Spain.

Isabel was doubtful, though. "If the Nazis have control of France, it won't be easy for Mom and Dad to get out." She felt like the school, as bad as it was, was the only safeguard we had.

"I know you're afraid to venture out, but we need to leave all this behind us. Mom and Dad need us, so we need to try to get a little closer to them. Our parents have always taken care of us, and now it's our turn to take care of them. This exiles organization can help us," I said firmly, letting it be known that I'd already made up my mind that we were going to the capital.

"How are we going to pay for the train tickets? We don't have any money," Isabel countered.

"I'll speak to the director. I don't think he'll have any problem with my ticket, but I need him to pay for you two."

"What are we going to do all alone in a big city?" Ana asked.

"A few weeks ago I wrote the organization, and they've found a spot for us in one of the shelters. There are a few homes in the capital for the Spaniard kids. It's nothing fancy, just food and a weekly stipend for our expenses. There we can start the process of locating our parents in France and trying to bring them back to Spain."

Lisa, who had been quiet up to that point, asked, "Can I go with you? Marco, one time you said horizons can change, even for the poor. Here in Morelia, I've got nothing. Maybe I'll find something better there."

I didn't answer her right away. She couldn't stay in the shelter with us because it was only for Spaniards, and the big city might be dangerous for an outsider. After studying her face a moment longer, I said, "I don't know if it's a good idea. Plus, how will you pay for your ticket?"

"I've got a little stash. I won't slow you down or be a bother. Once we get there, I'll find work and somewhere to stay. I'm not afraid of working for my food. It's what I've done all my life."

"What about your parents?" Isabel asked.

"I swear they won't complain about one less mouth to feed. Plus, if I find work soon, I can start sending them money. My brothers and sisters—turns out they have to eat every day."

The next day, I went to talk to the director. Our relationship had gotten better as time passed, and we had come to a degree of mutual respect for each other. Fewer students remained at the school, and Reyes Pérez knew that when the new government came into office, the school would probably get a new director.

He smiled when I stepped into his office. He had the papers ready for my transfer, but he was not yet aware of my plan to bring my sisters as well. I explained the situation, and he understood our desire to not be separated.

"Well, in life, there are seasons of beginnings and seasons of endings," he said. "This hasn't been easy, but nothing that's really worth it is. The hardest school of all is life itself. Here we've instilled in our students discipline and an appreciation for rules and work. They don't seem like very enjoyable lessons at first, but to educate men and women, first we must educate boys and girls. We've developed in you all an internal strength—a resilience that will help you overcome any number of problems and difficulties. I do hope you find your parents. If they've managed to escape the inferno Europe has become, they're some of the lucky few. I just hope the blows of that terrible war don't reach the Americas."

"Thank you so much, Mr. Reyes Pérez. I need to ask you for one more thing. Could you please cover the cost of my sisters' train fare?"

He studied me a moment, then unlocked a desk drawer with a key attached to his belt. He took out a few bills and, handing them to me, said, "I hope fortune smiles on you. Life is riddled with obstacles, but at least you three have each other. I'll ask the cook to pack you some food for the journey, and we'll get you some new clothes. You can't show up in the capital in those rags."

I left his office as light as a feather, though a host of other emotions were roiling around inside me. That horrible place had been our home for over three years. In Morelia, I'd fallen in love for the first time; I'd known friendship, betrayal, and fear; I'd become a man. Ana and Isabel had friends who were like sisters to them. A few of the teachers had poured themselves into helping us. President Cárdenas had been our mentor and protector. Now we'd be under the protection of the Republican government in exile, but we'd never forget what Mexico had done for us.

When I got to the dining hall that night, I realized that word of our leaving had gotten out. All my classmates stood and hugged me one after the other. It was dizzying to think that after so much suffering, after years of fear and uncertainty, we had become one big family. Tears flooded my eyes as the last boy embraced me. My sisters had received the same welcome when they walked into the cafeteria that evening. One of the students gave us a little souvenir he'd carved into a piece of bark.

Another student got up and said, "My friends and brothers and sisters of Morelia, today we're saying goodbye to three of our own. We crossed earth and sea to get to this corner of the world. We were lonely and wretched, lost and scared, but we've gone through it all together. Most of the ones who arrived with us aren't here anymore. Death snatched some of them too soon, almost at the start of their journey, while others have left in search of a better future. Those of us who are left keep waiting for news from our parents. We want to go back home, though some of us have learned that now our home is with our Morelia companions, both those who have stayed and those who have moved on."

He hugged me, then I stood to share a few words. "It's difficult to leave this place and all of you. You're not alone. You're part of one big family, but Isabel, Ana, and I must go look for our parents. It's the only way for us to find true happiness one day. We've laughed, cried, and danced with you all. For a while, fate brought us together, and now we must go our separate ways. If life doesn't bring us back together again, I want you all to know it's been a gift to share this journey with you. There will always be a place in our hearts for each and every one of you. Viva Spain! Viva the Republic!"

Everyone shouted out the old chants no one dared say aloud in our country anymore. We had become the last remaining threads of a world that was dying out, consumed by the fire of its own desperation. We were what got washed up to shore after a shipwreck, the remains of an idea of a world that wanted humans to live in unity but that, instead, had devolved into splintered groups fighting one another, an idea that had hoped to build a new society from the ashes of the old but that had succumbed to its own contradictions. My parents were now the only part of that world that interested me, the only part I wanted to save, even as the rest burned up on the pyres of hatred and suffering.

# Chapter 34

# The Train to Germany

On the Road to Mauthausen
August 24, 1940

Not even three weeks after we boarded the train headed for Mexico City, our parents boarded a different train with an uncertain destination. After much negotiation between Franco's and Hitler's governments, the Spanish dictator had ordered his minister of foreign affairs to send some 927 Republicans captured by the Nazis in the Les Alliers refugee internment camp near Angoulême for forced labor. The train traveling slowly north was packed with families, men, women, children, and elders. Thirst left them breathless, the suffocating heat zapped their remaining strength, and the stench of defecation permeated everything. The few stops the train made were opportunities for scant rations of rancid, worm-infested food. The children were dehydrated, and the elderly barely stirred in the corners where the Nazis had thrown them a few days before.

When prisoners asked where they were being taken, the guards answered that they had to take a circuitous route back to Spain because of the bombings.

For most, a return to Spain spelled out near certain death. Executions at the hand of shooting squads after summary trials were the norm throughout the country. The conquerors' thirst for vengeance seemed insatiable.

None of the passengers could have imagined how hell had spread over the face of the earth before universal indifference. The train traversed beautiful forests and fields restored after the fleeting war of the western front, while the Spanish Republicans inside wept for their distant lands. They dreamed of yellow fields of grain, the warm summer sun, the grapes ripening for harvest. Yet the gray sky of northern Europe revealed the true heart of darkness.

When they tried to escape to go west, my parents had been transferred from the camp at Rivesaltes to Les Alliers. Thus, they found themselves on that convoy and, after four horrific days of travel, reached a station none of the passengers recognized. It was Mauthausen, near Linz, in Austria.

When, with 927 Spanish Republicans on board, the train arrived at the station near the concentration camp, everyone was shaking. The Nazis threw the doors of the cars open and shouted their questions to children in German: "*Wie alt? Wie alt?*" No one yet understood why the soldiers wanted to know how old the children were.

The soldiers pulled the younger, healthier men out of the cars, along with boys over fourteen years old. My mother clung to my father. "No, please!" she screamed when a soldier grabbed my father's arm. Dad turned his dazed, fevered face up to the soldier, and the German dropped him. They didn't want invalids at the camp.

The scene in the train cars was merciless. Mothers clung to their sons in the midst of screaming and blows; boys wailed and kicked as soldiers hoisted them into the air. Adult males got out on their own, pushed by soldiers holding loaded guns.

Nearly half the men got off the cars, while the rest of the passengers shrunk back in a huddle, putting distance between themselves and the station. Everyone intuited that death waited at this stop and that there would be no return from this dark region of Austria.

The car doors slammed shut as abruptly as they had opened. Those few dramatic moments had exhausted everyone. A long silence ensued, interrupted only by the sobbing of wives and mothers. After keeping their loved ones alive throughout the war in Spain and the trials in France, now they had lost them forever.

My mother stuck her head out one of the windows, and an old man wearing a green Alpine hat said in French, "Poor dears, you'll never see your men again."

My mother turned back to my father, who seemed at the brink of death. She wept bitterly. At least he was still by her side.

The train began to move again, and four more days passed as they crossed Germany and France. Despite the cars being less crowded now, pain and desperation were emblazoned on the faces of those who would become premature widows, of the mothers whose sons had been ripped out of their arms, and of the young girls whose childhood had now disappeared too soon.

The arrival in Perpignan was not joyous. As soon as they crossed the Pyrenees, the passengers would end up in Spanish concentration camps or jails. No refuge existed for Spanish Republicans. Fascism had stolen first their Republic and then their country and now demanded the only thing they had left: their lives.

Part 4

# To the Motherland

Chapter 35

# A Ship to the Homeland

O ur trip to the capital was exciting. My sisters and I thought that, after three years in Mexico, nothing could surprise us, but Mexico City managed to impress us with its beautiful avenues, luxurious buildings, and imposing statues of freedom fighters and revolutionary heroes. It actually felt like several cities in one: the colonial capital built over the ruins of a great Aztec city, the elegant nineteenth-century capital city, and the modern city that seemed to gobble up everything in sight. Millions of people circled throughout the frenetic place every day: landless peasants coming from every corner of the country, immigrants from all over the world, employees of the countless federal bureaus, and the people who actually lived there and made up the heart of the capital's inhabitants.

My sisters and I loved it. We had grown up in Madrid and were used to the hustle and bustle, the noise of cars, and the crowds moving every which way. Mexico City made Madrid look like a quaint little neighborhood. The streets that shot out in straight lines, the wide avenues covered in trees, and the exquisite houses of the city's important personages dazzled us.

The shelter we were to stay in was on Alfonso Herrera Street in the San Rafael neighborhood. It was run by a Spanish couple, Alfonso Sánchez Vázquez and his wife, who welcomed us warmly. The rest of the students staying there were boys, but the Sánchezes had made a special exception for us and were allowing Isabel, Ana, and me to share a room. Isabel and I would go to school at the Luis Vives School, created especially for the children of Spanish exiles. Rubén Landa, a good but strict teacher, was the director. Mrs. Sánchez, who was also a teacher, would teach Ana at the house since she wasn't old enough for high school.

Our friend Lisa made a home on the outskirts of the city and had to take two different buses to get downtown, where she worked in a restaurant. We usually saw her on Sundays. She would tell us about her week as we walked through the Zócalo and admired the Palacio Nacional and the huge cathedral. Late in the afternoon she would go back to our house with us before returning to the unsightly room she had managed to rent west of the city.

That crisp afternoon in November, the air coming in from the mountains chilled us to the bone. The weather reminded us of autumn and spring days in Madrid.

"Are you going to talk to the ambassador from the Republic tomorrow?" Lisa asked. She was scared that any day now we would jump on a boat and sail away forever to Spain.

Isabel nodded. "We need to know if they've found anything out about our parents." By now, Isabel was a pretty young woman who looked so much like our mother. Every time I looked at her, I thought of Mom.

"I get it. Your relationship with your parents is different from mine with my parents. It's not that I don't love them, but I don't mind being far away from them. I think the time comes when people just have to make their own lives."

"At least you know your parents are okay. Ours are lost somewhere in France where the Nazis are in control, or maybe in Spain, where the regime hunts down anyone who fought for the Republic," I said. I knew I was being unfair to Lisa. Her life hadn't been easy, nor had life for her family. Poor, landless farmhands had many more mouths to feed than they could ever hope to provide for. Lisa's situation was a lot like that of the laborers of Andalusia and Extremadura.

She shrugged off my tone. "Well, I hope you find them."

It wasn't our first time going to the embassy to ask about our parents, but this time we had a little reason to hope. The director of the school, Rubén Landa, had said that in recent weeks there had been news of the Nazis sending a train of Spanish refugees back to Spain from France.

Lisa stopped in front of our house. Despite being a bit run-down, the ramshackle place was the closest thing we'd had to a home since we'd arrived in Mexico.

"See you next Sunday?" she asked, her voice tinged with sadness. She kept expecting to show up in the Zócalo one day and not see us.

"Yes, of course, we won't leave without saying goodbye," I answered.

"Don't forget how I'd love to go to Spain with you three. You're closer to me than my own family."

Ana squeezed her tight in a hug, and Isabel kissed her cheek. I gave her my biggest smile as I opened the gate and she walked away. My sisters and I went in the little yard and stayed by the front door talking.

"Oh, it makes me sad," Isabel said.

"Lisa is so sweet," Ana added.

"But she can't come with us. Spain isn't exactly safe right now."

Isabel cocked her head at me. "Do you think it's a good place for us to go? We're the children of fugitive reds. I don't expect they'll receive us with open arms. Plus, people who've just come from Spain recently talk about how everyone's starving to death in the streets and that winter last year was just miserable. Hundreds of people died from the cold, and tuberculosis has spread like the plague. What if there is nothing for us at home? In Mexico, if we finish two years at a vocational school, we can get jobs in an office or at a bank. You could even keep studying at a university. You're good enough to get a scholarship from the government."

My sister was right. Life was easier in Mexico, but sometimes we have to choose between happiness and survival. My conscience would never let me be if I didn't make the effort to find our parents. I shrugged and shook my head wearily. "Well, at the least, I need to go look for them. But you two can stay here."

"No, we promised them we'd stay together," Ana said, frowning. The mere thought of each of us going our own way was unbearable to us.

We went inside, and Mrs. Sánchez called us to supper. There were about twelve students that night. We knew two from Morelia, and the others had come from Spain more recently.

As we sat around the table, Dr. Alfonso told us the news from the war in Europe and the situation in Spain. "It seems the Germans are trying to invade Greece, though what's even more interesting to me is the possibility of Spain entering the war."

"But the Spanish people can't make it through another war!" Juan, one of the other residents, interjected. He had lost his parents in the massive flight of civilians from Valencia to Alicante in the final days of the civil war. He was another of our companions who was now all alone in the world.

"If our country goes to war and Germany loses, the Allies would invade the peninsula," the professor said.

His wife shook her head with a tsk. "Those are false hopes. The British are the only ones holding out. The French have sold themselves to the Germans, and the rest are already under their power."

"But, my love, there's still Russia."

"Are you forgetting that the Soviet Union made an agreement with Germany to divide up Poland? If I've said it once, I've said it a hundred times: Communism and fascism are two sides of the same coin." Then commenced a political debate between the two.

Meanwhile, Juan leaned over to me and whispered, "I know you're hoping to go look for your parents. There's a boat departing to Spain next week."

"Thanks, but we still haven't made up our minds. What can two teenagers and a girl do to find their parents somewhere in France or Spain?"

"I know. I know, but I swear that if my parents were alive, I'd cross heaven and earth to look for them."

Dr. Alfonso took a sip of wine and looked at all the students. "I heard that on Friday a group of students got into a fight with the *gachupines*."

"They started it," said Peter, another of our housemates. "Those fascists are always looking for trouble."

The *gachupines* were the children of Spaniard fascists or descendants of the Spanish monarchy living in Mexico. Their school was almost right across the street from ours. Each day when we got out of school, we would exchange insults—which sometimes devolved into fistfights. The Francoist Spaniards would denounce us to the authorities and pressure the Mexican government to deport us to Spain.

"Well, let that be the last time. The fascists may be savage brutes, but we are the authentic representatives of the legitimate government of the Republic."

We all hung our heads, though we knew that the fights would recommence the very next day. We couldn't let ourselves be humiliated by the sons of cowards who hadn't fought in the war but who now strutted around like die-hard patriots.

"You're going to the embassy first thing tomorrow morning?" Dr. Alfonso said, looking toward me and my sisters.

"Yes." I nodded. "They might know something about our parents."

"Let us hope so, my son. Hopefully good news."

After supper, we got ready for bed. Ana and Isabel brushed their teeth, then got into one of the beds while I curled up in the other.

"What do you think they'll say tomorrow?" Ana asked. She was nervous about the possibility of news and couldn't sleep.

"I have no idea. We can only hope for good news."

The next day, we didn't need any help waking up. My sisters jumped out of bed and were ready in ten minutes. We ate a quick breakfast, then walked to the embassy, going up to the floor that served as the main office. The line of people waiting to be seen that day stretched out to the street, but we were the first called since we had an appointment.

The ambassador received us kindly in his office, which was packed with boxes and files. The whole place had a hasty, makeshift air about it, and no one had near enough resources for the hundreds of Republican refugees streaming into the city every day.

José María Argüelles had a quixotic look. It was easy to picture him wearing a helmet and armor and swinging a spear at the giant windmills. That was, essentially, what he was doing: trying to squeeze enough hope out of severely limited resources for the thousands and thousands of Spaniards who had arrived in Mexico.

"Sit down, children. I can assure you this will be the bright spot of my day. I have some good news and some bad news."

We sat on the edges of our seats. My heart raced. I took Ana's hand, and we waited impatiently for the ambassador to go on.

"You already know that Spain is in a very, very bad state. Rampant hunger, chaos, poverty, and killings. What can I say? Thousands of Spaniards are prisoners in concentration camps. International public opinion isn't speaking out about these things, as it's more focused on the outrages of the Nazis."

"Yes, yes," I said as quickly as possible so he'd get to the point.

"Well, the situation of the Republicans in France isn't much better. Some fought in the Foreign Legion, others were used as cannon fodder by the French army, and many others were forced to dig trenches along the front. The Nazis are deporting most Spaniards to Germany and Austria, to concentration camps to do forced labor. All of this is in blatant disregard for international treaties, and the despicable dictator Franco does nothing to stop it. In fact, he encourages the deaths of his countrymen."

"Are our parents among the prisoners sent to Germany?" I asked, worried.

"No—well, sort of. It seems they were taken in a convoy destined for Mauthausen, a camp in Austria. When the convoy arrived, the men and boys older than fourteen were taken off the train. The rest were sent back to Spain."

"Was our father . . ." Ana began, her voice trembling.

"We're not sure why, but it seems your father returned to Spain on the train. We managed to get the list of names thanks to a resistance worker. Both of your parents are in Spain. Everyone who returned on that convoy was sent to concentration camps run by Franco's army."

Isabel squeezed my other hand while Ana jumped up and said, "So they're alive!" Her happiness was painful to observe.

"Yes, but they're in a very dangerous situation. Life in the camps is incredibly harsh. The food is bad, prisoners are mistreated, and they are forced to do hard labor. Countless prisoners end up sentenced to execution by the military courts."

Ana seemed to understand then that, though they were alive, our parents were in desperate straits.

"We wanted to ask you for something," I said.

Argüelles propped his chin in his hands and looked at us with sad eyes. "What is it?"

"We want to go back to Spain. We heard there's a boat leaving Veracruz next week."

He didn't seem surprised, just sad for us. "If your parents are in a concentration camp, you won't be able to see them. How will you survive there? We know the Francoists are locking up thousands of orphans—or children whose parents have been imprisoned—in the orphanages, and they're giving the younger children up for adoption. It's a terrible scene."

"We know, but we want to be there when our parents get out."

Argüelles raised his eyes in surprise. He must have mistaken my desperation for bravery. Life made no sense without our parents.

He picked up his pen and signed permission for exit so we would have no issues boarding the ship as minors. He also gave us money for the tickets.

"Deep inside I'm jealous," he said, bidding us farewell from the door. "I'd rather be locked up in my beloved country than in a palace far away from Spain. But someone's got to pick up the pieces of what remains of the dream we used to call the Spanish Republic."

Chapter 36

# Paths Crossing

Mexico City
November 30, 1940

My mother had not gotten to see the port outside of Bordeaux
from which we embarked to the Americas. Her boat was to
set sail from one of the few ports still beyond Nazi control. That
morning in Marseille, beside my father, she sensed she should've
gotten on the boat much sooner. For her, being separated from her
children was like walking around with her internal organs on the
outside. Empty, sad, and at the frayed edges of her strength, she had
managed to drag herself through the horrendous years of the civil
war, the flight to France, and the train ride north and then back
again—an experience she still could not allow herself to actually
remember in detail. She was haunted by the images of women bereft

of their husbands, mothers whose sons had been wrenched from their arms by the Nazis. She and my father had barely survived the trip back. After eight days in a disease-ridden cattle car with barely any food or water, they were on the brink of death. Yet even worse was the grief of the women who had lost husbands and sons. Mothers are always the rawest victims of war. What they love most in this world—their children—is ripped away from them. Their children starve to death, are tortured, or are simply killed outright, and sometimes the mothers receive the broken, beloved bodies back again in a shroud, wrapped in a flag incapable of drying all the tears. Other mothers never again see the bodies of their precious ones, disappeared forever in mass graves or cast off into ditches like dogs run over on the highway of fate.

When that train from Mauthausen reached Perpignan, one of the French gendarmes who spoke Spanish announced from outside the train car that they were being sent back to Spain. My mother told my father and a small group of friends who had traveled with them on the train, and they discussed what to do. That night they started to pull out the nails in a corner of the train car. It took several hours, but by five o'clock in the morning they had managed to loosen two strips of wood. Nazi soldiers were guarding the train station, so they decided to wait until seven o'clock when the train began to move. As soon as it was leaving the station, but before it was going too fast, they would let themselves fall down onto the tracks and wait for the rest of the cars to pass.

My father was the first to jump. He was still weak and feverish, but the desire to escape was greater than his lingering illness. My mother was next, and she didn't bat an eye at the danger. Yet the other four people who were to follow lost their nerve. They pinned their hopes on the notion that the Spanish authorities wouldn't be overly harsh with them once they returned.

My parents made it to a forest and then walked until they came upon a village, where some shepherds led them to an abandoned house halfway up a mountain. A few days later, they got in contact with French Resistance workers who took them to Marseille. There, a Mexican consulate issued them a visa and passage to Veracruz.

༺ঔৣ༻

While Isabel, Ana, and I were packing our scant luggage for Spain, our parents were a few hours outside of Mexico. That afternoon, our comrades at the refuge house had prepared a going-away party for us before our trip the next day. The train to Veracruz left early the next morning, and we wanted to get to bed early.

Our last dinner in Mexico City was really special. Though we were eager to leave, the place had become a semblance of home over the recent months. We would miss our friends and teachers. We were also pained to leave the land that had welcomed us at a very difficult time in our lives.

Alfonso Sánchez and his wife had worked hard to prepare special dishes, including a delicious chocolate cake. When the party was over, we all had full stomachs. A few of our housemates played songs on their guitars, and we had the strange sensation of feeling just a little bit closer to our homeland.

Juan, whose room was right beside ours, left the gathering earlier than most. With the sad smile of someone who's lost a reason to keep living, he said, "I hope you find your parents and that you can be really happy." Then he went upstairs while the rest of us remained at the party awhile longer.

"Well, dear children," said Dr. Alfonso, "you're headed back to Europe at a dismal time. Fascism is perilous, so please be careful. Once you're in Spain, don't trust anyone. In Madrid, you should go to the offices of the Service of Militarized Penitentiary Colonies, the organization that oversees the concentration camps. There are over a hundred camps throughout Spain. Some say that Franco rules the country like a military machine, but actually he rules as if it were one big prison. Do not, I repeat, do *not* tell people you are the children of prisoners. If you do, they'll stick you in an orphanage. Say that you're looking for your aunt or some other relative. Do you have anywhere to stay in Madrid?"

"Our grandparents live in a town outside Madrid, but first we could try to get in touch with some of my mom's theater friends."

"Well, give me a hug," our professor said, his eyes cloudy with tears. His wife came up and kissed us gently, wishing us a safe and successful journey. The rest of our comrades bid us farewell with a mixture of envy and grief. Most had already lost their parents in the war.

We went up to our room. My sisters changed their clothes, and I read for a while. I was too nervous to rest, and I didn't want to oversleep and risk missing the train and then the boat. Nor was I particularly looking forward to crossing the ocean again after our last experience. But what truly worried me was what we would do once we got to Spain. The boat would take us to Lisbon, in Portugal. Then we'd have to take a train to Madrid. We'd need to cross the border without raising suspicions, using falsified passports the Republican ambassador had given us, and then we'd have to hide out in the city until we could determine our parents' whereabouts.

I was starting to nod off when I heard a loud thump in the room beside ours. I jumped out of bed and ran to Juan's door. I knocked. There was no answer. On a premonition, I opened the door. Juan was dangling from a necktie tied to the ceiling lamp. I grabbed his legs as he swayed. He was very heavy, and I could hear his fatigued breathing, but I didn't want to look at his face.

"Help!" I cried, hoping that one of our housemates would hear me. It was Isabel who showed up. Between the two of us, we managed to lift his body some. Then Pedro showed up, half dressed. A chair lay on its side on the floor, and he stood it upright and climbed up to cut the tie down with his knife. Juan's body fell upon us, and we all tumbled to the floor. I looked at my friend's blue face and realized the knot was still compressing his throat. I loosened it as quickly as I could. His eyes bulged in a terrible expression, but he was still breathing.

"You're going to be okay," I said, blinded by my own tears. Juan looked at me weakly, and then his eyes closed. He had no desire to stay here on earth. In the grip of harsh loneliness, he lacked strength and hope.

"Juan, please don't die," Pedro said, embracing him. They were good friends who had escaped together on one of the last boats out of Alicante, right before the Francoists took control.

Alfonso and his wife ran into the room in their bathrobes and tried to revive Juan, but it was no use. The breath of life was leaving him even as the comrades surrounding him could not accept what was occurring. Ana was the last to come into the room. She took one look at Juan and ran out crying.

"Help me get him onto the bed, boys," said Dr. Alfonso. "Tomorrow we'll call the authorities. Now you should all go back to your rooms."

Almost everyone left, but Isabel, Pedro, and I stayed behind. "You really should go," Dr. Alfonso said.

"I'll watch over him tonight," Pedro said.

"Pedro, Juan is dead. You can't do anything more for him."

"I know, professor, but I want to hold a wake for him. The two of us, we were all alone in this world, together. I don't want him to go through another night on earth all by himself."

We left Pedro sitting in the chair. A sheet covered Juan's lifeless body. Walking back to our room with Isabel, I wondered if anything about a person survived once he was dead. I liked to think so. Life felt so short and riddled with dissatisfaction that immortality seemed like the most logical possibility to me. After tucking Ana and Isabel in as if they were little girls again, I dropped into bed like a heavy anchor.

I closed my eyes and thought about Madrid before the war, when the world seemed to make sense and you could hear people chatting in cafés and see them sauntering carefree down the street or dancing at summer festivals. Would that world ever exist again? I still did not grasp the fact that, as each day came and went, the past dispelled like fog to make way for the present. Earth is a huge valley of dry bones buried where, generation after generation, people struggle and live with the same false sensation of being the only ones, never discovering that they are just one part of an endless chain, mere links in line, and that others will take their place as soon as they disappear forever.

# Chapter 37

# The Return

Veracruz
December 2, 1940

It's never easy to leave part of your life behind. Usually we don't appreciate what we have until we lose it. Mexico had been a home for us. I had found love there; in Morelia, I'd forged bonds of friendship that would live forever inside me, but I knew I had to leave it then, that I had to let all the people who had joined me on that difficult part of my journey fly free. It's not fair to shut lovely birds up in a cage. It's best for them to fly away, though it overwhelms us with sadness. We always want to get back to the places where we were happy. In Mexico, I'd been happy in a way, but Madrid was still the place of myth for me, the setting of my childhood where everything fit together and even sadness wore a halo of joy.

I recognized how nostalgia would be hot on my trail for some time, like a long winter in which sunlight refused to peek through the gray clouds. But one day, when I least expected it, when I'd gotten used to muted days, the sun would come out with all its strength and burn the gray days up into pure light.

The port of Veracruz was as active as three years before. I was no longer the scared, timid child that had come to Mexico escaping the war with a heart broken from being separated from my parents—yet much of that child was still with me. Growing up doesn't mean forgetting; it means adding new layers of the past until we become the same person over and over again. My sisters followed me, suitcases in hand. The port of Veracruz had acquired mythical status in their minds, the memories of the place too magical to have actually existed.

We went up to our boat. It didn't seem as large as the *Mexique* had been, but it did look newer. We had second-class tickets, but at least we could all travel in the same cabin, not like last time. Before we boarded, we took a last look around at the palm trees on land. We were roasting in the heat since we'd dressed in wool suits more appropriate for Europe than for the Caribbean. As we went up the staircase, we were unaware that our parents were walking just below our boat, in shock at the exuberance of the Americas and trying to take in every detail of the landscape. Our paths crossed without touching, a macabre trick of fate.

Life is a search, though without knowing it we long to return to the nothingness from which we came, confused by the game everything on our path turns out to be. After every decision, we face countless rejections. It doesn't occur to us to feel nostalgic for the kisses we didn't give, the people we didn't meet, and the hugs that will never embrace the souls of those we'll never cross paths with again—though it is much, much sadder to never again see those we long for.

Our boat set sail in the afternoon. The sea was calm, and the water opened before us seemingly eager to whisk us away from all past happiness as soon as possible. We looked out at Mexico for the last time from the deck. When we leave a place, we never really know if we'll ever return, even if we live with the arrogant, unconscious audacity of believing we will.

The ship made its way into the immense blue where sky and water got jumbled together, the horizon stretching out to tire our eyes with the infinite monotony of the distance.

We ate a light supper, then went to our cabin. After chatting a little while, we fell asleep easily, all three of us exhausted.

It was a relatively easy journey. We stopped briefly in Havana, just as when we had come, but this time we got to disembark and spend a few hours in the city while the ship was docked. Then we continued through peaceful waters until, ten days later, we came to the Azores. A few days later, we were docked at the imposing city of Lisbon.

It was utterly strange to be in Portugal's capital. They didn't speak our language; the white buildings covered in elaborate ceramic tiles were so different from the granite buildings of Castile and even more drastically different from the red brick of Madrid; and yet, at the same time, it had the feeling of home.

A trolley took us to the Praça do Comércio, and from there we walked to Bairro Alto. We had to spend the night in the city since our train to Madrid didn't leave until the next morning.

We left our luggage in the pension. We had just enough money to buy dinner and breakfast the next morning. As we walked, Portugal's cobblestoned capital city was so calm it nearly unnerved us. The rest of Europe was in upheaval due to the war. Meanwhile, the people of Lisbon were busy preparing for Christmas. It was a perfect evening. We made our way down the hills toward the city's center and found a cheap restaurant where we ordered fish. Watching the street from the window of the restaurant, Ana began to cry.

"What is it, Ana?" I asked.

She'd been unusually taciturn throughout the whole journey, spending her time reading or taking long walks along the deck. In a way, she was more Mexican than Spanish, with fewer memories of our parents and Madrid than Isabel and I had.

"I just feel like I'm not really alive."

I didn't understand her at first, but then I got what she was saying. It took Isabel longer to understand.

"What do you mean?" Isabel asked.

"Life is like a flash of light between nostalgias."

Her comment left me breathless. I knew my sister was bright, but to hear something like that from a ten-year-old was uncanny. She'd been forced to grow up quickly and would soon have to leave behind all vestiges of childhood innocence, but what she'd just said seemed like something wise old men would be chewing on for years.

Isabel arced her eyes. "You're quite the philosopher."

"What I mean is," Ana said, her eyes scrunched up in an effort to put her intuitions into words, "we always long for what we've lost. At least you two actually remember it, but I just feel nostalgia for your memories, not really for mine. Plus, we can feel nostalgic for things we'll never experience again, which is why the present is just an instant, one second of certainty. Though the worst part is that while we have that certainty, we're hardly even aware of reality; it just feels confusing and slippery."

"For you, Mexico is the past, and Spain is the future," I answered.

"Yes and no. Spain is the past, even though I don't remember it much, and Mexico is also the past, but it's the only thing I've really got. Tomorrow I'll arrive in the place we left over three years ago. We've tried to live life like a parenthesis, but I'm afraid the only thing I'll be left with will be whatever I felt there, in Morelia."

We walked along the sea and sat on a stairway that led down to the water. I couldn't stop thinking about what Ana had said. I was scared to go back to Spain, scared to find out our parents were dead, scared and anxious about the future; but what really tormented me was the inferno of having to choose just one path and ignore all the rest. I was feeling nostalgic for all the lives I would never lead, all the opportunities I had denied myself by deciding to return to Spain.

Chapter 38

# Spain

Madrid
December 20, 1940

The brilliant white snow blanketing the city was an ironic mis-representation of the darkness of the reigning Francoism. The population was out begging in the streets. The fallout of all the bombing was still evident on Gran Vía. Joy had disappeared from Madrid like the summer heat. At least the bodies of the men and women shot or beaten to death no longer filled the place with the stench of death as they had in previous months. The few street dogs that remained were prime prey for Madrid's hungry poor, and the mongrels that escaped alive fed on the cadavers the municipal undertaker had no more resources to deal with. Spontaneous assassinations, brutal reprisals, uniformed people in the street, and the fear of being dragged off at night never to return—it had all turned Madrid into a sleepless place. The streets were dark, and there were no Christmas decorations beyond a splintered, bullet-holed nativity in Puerta de Alcalá and a few meager garlands in Puerta del Sol.

We had crossed the border without much trouble. Most people were trying to get out of Spain, not in. With our false papers and the excuse of coming from Mexico to visit an aunt who lived in Madrid, the customs officers stamped our falsified passports and waved us on down the line.

Atocha Station was still intact. We walked through the plaza and down Atocha Street. I was holding a piece of paper with the address of Jacinto Guerrero, the director of my mother's theater troupe from ages ago. He knew us well, especially me and Isabel, but in that version of inhospitable Madrid where anyone might betray you for a plate of weevil-infested beans, it was better not to trust anyone. Informants lurked in every building, and neighborhoods were organized by the Falangists, with neighborhood and building bosses who kept tabs on every move made by every inhabitant.

We rang the bell, and an elderly maid opened the door. She was gaunt, with thin, parchment-like skin. She looked like a ghost.

"Who are you? The master is busy . . ."

"We're the children of Amparo Alcalde, one of his star actresses." The maid looked us up and down.

"You're the children of 'la Amparito'? I can't believe my eyes. Goodness, how you've grown. You won't remember me, but we worked together when she was just starting out. Jacinto hired me here after I retired. There's nothing for an actress but hunger and poverty once youth passes. But that's neither here nor there. Come in, come in. You must be exhausted. Have you come far?"

"From Mexico," Ana answered.

"You're the little one. What was your name, now? Was it Ana?"

"Yes, ma'am," Ana answered.

We followed her down a long hall with the walls covered by old posters of theater shows. The woman took us to a living room and had us sit on the couch.

"Jacinto usually doesn't get up 'til around noon, but I'll tell him you're here. While he gets ready, I'll get you some powdered milk and biscuits. The director's got connections, and the authorities give him a few products it's impossible to get with ration cards."

The woman went off in a hurry. We were surprised she could move so fast. She must have been younger than she looked. We sat and raised our eyes at one another. Things seemed to be going better than we could've hoped.

A few minutes later, she brought out a silver tray with cups of milk and biscuits. We devoured them, not having had anything to eat on the train.

Then Jacinto came in. He was much heavier than the last time I'd seen him at the theater, and getting fat in postwar Madrid was a luxury only a few privileged people could afford.

"Good gracious, the children of Amparo, one of my best actresses. So there's something pure left after all in this devil of a city. How is your mother? Is she here? I knew your father belonged to the Socialist trade union, but if she's not registered, I could hire her immediately. I'm premiering a new piece by Jardiel Poncela," he said, gesticulating wildly. His maroon silk robe fluttered above his expansive middle as he bent to kiss our cheeks.

"We don't know where she is. She sent us to Mexico during the war, and we've just arrived back in Madrid. In Mexico we learned our parents might be in a concentration camp."

"Shh! Don't say those words. The walls have ears. You're not safe here. Did anyone see you come into the building?" he asked, nervous.

"A custodian outside the door," Isabel said.

"That's fine. I'm not worried about him. I give him food every day. The poor fellow is very down on his luck. Anyway, I've got a storehouse where I keep all the costumes and props and such. You'll be safe there for the time being. We can't be seen together in the street, but I'll come by every day to greet you. Here," he said, handing us some money, "this will get you by for a while. Everything's rationed these days, but you can get a lot on the black market. Don't tell anyone who you really are. I hope you find your parents soon."

"Thank you," we said, and I put the money away.

Jacinto leaned toward the window and peered out the lace curtain. "I don't see anything amiss, but you'd better go out with Angelines when it gets dark. For now, finish eating." Jacinto walked out, and we three looked at one another in alarm. We hadn't been conscious of the danger we faced in Madrid up to that point. If we were detained, they would surely separate us and send us to an orphanage.

The maid led us out just as the few surviving streetlights were being lit. We walked for fifteen minutes through the somewhat deserted streets to the neighborhood of Lavapiés. She stopped in front of a small building and led us inside. It seemed to have once been a store but was now full of dresses and costumes hung up on hangers. It was more like a forest of clothing of all styles and eras. At the back there was a room with two pallets, as well as a half bath.

"Don't go out for the time being, please," Angelines said. "Jacinto should get the lay of the land first. He'll ask around about your parents. He's got plenty of contacts. I've got your supper and some breakfast here in this basket. Goodbye for now, my children. May God keep you."

She lit a candle so no light would be seen from the street and then left us. We lay down fully dressed on the pallets. That was our first night back in Madrid, feeling once again like strangers with no place in this world. And we weren't wrong to feel that way.

# Chapter 39

# Imprisoned

Madrid
December 23, 1940

The days crawled by with painful monotony in that abandoned warehouse, and our hopes that Jacinto would discover our parents' whereabouts were slowly vanishing. Though he had promised to come see us, he hadn't been by even once. Angelines did come every day, bringing us food, books, and blankets to shield us from the freezing cold that gripped the capital.

We had nearly lost all hope when one morning, close to Christmas, Jacinto came by to tell us what he'd learned. He was dressed extravagantly, just shy of ridiculous for a city that reeked of gunpowder and holy water. "My dear children, forgive me for not coming to see you before, but the performances are in full swing. The Falangists, not content with the blood and suffering of their enemies, are greedy for comedies, so I've been at it nonstop. From what I've learned from my contacts, there are over a hundred concentration camps spread throughout the country, though the smallest and most hastily constructed are starting to close. They're taking all sorts of people to the camps, especially political dissidents, but also religious minorities, homosexuals, gypsies, and anyone who doesn't fit within the Francoist vision of the new Spain. My contact has been scouring the files for three days. As you can imagine, things are more than a little chaotic, since the entire government has been turned upside down. Plus, some of the camps are run by Falangists, others by Requetés, and others by local governors or the military."

We looked at him impatiently. He was going 'round and 'round without getting to what really mattered.

Then he cleared his throat. "Well, it seems that your parents arrived a few days ago to the port of Bilbao on a boat bringing coffee from Mexico."

"From Mexico?" I asked in disbelief.

"Yes. Apparently they went to look for you there, and when they couldn't find you, they came back. Once here, they were arrested by the immigration police and taken to the local authorities. Your mother was placed in a women's prison on the outskirts of Bilbao, and your father taken to one of the worst concentration camps, Miranda de Ebro, between Bilbao and Burgos."

We sat there stunned in the tension between joy and grief. At least they were alive, and they were in Spain.

"Can we see them?" Ana asked. "When will they get out of those horrible places?"

She had no way of understanding how serious it was that our parents were imprisoned. Hundreds of people were killed by government orders every day. Franco's desk was littered with death sentences he signed with glee. The rest of the world was too busy with the war in Europe to pay attention to what was going on in Spain. The only voices speaking out against the mass killings were a few ecclesiastical authorities and more moderate politicians.

Jacinto shook his head, compassion in his eyes. "No, darling, they can't have visitors. The concentration camps aren't like jails used to be, where thieves and anybody who broke the law would go. Prisons aren't like they used to be either. The people locked up inside have no rights. They're under military guard and are considered traitors. They are forced to do labor in order to eat, and living conditions are abysmal."

Ana started to cry, and Isabel tried to console her but was barely keeping herself together. I wrestled with my breath and finally managed to control my voice enough to ask, "What have they been accused of?"

"Sedition, treason, rebellion, violent crime. There's no proof they've done harm to anyone, but I'm afraid that military tribunals don't pay much attention to details."

"Can you do anything for them? Try to get them out?"

Jacinto was already putting himself at great risk by even asking about our parents. No one was safe amid that reign of terror and oppression. From one day to the next, the people lauding you for being a great playwright and theater director could turn around and report you to the authorities. Censoring, taking over businesses, purging companies, as well as making illegal payments to government employees to turn a blind eye, were the norm.

"Your mother's case is a bit simpler. There's no documentation linking her to any party or organization. They've accused her of lifting troop morale on the front, but that's not a serious offense. I've asked my contact to request an order for liberation and a dismissal of her case. He's promised me he'll do what he can. Your father is a different story. He was part of the UGT, the socialist party, and participated in the assault on the Montaña Barracks. He commanded soldiers and worked in Madrid's jails during the war. If we could find someone to testify on his behalf, someone he spared from death . . ."

It would be extremely difficult to find the people my father had rescued and even more difficult to get any of them to testify.

"My dad helped a lot of people, which is why he requested to be transferred to defending and protecting the Prado Museum. Some of the anarchists and communists were gunning for him," I said. That's what Dad had explained to me before we left for Mexico.

"We need names, people who would be willing to testify on his behalf."

Jacinto left before dark. He had brought us some rolls, shortbread cookies, and little soldiers made of marzipan, all of which were unbelievable delicacies in those days. My sisters and I huddled around the little table and had our supper.

"What are we going to do?" Isabel asked.

"We have to find those witnesses. I don't remember anybody's name, but maybe some of Dad's friends would know," I said.

"But it's too dangerous to go out," Isabel said. She had been scared stiff since the moment we'd arrived back in Spain.

"You two can stay here, and tomorrow I'll go out and try to find some witnesses. It'll be Christmas Eve, so I bet the control points will be a little more relaxed. I'll come back before dark."

Ana clung to me in fear. "We can't get separated. I don't want anything to happen to you. You know we promised Mom we'd stay together."

"But if we don't do anything, they might kill Dad. Mom will understand," I answered.

After supper, I read for a while. Angelines had brought me a book written by a British author named Charles Dickens. The misfortunes that befell the main characters reminded me a bit of what we'd endured in Mexico. I was thinking about my mother as I drifted off to sleep. She had begged me to never forget her, and I had not forgotten. Memories of her were some of the few things that helped me keep going.

The next morning, I dressed warmly and slipped out before my sisters woke up. I didn't want them to worry, but I was afraid that if I didn't go while they were sleeping, they would never let me leave.

It felt strange to walk along the streets, almost like being in a dream. My mind had long since idealized Madrid to mythical proportions, but there I was, walking along the very real streets and drinking in its beautiful buildings. The war had wounded the city but hadn't crushed its essence.

I came upon a priest who glared at me. "Despicable red! Haven't they taught you to kiss a priest's hand when you meet one in the street?"

Fear momentarily paralyzed me, but I bent to kiss his ring and then went on, shaking from head to foot.

I reached Plaza Mayor and then went to one of the bars my dad used to go to with friends after work. Only one of his old comrades was there. Those who hadn't fled or died were shut up in jails or in the regime's concentration camps, and the only one who seemed unchanged was the bartender. His beard was a little grayer and his frame a bit thinner, but he was the same quarrelsome, mean-faced old man.

"Mr. Ramón, you won't remember me, but I'm the son of Francisco, the printer."

He stared at me as if a voice from the distant, long-forgotten past were whispering to him. "You're Francisco's boy? The last time I saw you, you were knee-high to a grasshopper. Looks like war turns little squirts into men quicker than anything else. What are you doing here? I haven't seen your old man in a long time, not since the day the . . . the day the Nationals liberated us," he said, carefully choosing his phrases to reduce suspicions among his clientele.

"I'm not looking for him. I'm trying to find Sebas, his friend and assistant."

"Sebas? Now he's one I *have* seen. I think he's working on the presses for a Falangist paper. *Arriba* is what it's called, if I'm not mistaken. They're in the building where *El Sol* was."

"I know where that is," I answered. I quickly made my way out of the bar and walked down the freezing streets toward the newspaper's building. There was a tough-looking custodian at the door, but I decided to try my luck.

"Where do you think you're going, kid?" he grunted as I made to enter. I held a cup of coffee, which had been the only thing I could think of to get me in the door.

"I'm from the coffee shop down the street. One of the editors ordered coffee—I guess he didn't have time to come get it?"

The man's pockmarked face and dark mustache creased into a frown, but he let me through. I went to the elevator but pressed the button to go down to the basement, where I figured the printing presses would be. I opened the door and left the coffee cup on the stairs, then walked around the machines hoping to find Sebas, but I didn't see him anywhere.

"Excuse me, sir. I'm looking for Sebastián Bustamante," I said to one of the operators.

"Sebas? He's upstairs, in editorial. He took up a proof of the afternoon's front page."

I took the elevator back up as fast as I could, knowing that the guard at the door would get suspicious if I didn't leave the building soon. I looked all over for him among the journalists. Most wore Falangist uniforms, and my skin crawled at being so close to them.

"Sebas," I said, finally finding him with a ream of paper in his hands.

My father's former assistant stopped short when he saw me. "Marco Alcalde? Am I seeing a ghost? Come with me," he said, taking my elbow. He didn't want to talk in front of all the Falangists. "I thought you and your sisters were in Mexico. Your parents were going to try to find you."

"I know, but . . . it didn't work out. Now they're both locked away, and I need your help."

"My help?" His brows knit together in confusion. "Don't think that just because I work here I know people who can pull strings."

"That's not what I mean. I need to find some of the people my dad helped. You know he didn't support the massacre of the fifth column."

Sebas furtively glanced all around. "This isn't the best place to talk. Tell me how to find you, and I'll bring you a list."

I hesitated for a moment, then gave him the address of the warehouse in Lavapiés before returning to the elevator. Sebas went back to one of the tables and started talking with a journalist.

I left the building and walked down the streets that were now quite crowded. My heart soared as I went along Gran Vía toward Plaza de España. For a mere moment I let myself cherish the place. I dusted off the dregs of memory of what it was like to wander aimlessly through the streets for the sheer pleasure of the hustle and bustle of a big city, losing myself to the invisibility of being in a crowd.

# Chapter 40

# Split Up

Madrid
December 24, 1940

Our past few Christmases had been more bitter than sweet: far from home and from our parents, surrounded by strangers, and heavy with the galling sensation that we would never be reunited as a family. As I walked back to the clothing warehouse, for the first time in years I let myself dream about future Christmases. I saw the five of us sitting around a table eating a good meal and opening presents on Three Kings Day. Little by little the streets were emptying. People were rushing home to celebrate with their families. I walked to the warehouse building and pulled out the key, but the door was ajar. Fear prickled up my spine. It was dark inside, and the suits and costumes seemed like ominous ghosts as I walked to our room at the back. I jumped when I saw two men wearing gray raincoats. I looked all around but didn't see Isabel or Ana.

"Marco Alcalde, I believe? Looking for your sisters? Don't worry, they're safe. Tonight they'll sleep in a nearby convent with the nuns and tomorrow will go to an orphanage."

My blood froze at those words. How had they found us?

"Why did you take them? They're not orphans. They're under my care."

One of the men stood, and I took a step back.

"Your parents, blasted reds, sent you three to Mexico in 1937. You're some of the Morelia children. Some have already returned, and more are on their way back. But you three left Mexico and reentered the country illegally. We found your false passports here. Do you know how serious a crime that is?"

"We had no choice," I said, gasping. My mouth was dry. I wanted to bolt, but my legs had turned into stiff boards.

"How old are you, sixteen? For now we'll take you to an orphanage, but next year, if you don't behave, you'll end up in jail. Now, let's cut the chatter or we'll miss our Christmas Eve supper."

I turned and ran, but before I got to the door someone else stepped out and blocked my way.

"Sebas?" I cried out in disbelief. "How could you?"

My father's former assistant looked at me with the disdain one might save for a sewer rat. "Times have changed, kid. It's nothing personal. These people don't care if your dad saved a few priests or rich guys from Salamanca. He's a dangerous red and there's no place for people like him in the new Spain."

I looked at him with contempt, knowing his reporting us had probably secured him some sort of promotion or benefit. My dad had done everything for him: taught him a trade, treated him like family in our house—but human loyalty is conditional.

"You're despicable!" I screamed, spitting in his face.

The policemen grabbed my arms and dragged me out of the building. It had started to snow, and I could hear the music of Christmas carols in the distance. I thought about my poor sisters, our worst fears coming to fruition on a holiday that should have been a celebration. I envisioned my mother locked in a cell of the women's prison at Bilbao, at her wit's end for not knowing where we were; and I imagined my father bowed over in Miranda de Ebro, utterly incapable of protecting the family he'd lost.

We walked to a car parked in front of the warehouse. They shoved me into the backseat, and the car headed for Puerta del Sol. They locked me in a cell at the General Security Administration until I could be transferred to one of the regime's orphanages. I looked out the partially frosted window. My family was spread throughout the country, and within days we would all be locked up far away from one another. I tried not to descend into despair. I said a short prayer, regardless of whether or not anyone would hear it. I simply begged to be together with my family again. Then I thought about the millions of people that night who would be missing loved ones around their table: husbands, wives, fathers, mothers, brothers, sisters, sons, daughters, friends, or even acquaintances who would never again celebrate Christmas with them. I barely felt the tears pouring down my frigid cheeks. My chest hurt as if I'd been stabbed, and I wanted to give up right then and there, let fate have its way with my stubborn will. But hope was all I had. It was the only thing I could hold on to—the same hope that lived in the hearts of invalids whose lives hung by a thread, the hope that fluttered in the hearts of parents who received a letter from children feared dead, the hope that nourished those who would have nothing to eat that night, the hope that remained for the prisoners in jail hearing the shots of the nearby firing squad. At that moment I understood that, in the winter of 1940, the lives of millions and millions of people were dangling from the thin, fraying thread of hope.

Part 5

# The Layers
# of Loneliness

Chapter 41

# Paracuellos

Paracuellos
December 26, 1940

After two nights in a cold, dirty cell, being released was a Christmas gift. The whole time I'd been tortured by thoughts of what had become of my sisters. If the Francoists had set up over a hundred concentration camps for adults, I figured they must have something similar for children. Besides the thousands of orphans, tens of thousands more children had parents who were locked up or in exile. The state had taken charge of them, and what could have been considered an act of charity was exactly the opposite.

A couple of police officers took me to a small van parked in the alley behind the building where I'd been held prisoner, and they sat me down next to four other teenage boys, slamming the door before I was fully settled. We wound through Madrid's snow-covered streets heading toward the road to Aragon and less than an hour later arrived at a town on the outskirts of Madrid. The vehicle pulled into an area surrounded by a high brick wall and parked in front of a dirty, run-down building.

"Come on, you filthy reds!" one of the policemen yelled as he dragged us out of the car. Four guards in Falangist uniforms were waiting for us at the door.

The director was named Juan Rufián—an "old shirt," as the Falangists called the veteran fascists who hadn't signed up with the party just because of the benefits it provided under the new state. The original Falangists, despite having been combined by Franco with other parties into one umbrella party called the Falange de las JONS, maintained their fascist principles and believed that Spain could become like Italy or Germany. Most of Franco's ministers, many of them military monarchists, looked askance at the fascists, but the dictatorship needed Hitler's support and therefore gave them a bit of leeway to show the world that there was true ideology behind the cruel, foolish civil war.

Juan Rufián looked each of us up and down, inspecting our teeth, arms, and pupils. "They'll do for work," he said. "Many of the reds are pure trash. As Antonio Vallejo-Nájera makes very clear in his writings, Marxism is a sign of mental illness." Several of his comrades chuckled at that.

A priest wearing a cassock walked up, the Falangist symbol of the yoke and arrows on his lapel. Father Onésimo Sánchez was charged with indoctrinating us and turning us into good Catholics. Though hardly any red children had been baptized, the mere fact that we were Spaniards automatically made us Catholic in his mind.

They pushed and shoved us to the infirmary, where we were ordered to undress for a doctor to examine us. For all of the boys

I'd been grouped with, it was painfully embarrassing to strip naked before all of those men, especially the priest.

"Have you had breakfast?" the director asked.

We shook our heads, none of us daring to speak.

"Well, too bad, because we don't fatten up reds here. Fermín, shave their heads and show them to their palace suites. Here you'll work for your food. The new Spain we're building isn't going to give your lazy tails a free ride."

The one called Fermín was a working-class Falangist, chief servant, and errand boy. He was like a useful pet to the Falangists. He could've left the orphanage the year before, but they kept him around to do the dirty work.

He led us to a filthy, cockroach-infested room that would be our living quarters. Then he ordered us toward the workshop, despite our empty stomachs. In the workshop, a cramped and squalid little hut, we were to make rope. The workshop boss assigned us various jobs, and we worked in silence until lunchtime.

That wretched orphanage was nothing like the school in Morelia. Even though the first director of the Spain–Mexico School had hated us and the second treated us like we were in the military, the orphanage in Paracuellos was a prison of the worst kind. I came to learn firsthand how fanaticism drives humans to commit unimaginable atrocities.

At lunch, I sat beside one of the youngest boys, who couldn't have been more than nine years old. People called him Blondie.

"Did you just get here?" he whispered.

"Yes. What is this place?"

"It's hell. Social Aid set up centers like this all over the country. The fascists call them 'homes for war orphans.' But I'm not an orphan. My mom's alive, in jail. We were there together for a few months. I thought that was bad, but . . ." He shook his head. "This is a million times worse."

"Who's talking?" Fermín said menacingly.

Terrified, we stopped our conversation. After the meal, we went back to work until dinnertime. They allowed us to wash up and then we were to go to bed. In whispered spurts throughout the afternoon, I had learned from Blondie that we were forbidden from speaking, playing, singing, gathering in groups, or doing any spontaneous activity. Life was organized around work from the moment we awoke to the moment we laid down at night. Only on Sundays would we have a modicum of free time, when we were allowed to be outside in the yard after the obligatory Mass.

After washing my face, we had thirty minutes before lights out when all noise would be forbidden. Blondie came up to my bed.

"What is going on in this place?" I asked, bewildered.

"They say it's an orphanage, but it's really one big torture chamber. I can't remember anything from before the war. That's as far back as my memories go. I lived in the Vallecas neighborhood with my parents, who were anarchists. Toward the end, anarchists were hunted down in Madrid. The communists shot my dad, and my mom and I were all alone. There was nothing to eat, but at least we were together. When the Francoists invaded Madrid, some of our neighbors reported us, and they took us to Ventas, the women's prison. Mothers and their children were crammed into the cells together without water and barely any food. Babies were crying constantly, and the mothers weren't given diapers to change them. The stench was unbearable. Once a week the women could wash clothes, but they weren't allowed to dry them outside. They'd try to dry their babies' clothes with their own body warmth. Every day some were taken out to be shot, and the kids were just left there, dirty and alone. Other women would take care of them until the Falangists would come and cart them off. After a few months, they began taking the children away, starting with the youngest ones. The officers would rip the kids out of their mothers' arms, screaming at the women and beating them back. Eventually they took the rest of us away too. I'm too old for anybody to want to adopt me, but the younger kids were given to regime families."

I gawked at him in silence, unable to believe what I'd just heard. What kind of people would commit such atrocities? It was one thing to punish the parents, even though the only thing they'd done wrong was to support the democratic government of the Republic. It was something else entirely to steal their children.

"Go to sleep!" Fermín barked, slamming off the lights.

"Where are you from?" Blondie asked me. "You've got a funny accent."

"From Mexico," I said, my voice barely audible.

"Mexico? Where's that?"

"In the Americas."

"What? Why did you come to Spain? There's nothing here. It's one big tomb, and we're all just a bunch of walking dead."

It took me a very long time to fall asleep that first night. I hated myself for insisting we leave Mexico, especially when I thought about how my sisters would be going through something just as horrible as my fate, or worse. I had to get out of there any way I could. After everything that had happened, I wasn't going to stand there with my arms crossed while my family was completely destroyed.

They woke us up by shouting at us. We had to rush to get dressed before eating a meager breakfast. Then we had an hour or so of elementary school classes, because the Falangists deemed our education was complete so long as we knew the basic mathematic functions and how to read. The rest of the day was spent in the workshop.

"This Sunday, one of the big bosses is coming," a boy named Rubio whispered to me at lunch. I was twirling my spoon through the worms and chickpeas mixed together in my bowl, but sooner or later I would have to eat it because we were required to eat everything served to us. We were told often how good and magnanimous Franco was; out of pure Christian love he fed the children of his enemies.

"Is that good or bad?"

"Depends on how you look at it. They'll give us better food and clean clothes, but our prison guards will be all uptight. If anyone steps out of line, they'll have his head. Know what I mean? The government gives this place money for each kid under their roof, but the director of course buys the cheapest stuff possible so he can keep the profit. Thus the dawn of the new Spain . . ." Rubio trailed off, paraphrasing one of the common Francoist slogans.

Just then, the priest came into the dining hall. "Confession is this afternoon. Come one by one, in order of your class roll. Understood?" he said.

Blondie started to shake—so much so that I asked what was going on.

"Just be careful of Father Onésimo. Besides being a cruel, fanatic Falangist, he's dangerous."

That warning scared me. I was seventeen years old and had seen a lot, but the people in that orphanage truly terrified me.

That afternoon, the workshop boss ordered me to take some samples up to the director, and I seized my chance to study the campus. The wall was really high, at least thirteen feet, and topped by barbed wire, except for one part where a mound of dirt piled at the base put the wall at about ten feet. Regardless, it looked impossible to climb, and the gate was always locked. The main building looked like it had once been a monastery. There was a fountain with dirty water, a large yard with both the Francoist flag and the Falangist flag, a chapel, a soccer field ruined by countless holes, and a garden where some of the boys worked instead of in the workshop. I went into the main building. I had hardly seen the first floor because our dormitories were upstairs. Of what was on the main floor, we were only allowed into the dining hall and, a precious few times a month, into the gymnasium.

The director's office was in the nicer part of the building. The walls were wood-paneled, making it feel much warmer than our bare brick walls, and the floors were carpeted. Portraits of Falangist leaders hung from the walls beside paintings depicting heroic scenes from Spain's history. The director had a secretary, and she and a couple of nuns who worked as nurses were the only females on the premises.

"What do you want?" the secretary snapped. She was mean-looking with thick glasses, greasy skin, and an ill-fitting Falangist uniform.

I cleared my throat and said, "The workshop boss sent me to show some samples to the director. He said he doesn't want to make any mistakes."

"Hang on," she said, standing with an exasperated sigh. She knocked at the director's door. "There's a kid out here with some samples," she called.

"Let him in," came the reply.

I was trembling as I stepped forward. More than respect, I felt pure terror for the man. I stood waiting by his desk while he read a newspaper.

"Give them here," he said, holding out his hand. I passed him the samples, and he examined them, wrote a short note, and handed me the piece of paper. "Sit down," he ordered. When I obeyed, he stood up and started walking around the office. It was decorated in a pretentious, almost ridiculous way, as if a lowly director of a charitable institution were considered one of the great leaders of the regime.

"I've read your file," he began. "Finally, they brought me someone interesting, not just your everyday starving red scum who can't tell his tail from his elbow. In 1937 you went to Mexico. You're one of those little Morelia brats. It seems you studied hard and finished primary school, then started high school in Mexico City. You're a smart kid. Vallejo-Nájera would say we might be able to save you. Maybe your brain hasn't rotted from the red virus. So why did you come back to Spain? Surely you were nostalgic. Nowhere else on earth is as beautiful as Spain."

I had no idea how to answer. Anything I said would likely be misinterpreted. "Well," I stuttered, "I did miss Spain a lot, but mainly I missed my family. I didn't know what had happened to them."

Juan Rufián perched at the edge of his desk and drummed his fingers on his chin. "Mmm, good answer. Family is an important value, though in your case it's been a bad influence. Your father is a socialist and a union man; he had an important role among printers in Madrid and was one of the assassins of our comrades at the assault on the Montaña Barracks."

"My father isn't a murderer," I blurted out without even thinking.

He slapped me hard across the face. "Your father is exactly what I say he is," he hissed.

"Yes, sir," I answered, my cheek on fire.

"You have two younger sisters and a mother who was an actress and also a red, a harlot like all actresses. But you could leave all that behind, you know. We need smart boys, boys who are brave and have life experience. I'll be watching you closely."

I had goosebumps, and the hair on the back of my neck stood on end.

"Mexico, one of our conquests . . . I'd like to see it someday. Well, we're building Social Aid centers outside the country, starting with Cuba, I believe. Maybe I'll request a transfer. I imagine the Americas are very beautiful."

"They are, Mr. Rufián. I've been to Havana."

He raised his eyes as if to say he could just imagine it. "Very well, go on. We'll talk again later."

I stood up and went to the door, but before I closed it behind me, he said, "Oh, I forgot to mention, your father's been condemned to death. All the murderers must be purged from our new society. To start fresh, we'll do away with all the evil that led our beloved country to the brink of disaster. Kill the dog, and the rabies disappears."

My heart stopped at his words. I held myself together until I got outside, when the tears came out in suffocating gasps. My father had survived the long, hard war; he had escaped Spain; and it was our fault he'd come back to Spain only to be killed like an animal.

The rest of the day was chaotic. I couldn't pay attention to anything, my mind locked onto Rufián's closing words. After finishing in the workshop but just before supper, it was time for confession. The only good part was that meant we got to stop working a little early. We were allowed to be outside, and even though it was freezing cold, being outside at dusk was better than being bent over our work.

A boy came up and sat beside me. "What I wouldn't give for a cigarette right now," he said wistfully.

"You smoke?" I asked. I had tried cigarettes a couple times in Morelia but hadn't liked the taste.

"Yeah, it calms my nerves. It's impossible to get them in here. Sometimes Chema gives me one, but not often. The pigs say we're supposed to lead clean lives. But if they really believed that, then they would give us decent food instead of that hogwash."

The food was scant and awful, but even worse was our constant thirst. We weren't given enough water, and there was never coffee. Lots of the boys collected snow and drank it once it melted.

"What are your nerves so worked up about?" I asked.

"Confession," he said, looking at me in surprise. "I hate it."

"Why? Aren't you Catholic?"

The boy grimaced, then cupped his hands around some snow and started drinking it as it melted.

"You'll see for yourself. Just . . . just beware the priest."

That put me on edge. The boy in front of me in roll call came out of the chapel, and it was my turn. I went in with my hands stuffed deep in my pockets. I'd never gone to confession and hadn't even been baptized.

The chapel was dark and smelled damp and sweaty. It was austere, nearly spartan, but my eyes landed on a huge crucifix and two wooden statues of the Virgin. There was a confessional along one wall. I went up hesitantly and knelt down.

"Hello, son."

"Hello, F-father," I stuttered.

"You have to make the sign of the cross," the priest said, the ghostly voice issuing from the other side of the lattice through which he was hardly visible.

I made the motions that I remembered seeing in the church in Morelia when I would go to Mass to see María Soledad.

"In the name of the Father, the Son, and the Holy Spirit," he said, annoyed. "Have you never been to confession?"

"No, Father."

"Have you been baptized?" His voice raised a bit more each time he spoke to me.

"Not to my knowledge."

"So you've never had communion. You're a pagan, like a Saracen. Heaven help me, how much damage these atheist reds have done. We'll have to take care of that. Go on, tell me your sins."

"Well, I'm not sure what sins you're talking about."

"Everything you tell me is confidential. Thanks to the secrecy of confession, what you tell me stays between God and us."

I hesitated. They'd warned me about this revolting man.

"I try to be honest and good, I don't wish harm on anyone, I try to help other people . . ."

"Those aren't sins. Have you had impure thoughts? Have you touched yourself?"

"What? No!" I said, recoiling from the lattice.

"At your age, that's impossible. If you're not sincere, I cannot help you."

"All we do here is work. The only thing I think about is getting out and finding my family."

The priest pulled back the lattice and said, "God will punish you with eternal fire unless you confess!"

I looked at him in fear, and he slapped my face.

"Get out of here!" he yelled. "I'll make my report to the director, and you'll get what you deserve."

I ran out of the chapel, scared and confused. I couldn't understand anything that had just happened. Why would I talk about my life to a stranger? If God existed—a matter I was not at all sure about—I'd take care of telling him what I wanted to tell him.

I spent the night in a small closet where they locked up boys who misbehaved. I could hardly even sit down, and there was no light and nothing to eat. All I could do was think. I tried to sleep, to forget everything and give myself over to the world of dreams, but Rufián's words kept tearing through me like machine-gun fire: my father had been condemned to die. The world I knew and loved had almost completely fallen apart. The dark, macabre place we'd returned to was so different from the country I remembered that it was hardly recognizable, even though I'd only been gone a few years. Never in my worst nightmares had I imagined Spain becoming hell on earth where a man's life was worthless and Franco's black crows sought to rule people's souls. With my shattered heart, I tried to recall happy moments, to think about our small apartment so full of love. I wept bitterly. I had lost it all. All of it. I could no longer hope things might go back to how they used to be.

# Chapter 42

# Hell

Paracuellos
December 28, 1940

They let me out of confinement the next day. My whole body throbbed in pain, and I was hungry and thirsty beyond description. The boys in my group gave me some of the black bread they kept hidden to help mitigate their constant hunger, and their kindness touched me. I was allowed to wash up and then sent to class. It was hard to pay attention, but I tried my best.

Our teacher, José María Pérez, whom most of the boys called Chema, was one of the few adults at the orphanage who treated us with any degree of humanity. He announced, "Tomorrow, Sunday, the Social Aid national delegate will be making a visit to the school. His name is Don Manuel Martínez de Tena, and I expect you all to be on your best behavior. We must make a good impression. Due to her duties as a wife, our founder, Mercedes Sanz-Bachiller, can no longer fulfill her role, but the fact that there's a roof over your heads this winter and food on your plates every day is due to her." He paused and looked at me. "Marco, you're not looking well. Go back to your room. I'll let the director know."

I did feel truly horrible. I gathered my things and went straight to my dorm, where I fell immediately into a deep sleep. I'd been asleep maybe an hour when some noises woke me. I was scared, because no one was supposed to be in our rooms right then. I crept to the bathroom and heard Blondie's voice.

"No, please, Father Onésimo, please stop," he cried in distress. I nudged the door open just a crack. The priest's back was to me, and Blondie was in front of him. That's all I saw. I closed the door and went back to bed, buried my head under my pillow, and sobbed.

The next morning, as promised, we had the day off. It was almost like a holiday, though we did have to go to Mass. As the vile priest spoke, I couldn't stop thinking about the scene I'd witnessed the day before in the bathroom. Though I wasn't quite sure what I had seen, it made me feel sick nonetheless. I glanced at Blondie. Deep gray bags under his eyes dimmed their crystal blue. He met my gaze for a second. He knew I'd seen them.

"Dear children of God, despite the sins of your parents, God loves you. The most holy Virgin watches over you as a mother from heaven, and Franco, the Caudillo of Spain, provides your daily bread. The forces of evil seek to destroy our beloved country, the spiritual stronghold of the West, but providence has saved us from communism. Now our comrades in Germany and Italy are waging their crusade against atheism. Very soon that terrible and malevolent ideology of the demon Marx will be wiped off the face of the earth. Let us pray for those who govern us, that God would impart his wisdom and prudence to them." He droned on and on.

When Mass was over, Chema came up to me. "Can I trust you to wait on the director's table? If you do a good job, I'll give you a prize afterward."

"What kind of prize?" I asked, dubious.

"You'll see," was all he said.

At one o'clock, a luxury Mercedes-Benz drove into the orphanage. A chauffeur opened the back door, and a man in a gray coat and hat stepped out. He was not wearing a Falangist uniform. Rufián stood ready to greet him at the orphanage door. He bowed several times, and he led them all to the teachers' dining room.

Two of my classmates and I were dressed as waiters. We poured wine, then served three different dishes before bringing out the dessert. It had been years since I'd seen some of the delicacies the teachers ate that Sunday.

"Thank you for welcoming me into your home so lavishly," Manuel Martínez de Tena said.

"It is our great honor to host the national delegate," Rufián answered.

"Oh, come off it, Rufián, call me Manuel. We've known each other for years. How I miss José Antonio—he would've built a real Falangist Spain, none of this nonsense like *paquita la culona* has brought us."

Everyone guffawed. Despite Franco's purge of Falangist leadership in creating the unified JONS party of which he was the unquestioned leader, many longed for Hitler's help to oust him so they could implement a truly fascist regime.

"Oh, things are bad, comrade," Rufián quipped. "Serrano Suñer, the *Cuñadísimo*, does whatever he pleases. You saw what happened with Mercedes—the woman was a true saint! But of course *Hermanísima* Pilar wants to control the entire Falangist women's division. What does that pig know about being feminine?"

"The important thing is that the reds are under control. Thousands are being taken out for a little walk, but we can't kill them all. Some will have to go back to the factories. Marxism deceived them, but we'll show them a better life with the Falangists." Manuel raised his glass to toast. "To the return of the Spanish Empire! Down with communism; viva the Falange!"

They all shouted as one. Cocktails followed dessert, and soon they were singing patriotic songs. Rufián waved me over.

"This little red was one of the Morelia rats," he told his boss.

"We're working on getting the rest of the minors transferred. The sons of the fatherland need to come back home. Those blasted reds even set up an embassy in Mexico and are trying to keep their government going—in exile! If it weren't so pathetic it might be an offense to the regime," Manuel said, the flush of his face showing the number of drinks he'd consumed.

"This little squirt came back on his own with his sisters," Rufián said, clapping me on the shoulder and letting out a hoot.

"Well done, my boy. If only others would follow your example! There are thousands of Spaniard children all over Russia, France, England, Belgium, Argentina, and Mexico. They're Spaniards stolen by the reds," Manuel mused.

"You can go now," Rufián said, shooing me away.

An hour later the visit was over, and it was time to clean everything up. It was late when we finished, but before I headed up to bed, Chema called me over.

"Well, I think you've earned it. I wanted to tell you that your sisters are in an orphanage outside Madrid, in San Fernando de Henares. They're fine, and they're together. You don't need to worry about them. When you come of age and if you have a job, you can request guardianship over them. That won't be hard for a bright boy like you. You officially come of age at twenty-one, but if you're able to provide for yourself before then, they'll let you see them."

I was breathless. "Thank you," I said, and I meant it. Perhaps, just perhaps, there was a chance to see at least part of my family again.

I went up to our room, where most of the boys were already asleep. I got my clothes and went to the bathroom to wash up. The first thing that surprised me was a light that was already on. I set my clothes down and got ready to shower in the ice-cold water. Then I saw the blood, trickling out from one of the bathroom stalls. I didn't know what to do. My heart raced, but my body was paralyzed. I forced myself to go up to the door, and I pushed it open slowly. I didn't want to look, but I had to know if the person inside was dead or alive.

Chapter 43

# Lies

Paracuellos
December 29, 1940

My screams echoed throughout the entire building. I jumped back and started to retch. All the boys raced in, and a boy named Daniel threw a sheet over the body while Fermín went to get the director. Rufián ran up in his bathrobe, wearing a ridiculous hairnet on his head. They asked me what happened, but I couldn't speak. Everything was swimming in my head, and I heard their voices like noises underwater from far away. Finally, Chema showed up and managed to get through to me.

He put his hands on my shoulders and asked, "What happened, Marco?" I couldn't stop crying and saying Blondie's name over and over.

"What happened to him?" Chema asked again.

"I don't know. I don't know. I just found him there, dead, with blood everywhere."

I couldn't get the image of my friend's pale face out of my mind, his wrists slit and the blood all around him.

"Suicide," the director concluded after confirming that Blondie was dead. "What a disgrace."

Father Onésimo appeared and rubbed some sort of oil on the dead body. Then he turned to us and said, "This little angel is in the presence of our Lord and Savior."

I couldn't stop myself: I retched again, this time all over his feet. The director sent everyone else away.

"Well, Marco, things have turned ugly. We'd better clear up the facts before the inspection comes. The poor boy suffered a terrible accident, and that's what the doctor will record. If they ask you, you're to say you found him with his neck broken. Is that understood?"

I couldn't believe what I was hearing.

"But—" Chema started to say.

"Don José María Pérez, there are worse positions than here at the orphanage, I assure you. If you wish to avoid reports about your incompetence, I suggest you not make things more difficult. The child has died as a result of a terrible accident."

"He took his own life," Chema said, very serious.

"Suicide, accident, natural death—they're all ways of saying the same thing. The boy died. I don't want our institution to be disgraced. The church is already leery of our centers, and they want exclusive control over the education of the children. The only thing Carmen Polo cares about is making the priests happy, and we all know how influential Franco's wife is in the government. Now, get Marco calmed down and send him to bed."

Rufián left the bathroom. Blondie's body still lay there on the floor, as if no one cared what had happened to him.

"Don't worry, they'll come take him away and clean everything up," Chema said, reading my thoughts. "I'm really sorry, Marco. I really am."

"I know what happened," I croaked, my voice hoarse from the tears and vomit.

"Did you see something?" he asked, curious.

"No, he was already like that when I found him, but the priest, Father Onésimo, he . . . he was abusing Blondie, and probably some of the other boys too. Poor Blondie couldn't take it anymore and—"

"What you're saying is extremely serious. Do you realize that? You're accusing a servant of God of committing terrible sins."

"I saw it myself the other day, when you let me come back to bed to rest."

"That's not possible."

"I saw it. They were here, in the bathroom. The priest—"

"Stop, stop it right now! You heard the director. It was all a tragic accident. You have to learn that to survive in this world you've just got to look the other way sometimes. Do you think I've always been a Falangist? My father was the captain of a Republican group, a red, and they know it. I'll always be an intruder in this world. But if you learn how to adapt, you can get along." Pain and rage were at war on his face. In the new Spain, we had to learn our place or else the regime would devour us all.

I shook for a long, long time after I crawled into bed, and I couldn't sleep at all that night. I swore to myself I would get out of that hellhole the first chance I got. I couldn't stand it one day more.

In the morning, they lined everyone up to give them the news. It was the second-to-last day of the year, and to make us keep our mouths shut, they promised us a party on New Year's Eve.

Once the doctor wrote his falsified report, the director wanted to bury Blondie as soon as possible. The boy's mother was in prison and would have no way of finding out, so Rufián knew no one would come for the boy.

Before lunch we went to the chapel for a mass for the departed soul. The students were all standing, dressed in our Falangist orphanage uniforms. The director got up and spoke from the pulpit.

"Today is a day of mourning for our entire boys' home. A member of our family has left us. Young Tomás is now in heaven with the Virgin Mary and all the saints. Social Aid was created to help the children of Spain, regardless of their parents' ideologies. Christian, Falangist values are above the sins committed by one's parents. You boys are here to become proper Spaniards and Falangists. The caudillo has given each of you a second chance. Viva Spain! Viva Franco!"

We dutifully answered his rallying cries, and then Father Onésimo got up to officiate Mass. He seemed less put-together than usual.

"Poor Tomás has left us, but we who remain behind in this valley of tears will keep fighting to spread the light of the gospel to the world. Franco won much more than a war; he waged a campaign to restore the people's true faith. Tomás is one small sacrifice burning on the sacred altar of this great, free Spanish nation!"

After the ceremony, four of the boys lifted the coffin and carried it to the small cemetery behind the chapel. The grave had already been dug, and it took me aback to see how deep it was. It felt like the ground would literally swallow us up after we died. They lowered the simple pine box with rope we ourselves had made in workshop, and we heard a thud when the wood met the ground below. Then, one by one, each boy threw a handful of dirt onto the coffin. The priest said a few closing words to bid Tomás farewell, then the groundskeepers started shoveling the rest of the dirt over the casket.

That afternoon broke our hearts. Hardly anyone talked in the hallways or rooms. I thought about Morelia and the day Paquito had been electrocuted. The entire student body had revolted against our wicked director. Back then we still had the courage to stand up to evil. But there in the orphanage, we were a docile, frightened flock.

Daniel came up to me and put his arm over my shoulder. We were sitting on one of the beds. I didn't feel like talking, but he kept at it.

"Just don't think about it anymore. It could've been you, or me, or any of us. Sometimes I think about it, about doing myself in, you know. I mean, just try to imagine how many people have died. But we're here alive, you know? Alive and kicking."

"Alive? You call this life?" I asked, my temper rising.

"You haven't been here long. I swear, things on the outside aren't much better. Both boys and girls sell their bodies for scraps of stale bread. Others die on construction sites for miserly wages. And most everybody is starving to death. At least here we get to eat and—"

"And get raped, stomped on, abused, and brainwashed into their fascist ideology and religion. Yeah, sure, this is *way* better."

"Well, what are the options? They won the war, so what can we do about it?"

"Resist, not let ourselves get trampled on. They can control our bodies and try to control our minds, but we still have our souls. And they can't have those."

"It's a pretty thought," Daniel said, sighing and standing up.

As he walked away, I thought over what he'd said. I knew he was right, but I didn't want to admit it. In spite of everything, I could not just stand there idly.

The next day, the last day of 1940, we had class in the morning, then workshop like normal, but they gave us a nice meal that night. The rice was actually fresh, and for the first time since I'd gotten to the orphanage, we had meat. It was pork, and it tasted divine. They even gave us half a glass of sweetened wine and something chocolate for dessert. All together we counted down 'til the new year, and they let us have twelve pine nuts since we didn't have any grapes.

By midnight, most of the professors were drunk. I had developed the habit of scanning the adults for the priest to always keep him in sight, but tonight I couldn't find him. I slipped out of the main building. It was bitterly cold. I saw a light on in the chapel and went in quietly. The priest was on top of somebody on a pew. In my hand, I gripped a fork I'd taken from the dining hall. I snuck up and, before he had time to react, jammed the fork toward his groin with all my strength. I twisted the fork, and he screamed like a madman and then passed out. The boy ran away as soon as the priest's weight was off him, and I stood there quietly, not sure what to do. Finally, I went back outside, got a ladder from the workshop, and took it over to the spot where the dirt was mounded up against the wall. The ladder wasn't tall enough to reach the top, but as I stretched my arms up, I could grab hold of the barbed wire. My hands started to bleed, but I didn't feel any pain. Then I let myself fall down the other side. My leg throbbed but not enough to keep me from walking. I didn't know where I was going. I only knew I had to escape from that house of horrors as fast as possible.

# Chapter 44

# The Party

Walking around lost can be better than being in the wrong place. Most people prefer the security of a terrible life over the uncertainty of starting down the road with no plan or clear destination. Yet, often enough, desperation rescues us from disgrace. Something inside us compels us to escape, despite the fear and doubt. It might seem like our basic survival instinct, but it's actually the exact opposite. It's essentially a struggle between instincts and principles.

At dawn, I found an intersection that announced I was near Alcalá de Henares. From there I knew I could hop on a train that would take me to Madrid. My sisters were in San Fernando de Henares, not far from Alcalá, but I couldn't just show up dressed like I was and get them out. I'd attacked a priest and run away from a state orphanage, and I was the son of a man condemned to die. I thought about going to my grandparents' house, but I didn't want to bring trouble to them or cause them any more grief. The only place I could think of where I would feel somewhat safe was in the house of my mother's former troupe director.

I jumped onto the train when it was already in motion and spent the thirty-plus minutes of the ride avoiding the inspectors. When I got to Atocha Station, I again had that strange feeling of being free. It's one of the most mysterious sensations in the world. It might seem like the natural state of human beings, but most of the time that's not the case. We're slaves to so many things, to social conventions that pressure us, to the moral principles we were taught as children, to imposed fears and taboos, to not living up to what our parents expect of us . . . In short, slaves to leading unworthy lives. Sometimes death seems like liberation, though at the core it's the ultimate abdication. As long as we're alive, we're fighting and struggling, and there's the possibility of changing and trying to transform the world. Dying, however, is life's greatest act of impotence; death, the final unvanquishable foe.

I got to Jacinto's gate and paused. I was thinking about my sisters and all the hope we'd had when we arrived in Madrid not many days before. The city seemed to slumber in the New Year's Eve hangover. Still shackled to desperation, I was hardly aware of the fact that a new year had begun. Desperation is atemporal, a kind of purgatory where minutes become years and centuries become an eternity.

I knocked at the door, and the maid opened after a minute or two. Angelines was shocked to see me, as if staring at a ghost. In a way, I did look like a ghost in that absurd Falangist uniform.

"Good heavens, what . . . How?" she began.

"I'm fine. Can I see—?"

"He's asleep. He got pretty drunk yesterday. It's New Year's Day."

I nodded and started to cry. "I need help."

She brought me inside. She fixed me some hot chocolate and cookies, and I started to feel much better after sitting down in the warmth.

"Jacinto got into some pretty bad trouble. Some friends got him out of it, but he was accused of harboring fugitive children."

"I'm so sorry," I said.

"You know how he is. Well, maybe you don't know, but he's very melodramatic. It's in his blood. Where are your sisters?" Angelines asked. Her question brought me back to reality like a hammer falling on my thumb.

I gulped. "Locked up in a Social Aid center. My mom's in prison, and my dad's been condemned to die," I said, dissolving into tears again.

"Oh, honey, I'm so, so sorry. These are wretched, terrible times we're living in. Thank God I'm old and don't have much longer to go. I hardly recognize this country anymore."

We heard some footsteps, and Don Jacinto entered the dining room. He rubbed his eyes when he saw me. "Well, New Year's brings mysterious gifts," he said, smothering me in a hug.

I told them what had happened since I'd last seen them. Jacinto's eyes were wide in disbelief as I talked about the orphanage and how the children were mistreated, especially the day of Blondie's death.

"After they found you three in the costume warehouse, they asked me so many questions—but thanks to my connections, nothing came of it. You know how angry I was about your mother's situation in the women's prison. I haven't been able to do much, for which I'm so sorry. She's not been sentenced to death, but for now she'll have to stay there."

The tears came again, great gasping waves of them. I couldn't take it anymore: my sisters locked up in an orphanage, my parents imprisoned. I was completely powerless. Throughout those many years I had faced terrible things and managed to overcome them all, but the current situation was beyond my control.

"I'm so sorry, my boy," Jacinto said. "I could seek custody of your sisters, though I'm not sure they'd grant it."

"Thanks, but you've done enough for us," I said between sniffing and wiping my nose. "Sometimes we just have to leave things in the hands of fate."

He asked Angelines for a glass of port, longing to forget the things I'd just told them. The country where we lived no longer belonged to us.

"I can get you some money. Maybe with a little help . . ."

"Thanks," I said despondently. But money wasn't going to change anything.

Jacinto let me sleep at his house that night, and the next morning, before he or Angelines awoke, I slipped away. At first I wandered through the city, though every corner and each street recalled some happy memory from when I was young. People are never aware of happiness when they're experiencing it, only later—like walking through dense fog and sensing a glimmer of light, some small lamp to light your way.

I ended up walking around University City. The vestiges of war were so evident in that area of northern Madrid. Mortar shells and the craters of bombs were strewn about the place. Then I walked through a pine grove and came to a well-to-do neighborhood with high-end villas. Dogs growled and barked from behind the fences, baring their sharp teeth at me, but I hardly glanced at them. I felt completely absent, unconnected to my body, watching everything around me with the indifference of a death wish.

Eventually I sat down on a fallen trunk and stared out at the field and the villas of the new masters of Spain. Then I heard the voices of children behind me. Turning, I saw a maid pushing a baby carriage while little twin boys walked beside her. I watched them play for a few minutes, remembering when my sisters were younger. The memories got me crying again.

"Are you okay?" a female voice asked. I didn't bother lifting up my head. I knew the person would walk on by and leave me alone. But she didn't. "Can I do anything for you?" the voice insisted.

I looked at her shiny black shoes, dark stockings, and the hem of a pink satin dress. I shook my head, but then the woman bent down. "Are you hungry?" she asked.

My eyes were clouded with tears as I looked at her. I was a ball of anger. I didn't want any compassion from the victors. Instead I wanted to spit in her face, but I didn't have the energy.

"I live nearby. Those are my boys playing over there. Do you need work? My gardener is looking for some help," she said.

For the first time I looked directly at her, and her face seemed somehow familiar to me, but I couldn't remember where I would've seen her before.

Finally, she led me over toward the maid and the children, then we walked for a few minutes and stopped before a high wall. The wall was painted black and gold, and two lions sat atop the pillars flanking the gate.

The woman led me to the gardener's small hut and introduced me. "Javier, this boy can help you with the grounds."

"But, miss, I need someone with experience. I don't have time to train this boy," the man huffed. Despite his age, he looked to be strong and able.

The woman frowned, then pushed me forward gently so I was standing in front of the gardener. "This boy looks strong and capable. I hope you teach him the trade well."

When the woman was out of earshot, Javier let loose. "That stuck-up witch! Treats us all like we're her slaves. The Gonzagas are one of these new regime families. Her husband's one of Franco's right-hand men, though a guy like the Caudillo only has right hands—nothing left about him. Anyway, where the hell did you come from?"

I didn't know how to answer. My head was still spinning. I had decided to just let myself float along since I had no idea what to do with my life. Maybe a job would help me get things in order and retrieve my sisters from the orphanage sooner rather than later. I cleared my throat and began, "I'm Marco Alcalde, and the lady—"

"Another one of these poor wretches from the country who's come to the city looking for a better future. Well, let me tell you, there's no future here, or anywhere else for that matter. The world has lost its mind."

He let me into the house and pointed to a pallet with threadbare blankets in the attic. "I'll get you some work clothes. You've got to remember four simple rules: First, never go in the master's house unless you're invited; second, never speak to them unless they speak to you first; third, do everything I tell you without complaining; and fourth, don't go in the yard when the Gonzagas are having a party. Is all of that clear?"

I nodded and tried to make myself invisible. The boys were still on holiday from school for Christmas and New Year's, and the mistress of the house played with them in the yard in the mornings. I hid behind the shrubs and watched them, thinking about my family. I felt a measure of comfort seeing the kids happy. Very few families could say the same about their children in our country devastated by war and hatred.

The masters held a party the night before Three Kings Day. It wasn't one of their bigger parties, Javier explained, just something for family. Luxury cars started arriving and parking at the front door in the afternoon. The women who got out of them wore elegant evening gowns, and the men, suits or the Falangist uniform. The butler greeted them formally in the entryway and led them to the great hall. The cloudy sky made the afternoon feel darker than usual, and night would soon stretch its shadows over the dead winter lawn.

Going against Javier's instructions, I slipped out of the small house where I now lived and got close to the back of the big house. Hidden in the shadows, I could see the great hall through the huge picture windows. The guests were drinking wine from fine glasses and eating canapés from silver trays. I watched for a while, not believing so much luxury and excess existed in such proximity to the poorest neighborhoods of the capital.

Children ran around wrapped presents circling a Christmas tree while older adults sat and chatted on silk-lined armchairs. The mistress of the house went back and forth between guests, gushing over each.

Furious at such waste while most of the population was starving, I turned to leave and ran smack into one of the guests. She was holding a cigarette and was frightened half to death by my sudden appearance.

"I'm so sorry, please forgive me. Don't be afraid, I'm just the gardener. I was just—"

"It's fine," the woman said, calming down from her fright and waving away my apologies.

"I'll be going now," I said.

"Do you like the party? I despise these superficial gatherings. But my husband's brother is a very powerful man and likes to show it off every chance he gets."

As she spoke, I had the strange sensation of déjà vu. I had heard that voice before, though I couldn't remember where.

I kept my opinions to myself. It was difficult for me to believe or trust a woman dressed in something that was worth more than what a worker could earn with a year or more of hard work.

"Sorry to bother you," she said, noting my face pinched with annoyance.

"Forgive me, I should be going."

I was walking away when she called to me, "Marco?"

I turned, terrified. How could she know my name? I hadn't mentioned it.

"How do you know me?" I asked nervously. I hadn't thought there were many people left in Madrid who knew who I was.

"You won't remember me. I was leaving class one day and you'd gotten lost in the middle of University City. My sister-in-law, your new boss, was with me that day. I took you to your house after we got a bite to eat. You told me your parents had been arrested . . ."

I froze. This woman was the girl who had taken me back home in the trolley all those years ago. How in the world had she recognized me after so long?

"You've changed a lot, but your eyes are hard to forget," she said, reading my thoughts.

"Miss . . . ?"

"Rosa Chamorro, though now I'm Mrs. Artola. I ended up getting married to a . . . friend."

"I think I should go now."

"Yes, and I should get back inside. Here," she said, taking something out of her tiny purse. It was a card with her phone number and address. "Call me if you ever need anything. My husband has helpful contacts." Then she walked away, her silky dress swaying.

As she came into the light of the great hall, I had the feeling that my luck might be about to change. I went back to the gardener's hut practically skipping with joy inside. I marveled at how fate toyed with us. Two casual but life-changing encounters six years apart with the same person—a truly uncanny coincidence.

# Chapter 45

# In the Name
# of the Father

Madrid
January 8, 1941

I wrestled a long time with the choice, but I finally decided to call
Rosa. I felt more eaten up by worry and fear for my family each
day that went by. Unfortunately, Rosa didn't answer, but one of the
women in her employment did.

"Good afternoon, Artola residence. How may I help you?"

At first I didn't know what to say. Just as the woman was about
to hang up, I said, "Hello, good afternoon. This is Marco Alcalde,
and I need to speak with Mrs. Artola."

"Just a moment, please," was the reply.

Those few elapsed seconds lasted for ages. I half wanted to hang up the phone, not sure how Rosa would respond to what I was going to ask her.

"Good afternoon," came Rosa's young, cheerful voice.

"Hi, this is Marco."

"Yes, Lolita told me. How can I help you?"

"Can I see you? I need to tell you in person."

She was quiet, as if studying her calendar. I could hear a piece of paper being turned.

"How about this afternoon at the Café Comercial? You know where it is?"

"Yes, in Glorieta de Bilbao."

"How about five o'clock?"

"Yes, I'll be there. Thank you so much." My heart was racing as I hung up the phone. I took a deep breath and tried to calm down. Then I looked at my dirt-stained clothes and worn-out boots. I couldn't go to a café downtown like that.

I returned to the little hut and went straight to Javier's wardrobe. I had just opened the door when I heard his voice behind me.

"And just what do you think you're doing?" he demanded.

"I need—"

"You need? No, you're robbing me. I'm going straight to the mistress and she'll kick you to the curb."

"No, please," I begged him. But Javier stormed out of the room. I chased after him and grabbed his arm before he could open the door to the big house.

"The first day I came to this house you told me that these people robbed our country and gave us the crumbs. It's true. My father is sentenced to die, my mother is locked up in a women's prison, and my two sisters are in an orphanage. The mistress's sister-in-law wants to help me, but I can't go downtown dressed like this. Please, help me."

Javier stared at me, unsure whether to believe me. "You're a hard case to crack. I've been hiding out here since the end of the war. I've also got a death sentence hanging over my head. During the war I killed my fair share of fascists, but I didn't have time to escape to Valencia when Madrid fell. I somehow managed to get work here. The lady didn't ask me many questions. Despite what I said, she does have a good heart. But her husband is the very son of Satan himself. I think I've got something that might fit you. The mistress gave it to me a while back, but I've got no time for suits and fancy clothes."

We walked back to the hut and he brought out a nice suit jacket and some shoes that, though worn, looked like they had been expensive. He helped me get dressed.

"I had a son around your age. He was young like you, not yet a man. He got called up in the final months of the war in the 'baby bottle draft,' as they called it. He didn't make it out alive." In the mirror, I could see tears in the gardener's eyes.

I thanked him and walked to where I could take the trolley to Cuatro Caminos. From there, I took the metro to Bilbao Station. As I walked along the busiest streets of the capital, I kept glancing at my reflection in the shop windows. I paused at the door to the café, took a deep breath, then pushed the revolving door open and walked in. As I looked around, a waiter dressed in a tie and white jacket came up and asked if I was looking for anyone.

"Yes, I . . ." Then I saw Rosa raise her hand from a table at the back, and I headed toward her.

I shook her hand and, as I settled into the seat, she commented that the suit looked good on me.

"Thanks," I said, blushing.

I ordered coffee and looked out the window to the street. It was hot inside the restaurant, and I began to sweat under the heavy jacket.

"You mentioned that you needed something," Rosa said, smiling.

She still looked as young and pretty as the first time I'd seen her. Now she was wearing a suit befitting a married woman, but the clothing didn't seem to rein in her young, rebellious spirit.

"I don't have a favor to ask for myself. But my family . . ." I swallowed hard to keep the tears at bay.

"What is it?" she asked, taking my hand tenderly in hers.

So I told her our story. I narrated everything from the past few years: war, hunger, exile, the difficulty of being separated from our parents, our return to Spain, and being separated from my sisters. Rosa's big eyes held deep sadness. I wondered if she wasn't happy either. It seemed that after the war we were all playing roles we didn't want but which circumstances forced upon us.

"I'm so sorry," she said. "I had no idea your life was so difficult. The war has been hard on everyone, but we all try to get over it the best we can. My parents . . ." she began, choking up.

I took a handkerchief out of my jacket pocket and held it out to her.

"Thanks." She dabbed her eyes. "I didn't mean to cry. In fact, it's been ages since I've cried. I know I'm lucky. My parents died in one of the bombings, though sometimes I think it's the best thing that could've happened to them. The war was so horrible here in Madrid. I was living in the Salamanca neighborhood, and chekas and other groups of robbers attacked our homes all the time. One time they broke in and . . ." She buried her eyes in the handkerchief. Seeing her crying like that, I realized how easy it was to jump to conclusions about someone based on appearance. It turned out that the victors also had painful stories to tell. "Well, it's better not to remember those things," she continued. "God gives each of us a second chance. Maybe he's kept us alive for a reason, so we can help remedy some of the suffering and pain."

"I don't believe in God, but I do believe with all my heart that we should try to leave all this hatred and pain behind," I said. It wasn't easy for me to say things like that, but resentment was eating me up on the inside. If I didn't fight against it, no room would be left in my heart for anything but hatred and contempt.

"My husband works at the Department of Justice. They're slammed with work, and we hardly see each other, though honestly that's just fine by me. Ours was a marriage of convenience. My aunt, Susana, managed to convince my mother-in-law that I'd be a good catch. My parents had a lot of land in Jaén. I would've rather stayed single, but I was too chicken. Nowadays women are second-class citizens, and the laws of the new regime don't let us do anything unless we have men by our side. I spend my days going to charity projects, plays, and fancy dinners."

"I'm sorry," I said, confused. That didn't sound like a hard life to me. I still hadn't grasped the concept of living trapped in a golden cage. Rosa's dreams of studying and being a journalist had gone up in smoke alongside the dreams of millions of Spaniards. No one dared to dream anymore; we were just content to survive.

"I'll ask my husband to see if they can get your mother out of prison. Getting a pardon for your father won't be as simple, but if it's true that he helped that many people, we might be able to do something. If your parents get out, they can request custody of your sisters."

We left the restaurant and said goodbye at the entrance to the metro. The next day I was to go to the Department of Justice and speak to Rosa's husband. I couldn't sleep that night. I asked Javier to be excused from work that day and was standing at the building door by nine o'clock. I was fortunate that Rosa's husband had included me on his official schedule for the day, and the guards didn't ask me for any documentation when I entered the building. I went up to the fourth floor, and a secretary asked me to wait for a moment.

It took every ounce of self-control I had to overcome my desperation and wait calmly in that small, windowless room for nearly three hours. Right before noon, the secretary said, "You can go in now."

Rosa's husband was shuffling through papers as I entered his office. "Have a seat," he said.

"Thank you for being willing to see me." I sat stiffly in one of the chairs.

"It's my wife you should thank. She's got a big heart. So apparently you two met before the glorious uprising?"

"Yes, sir," I said tensely. His features did not endear me to him. He was the perfect Falangist stereotype with his slicked-back hair, thin mustache, and pinstriped suit.

"I'm going to shoot straight with you. It doesn't bother me one bit if we kill off all the reds we possibly can. The state has to make sure that what just happened in Spain never happens again. Fascism and communism are in constant war. It won't be long 'til we can support our natural allies against Russia and the worn-out bourgeois democracies, but in the meantime, we need to clean out the reds from this country. Even so, I'm not as radical as some of my comrades. I recognize that if we kill off all the reds there won't be enough people to harvest the fields or work the factories. We've got to weaken the working class but not fully exterminate it. The workers themselves aren't ultimately guilty of their own alienation; bourgeois capitalism drove them to it. You'll understand all this once we've been able to put our social measures in place. Not even God will be able to recognize this country."

I listened to his speech in silence. When he had run out of ideologizing steam, he added, "Your mother's case is pretty simple. She's a red that runs her mouth a lot, but she doesn't seem dangerous. I'll write to the women's prison in Bilbao asking them to let her out. But your father's case is more complicated. The death sentence against him is about to be carried out any day now, which means time's run out for appeals or pardons. Military justice is very strict on these matters. I asked the minister to sign a pardon, but you'll have to take it yourself to the camp at Miranda de Ebro. The camp's tribunal will have to rule on your father's freedom and the commutation of his sentence. Do you understand?"

"Yes, sir."

He handed me a folder with the yoke and arrows symbol printed on the front.

"I hope your father knows how to serve the new state. He won't receive a second chance; we're gifting him with a new life. He can't go back to the printing press, but at least he won't die before the firing squad," he said, standing up to signal that the meeting was over.

Going down the elevator, my head was buzzing with thoughts about my parents. In my hands I held the documents that might save my father's life. I headed to the gardener's house to pack my few belongings and take the first train I could. Time was of the essence. I could feel my head splitting with the choices: Should I go to Bilbao for my mother or risk going alone to Miranda de Ebro for my father? What if he were already dead and I wasted two days in which my mother had to suffer longer in prison? But what if they took Dad out for a walk while we were en route from Bilbao? I had no good options and too little information. In the end, I decided to take the first train to Bilbao.

Javier was eating in the small kitchen when I entered. I didn't have to say anything, just simply held out the folder and nodded in shock. He stood up and hugged me. "I hope you make it. At least somebody will find justice in this godforsaken country."

"Thank you," I said from the bottom of my heart. Then I gathered my meager things for the trip.

I was walking out the door when I ran into Rosa. "My husband called to tell me about your meeting. I figured I'd find you here. I wanted to give you some money and wish you well."

"But . . ." I began. I didn't want to take anything else from someone who'd already done so much for me, yet I was in no position to refuse the help. "Thank you, thank you so much. I can't ever thank you enough," I said, trembling as I put the money she held out into my pockets.

Then she hugged me. At first my arms were stiff against my body and I didn't know what to do, but finally I relaxed and accepted her simple act of affection. It had been a long time since anyone besides my sisters had expressed genuine feeling for me.

"Go on, now. Do not waste time," she said, stepping back and wiping her eyes.

I took the trolley to Norte Station, bought a one-way ticket, and within a couple hours was on the train. I sat in a third-class car and stared at the scenery for hours. Javier had packed me a sandwich and a wineskin. After I ate a bit, I nodded off. The train arrived in Bilbao after night had fallen. The dirty, gray city greeted me when I left the station in search of somewhere to stay. Trying to fall asleep between the smelly, threadbare sheets, I dared to let my mind dream about the future just a bit. What would my mother be like now? Would we actually be all together again as a family? I'd never been so close to making it happen.

I got up early and was so anxious I didn't even eat the pitiful breakfast the pension kitchen provided. I took a bus to the women's prison and waited in the long line to go inside. Finally, I was led to the director's office.

"Mr. Marco Alcalde, I read the pardon for your mother, Mrs. Amparo Alcalde. I don't quite know how you pulled that off, but I suppose that if you know the right people, you can get anything. Don't think you're off the hook, though. She may walk away from these four walls, and I can't do anything to stop it, but you can't make one false move without us finding out. No enemy of the state can sleep soundly at night. If it were up to me, I'd shoot the whole lot of these reds, but I've got to follow orders."

The director signed for my mother's immediate release and told me to wait in a room nearby. Two eternal hours dragged on before I heard the door to the waiting room open. A guard brought forward a white-haired woman. I had to stare at her for a long moment to find anything of my mother in those sunken eyes and the deeply wrinkled face. I stood and ran to hug her. She opened her arms to me and moaned as the warmth of our bodies recognized each other, the body that had sheltered me so many nights during a nightmare or a fright. I felt tethered to the world once again.

"You didn't forget me," she said through happy tears.

"Of course not! You told me to remember you, and not a day has gone by in all these years when you weren't the first thing on my mind."

Time slowed down, and we continued the embrace. The images of everything I'd lived through since our separation flew rapid-fire through my brain. The worst thing of all—worse than the loneliness, the mistreatment, the fear, the anguish—had been the distance between us. I fought to believe our embrace was real and that I wasn't dreaming. I couldn't believe I was finally home again.

# Chapter 46

# Bilbao

Bilbao
January 10, 1941

My mother felt mainly relief at finding herself outside the walls of the prison. She was skittish and frightened, as if her confinement had crushed the fight out of her. We went to the pension where I'd stayed the night before and ate at a small bar nearby. We talked for endless hours about the past four and a half years and how we'd always hoped to find each other again.

"I regret sending you three away. If I could go back in time, I wouldn't do it again. You've suffered so much, and even though things were absolutely horrible in Spain, at least we would've been together." The remorse on her face broke my heart.

"No, no, we made it well enough in Mexico," I said. Right then, I vowed to never let her know all that had gone on because she had suffered enough. "It was hard at first, but for the most part they treated us well. I think we learned things that will shape us for the rest of our lives. You and Dad did what you thought was best for us at the time."

She clung to my hand, and I could feel her bones just beneath her pale, papery skin. She was so thin, and her face looked decades older. "They took us on a train to Germany and forced all the men out to work in a concentration camp. We managed to escape and went to find you, but you weren't in Mexico." Her eyes were full of questions.

The guilt that had threatened to swallow me since we'd heard Jacinto's report of my parents' whereabouts now had me full in its grip. If I had obeyed my parents and not come back to Spain, none of these horrible things would've happened. We could've made a new life, together, in Mexico.

"I'm so sorry," I choked out.

"I know, darling. It's not your fault. You wanted to come back so we could all be together again. My goodness, I can't believe how handsome you've grown. And thanks to Jacinto and that woman, you got me out of jail."

"I have to tell you something important," I said. Up to then, I hadn't wanted her to know about Dad. She was quiet. The hypnotizing gleam of her big green eyes was the only thing left of the strong, young woman I had known her to be.

"Out with it! I can't bear the suspense anymore. Is it your father?"

"Yes. You know they took him to a camp."

That was all it took for her face to fall again, all the weight and suffering of the years returning full force.

"We were arrested at the same time."

"Well, in his case, a military tribunal has condemned him to death. I don't believe they have enacted the sentence yet, but Rosa's husband told me it could be soon."

Confusion danced across my mother's face, swirling between joy and defeat. "I presumed he'd surely been shot already, so maybe there's a chance . . . But why execute him now? Your father's saved so many people from certain death."

"I know, but military tribunals are really strict, and they condemned him for participating in the attack on the Montaña Barracks."

"Oh, ridiculous!" She nearly spat the words out, enraged.

People in the restaurant turned to look at us. The few regular customers sipping on cider or beer were speaking in hushed tones. The regime's spies could be anywhere, and no one trusted anyone.

"So tomorrow we'll head to Miranda de Ebro. There weren't any more buses going this afternoon. We'll get there in time, and it'll all work out. It's got to."

Mom breathed deeply from my confidence to calm her nerves. Then she took a sip of wine and finished her plate of food, sighing over every bite.

"I thought the war was the worst thing that could ever happen to Spain, but I was wrong. The postwar fallout is even worse. Those swine are ravenous for revenge. And the worst part of all is how they package everything in the pretty language of the Christian spirit and loving their neighbor, when really they're savage beasts. Our guards at the prison were Falangists, but there were also nuns who came by. I've never known any group of people to be so cruel and bloody."

"I'm so sorry," I said.

"In the prison they stole our souls. I think you should hear about it all; you need to know. These people know their biggest victory is convincing people to fear them. They had us living in complete terror. They had it in for me in particular from the moment I arrived. They seem to have a special predilection for stronger women, as if they are thrilled by breaking us. Not long after I arrived, one of my cellmates gave birth to a premature baby. The poor nutrition and the beatings made her go into labor early. We begged for a midwife to help her, but one of the nuns answered that we reds were like rabbits and didn't need any help. After a long night in pain, the baby was finally born. The poor wretch was so tiny. We put him on her chest, and the mother smiled when she saw her baby, in spite of everything. But it wasn't long before the mother started to bleed. One of the prisoners who'd been a nurse tried to stop the hemorrhage, but it was hopeless. We screamed for help and banged the bars of the cell, but no one came. The next day, two men took her away. We told them the child hadn't had any milk and begged them to take the baby to one of the women who was nursing her children there at the jail. The men actually showed a modicum of compassion for the creature and sent for a nun. It was Sister Diana who came, hours later, around noon. By then the tiny baby had lost nearly all the strength he had. Sister Diana looked at him and said with such spite that the red rat wasn't worth saving. She left him there in our cell, and he died in my arms. Sometimes I think that was the best thing for the child. Living in this hellhole has to be worse than whatever world awaits beyond."

I felt sick, though after what I'd lived through at the orphanage, such a story wasn't surprising. The regime's executioners had lost the last remaining shreds of their humanity.

"Another of the prisoners who was there with her two daughters, precious twin girls, went stark raving mad. A few weeks after she'd arrived, she was called to a room for an interview with a priest. Then they put her in the cell next to ours. The next day, two of the guards took her daughters to be adopted. My poor companion screamed that her daughters already had a mother, and she refused to eat after they were taken. She was dead within days."

"I'm so, so sorry," I said.

"I'm just so grateful you three are okay," she said, stroking my cheek.

It was very late by the time we went back to the pension. Perhaps we'd been delaying so that we'd be exhausted enough to fall asleep as soon as we lay down.

We woke very early the next morning, and after a light breakfast with weak coffee, we boarded the bus and were traversing the forests of Basque Country by dawn. A couple hours later we stopped at Vitoria and then went on to Miranda de Ebro. The bus dropped us off around noon and then continued its route to Burgos. The concentration camp was between the railway and the river. A ten-minute walk in the bitter cold led us to the main gate, which was guarded by soldiers.

"What do you want?" one of the soldiers asked. His jaw barely moved, and he seemed frozen stiff. He had a blanket thrown over his shoulders and a rifle in his hand.

"I've brought an official pardon for one of the prisoners."

The soldier frowned and called for his superior. The situation was extremely out of the ordinary. The corporal came out of the observation tower. He was a large man, and his skin was whipped red by the wind. A thick black mustache partially covered his lips.

"You brought a pardon? That's not how it works. Orders always come straight from the office. You go on back home and carry on," he said, turning back toward the observation tower.

"Corporal, this order is signed by the Department of Justice."

He turned back and held out his hand. I gave him the folder, and he studied the paper carefully, as if reading it were a difficult chore.

"Follow me," was all he said.

The soldiers opened the security gate for us, and we walked through the frozen mud down a row of white barracks until we reached a larger building with soldiers standing guard all around. They let us in, and the warmth inside the building was a welcome relief. The corporal went into an office and came out a few minutes later.

"Go in," he said, holding the door open for us.

Two men waited inside, one Spaniard and another who looked to be a foreigner and spoke with a decidedly German accent. "Sit down. Who gave you this letter?" he demanded, seemingly angered by the mere existence of the piece of paper.

I briefly explained how the pardon had come about. The Spaniard nodded but said nothing.

The German said, "Pardons always come straight from the office. They're *never* brought to us by the prisoner's family."

"I'm sorry, but that's what they told me to do in Madrid," I said, working hard to sound calm and unaffected.

"Paul," the Spanish officer said, "it seems there are some in Madrid who don't think we're doing our jobs properly."

"Well, no matter what, we have hardly any Spanish prisoners here. Most are other nationalities, former members of the International Brigades or foreigners suspected of spying. We'll look to see if your father is really here at this camp."

My mother kept her head bowed the whole time. The camp reminded her of being locked up in the women's prison.

Paul and the Spanish officer called the corporal back in and sent him to look up my father's name in the records.

"Everyone here deserves to die. The foreigners are squeaking by for the moment because the Caudillo doesn't want any diplomatic trouble with other countries, but there are very few Spaniards left," the German said dryly.

I hazarded to say, "My father was not a fighter. In fact, he saved many people in Madrid, people who were accused of treason or of working for the enemy."

The Spanish official took a step forward and looked hard at my mother. "Was your husband involved in a political party?"

Terrified, my mother looked at him, not knowing how to answer. Finally, she whispered, "Yes, like most people during the Republic."

"Did he have an official post?"

She nodded her head slowly.

"That's enough for the sentence to be carried out."

The corporal returned and whispered something in the officer's ear. The Spanish officer nodded and said indifferently, "I'm afraid there's nothing to be done. Half an hour ago your husband was taken out with other prisoners to the firing squad. By now the soldiers will have finished their job."

The German smiled at us, pleased at the turn of events. My heart was seizing, and my mother lost it. She stood up, grabbed the pardon off the table, and waved it around. "It's an order from the Department of Justice. You've got to stop the execution right now!"

The two men looked at each other in annoyed surprise. The corporal stepped toward my mother to take the letter from her, but I jumped in front of him.

"Calm down, Curro, let's not get out of hand," the Spaniard said. "It won't do any good, but take these two down to the execution site, and if it's not finished, have them find this—"

"Francisco Alcalde," the German finished.

We got out of the building as fast as possible. The corporal, Curro, was none too pleased with his mission and dawdled as much as he could. We got to the front gate and then walked toward the river. Before we arrived, we saw a truck parked among the trees. We kept walking down a path, and my mother broke into a run. I followed her, and the corporal quickened his pace a bit.

We could see a wall and a dozen soldiers lined up. One of them raised his hand, and we started screaming. The officer kept his hand raised and the firing squad took aim at the prisoners. When he heard our commotion, the officer turned and inadvertently dropped his hand. The soldiers interpreted it as the command to shoot, and a flurry of shots resounded off the wall. The officer screamed for them to halt, but the prisoners were already lying in pools of their own blood.

"Halt, I say!" the officer roared.

"Captain," the corporal called, finally showing some initiative.

"What is it, Corporal?"

"I've got orders to halt the shooting. There's been a pardon for Francisco Alcalde."

I panicked at the sight of the men and shook with the terror of what I'd just witnessed. Where was my father? Was he already among the dead?

The officer shrugged and moved toward the lifeless and bullet-ridden bodies. He leaned down over one and examined it. "He's still breathing," he said.

My mother screamed, and we ran. We ran toward the man he claimed was my father, and I lifted his head. The man opened his eyes and smiled. "Marco, my boy!" he rasped.

"Don't die!" my mother screamed through her tears.

"I'm sorry," he struggled to say, his life slipping away.

My mother clung to his chest while I held him from behind, but his body grew progressively stiffer.

"Where are my daughters?" he managed to ask.

"They're okay," I croaked. "They're alive." My voice was hoarse from crying, and my trembling hands were covered in my father's blood.

"They must be so big by now." He took a labored breath. "I won't see them anymore, but tell them their father loves them with his whole heart and that I'll always be by their side. Death is better; there's no place for me in Spain anymore. You, Marco, keep fighting. Someday things will change."

"Francisco, Francisco," my mother kept whimpering, kissing his face everywhere she could reach.

A stream of blood trickled out from between his lips, and his eyes locked. The weak breath coming out of him stopped, a flame that had flickered out.

They let us mourn beside him for a while. Beside him lay five other bodies that no one screamed or cried over, murdered on the altar of rage and vengeance. As we grieved, the executioners stood to the side, smoking cigarettes with such indifference. Their consciences were as light as if they'd just shot a deer in the middle of the woods for supper.

My mother refused to leave my father, even though she knew the empty, soulless body was no longer the man she had loved, the father of her children. I pried her fingers off and struggled to help her stand upright. "Mom," I said, "we can't stay here."

With great reluctance we started walking past the line of soldiers. Most were very young, and one or two had the pinched expression of something resembling compassion. They were victims in a different way: conscripted and forced to murder their own people, workers and poor farmhands like the families from which they'd come. As we walked away, coups de grâce echoed in the background.

We stumbled toward the railway and watched a line of prisoners leaving the concentration camp to go to their work site. We slouched deeper in sorrow at seeing their pale, haggard, bruised faces. My father had escaped hell, at least, but those men would keep enduring the abuses of the victors.

We didn't speak until we got to the train station. It was as though my mother was gone, her brain incapable of facing such grief.

"I'm so sorry," I said, crying. "I should have come here first instead of Bilbao. I—"

"Shh, don't," she said, hugging me. "You've done all you could have done." She did not cry. The reserves of her beautiful eyes had been used up.

"Remember all of this, everything," she said. "No matter how much time passes. The world has to know the truth. The victors always write the history books, and, when things have calmed down and new habits become routine, they'll deny all this happened. Don't let your father and everyone like him disappear into oblivion."

"I'll remember, Mom," I promised. Her words would haunt me my whole life, just like what she'd said in Bordeaux right before we were separated.

"It's devastating, Marco, when brothers become enemies. At the end of the day, the same blood has been spilled on both sides of the front: two Spains at each other's throats because of their damned ideals. Do we really have to do so much damage in order to live in peace? Each human life is more important than any ideology. We thought we could build a new world, an ideal country where injustice and inequality would be no more; but evil is inside the heart of every human being. Long before the war was over, we'd already lost by committing the same inhuman atrocities as our enemies. The innocent ones are always the ones who suffer most in the war, while the cowards who didn't go to the front kill from the rearguard in the name of God, of the Republic, of Franco . . . What difference does it make? Whatever name they use to justify themselves—their killing disgusts me."

The train plodded toward us across the frozen field, slowing to a stop in front of the small station where hardly a dozen passengers waited with us. We got on the third-class car, sat on the hard wooden bench, and listened to the sound of the steam engine as smoke puffed by the closed window. It was so cold, and people sat hunched together in search of any warmth possible. Everyone traveled in silence. There were no songs, no conversations, no laughter; the entire country felt like one big cemetery. My mother's eyes were closed, but I knew she wasn't sleeping. She was trying to go far, far away from there, perhaps back to the happy past when the five of us were a family, when life was all future and hope, youth and dreams. On that train ride from Miranda de Ebro to Madrid, I understood that suffering is our only lifelong, faithful friend. At every moment it reminds us that we're mortal and that around every corner we could lose all our happiness and long to curse the day we were born.

I bowed my head and tried to recall every good moment I'd had with my father and everything I'd learned from him. As long as I was alive, he would never fully die, because he'd be present in my movements and expressions and all my memories.

# Chapter 47

# Madrid

Madrid
January 11, 1941

It was late when we got back to Madrid, and we went straight to Jacinto's house. Angelines opened the door and let out a little scream when she saw my mother. The maid wrapped Mom in her bony arms and covered her with kisses. We went inside and sat on the sofa. Mom's reserves of tears had built back up again, and the floodgates opened when Jacinto came into the room. He didn't say a word, just hugged her. And then he hugged me. We didn't say anything about what had happened in Miranda de Ebro. There was no need to. We ate hot soup and bread all together in the kitchen. Jacinto sat next to us and stared back and forth between Mom and me the whole time but never spoke.

Finally, my mother asked, "So the theaters are open again?"

"Yes, right now I've got a show running and another in the works," Jacinto said, trying to smile.

"That's good. Laughter is probably more important than bread right now in our dead, soulless country."

"My dear Amparo, how I've missed you. The young actors hardly know the four basic rules of the stage. There's been no one to train them for years now. The older actors are no longer with us or are living in exile. I was tempted to go abroad myself, but someone's got to raise the curtain."

"You made the right choice," Mom said.

"Where will you go when you get your daughters back?" Jacinto asked, timidly proffering what we were all wondering.

Mom sat there deep in thought, as if the question had taken her by surprise. For years, she had been used to simply surviving; people can't make plans during a war.

"I have no idea. I admire you, my good friend, but I'm not sure I could get up on stage again, certainly not in Spain. The country I loved doesn't exist anymore."

Jacinto's shoulders drooped at her answer. Perhaps he had secretly hoped she would return to the theater. "Whatever you do, it'll be the right thing," he said, though it was clear he wished she would stay in Spain and, more specifically, in the acting world.

"The right thing? I'm pretty sure that nobody thinks about doing the right thing anymore. We'll go back to being the country of rogues, blessed virgins, go-betweens, and tricksters bent on shameless survival like we've always been. A complete scoundrel is in power, surrounded by crooks just as bad if not worse than him because they're not brave enough to wrest his power away."

"It's not cowardice, honey, it's self-interest," Jacinto clarified. "The regime has no ideology; it's all a façade. The only thing most of them care about is taking the biggest slice of the pie. The monarchists aren't clamoring for the king's return, at least not most of them; the military is well paid by their caudillo; the old shirt Falangists complain in private but fawn all over themselves in public just as much as the new shirts; the priests are doing what they've always done; and the rest of us tremble and pray we're not carted off to the firing squad."

We finished eating, washed our weary bodies, and went to bed. Mom tucked me in, then lay down in the bed beside mine. After a while, I could tell she was still awake.

"Are you asleep?" she whispered.

"No," I said, turning to face her.

"What do you think we should do? Stay here or try to go to the Americas?"

"I don't know. On the one hand, I'd hop on a boat to Mexico this very minute. I miss the people there. But at the same time, I don't want to leave. I don't want those murderers to steal my country."

"I know. You're too young to really understand that they've already stolen it. It's gone. The war took much more than hundreds of thousands of people; it stole our future. I've no idea how long Franco will be in power, but Spain will never, ever be the same. There will always be losers and winners, executioners and victims, brothers against brothers."

Perhaps it was youth that kept me from seeing what my mom could see, but even after everything that had happened, and even though I knew deep down that she was right, I didn't want to give up hope.

"There's no future here," she added. "I want you three to grow up believing you can do what you want to with your lives."

We drifted off eventually, and the exhaustion kept us in deep sleep until late morning. Jacinto made some calls to get us an appointment in the central offices of Social Aid downtown. Mom put on a nice outfit Jacinto pulled out of a closet, and I dressed in an elegant suit.

"Thank you for everything, dear friend," my mother said, sinking deep into Jacinto's embrace before we left.

"You can stay here as long as you need to, and you can work in the company again if you want. I'll pay for the kids' schooling."

She hugged him again. "Oh, thank God there are still a few noble souls in this world. I have to ask you for one more favor. I'll need money for the trip, four train tickets plus passage on the boat. And—"

"Don't worry about anything," he said. A moment later, he returned from his office with an envelope stuffed with cash.

"I'll pay it all back, I swear," my mother said.

"It's not a loan; it's a gift. Friendship is more than words. I wish you would stay, but I understand why you need to go."

They embraced again, and Angelines was crying as she held the door open for us. We waved goodbye one last time as we waited for the elevator.

❧

The Social Aid office was nothing to speak of, just two floors crammed with old filing cabinets, scratched-up tables, and Falangist paper pushers who either felt some sense of calling or who hadn't managed to get a better position in the new administration.

A woman named Doña Ágata received us warmly and searched for my sisters' files. She confirmed that they were still in the San Fernando de Henares orphanage and authorized their removal.

"We've taken care of the girls in your absence. I do hope the whole family can be together again," she said.

I was tempted to describe all I had endured in one of her wretched orphanages, but it was better to hold my tongue. We wouldn't be safe until we were far away from Spain.

An hour later, we were in San Fernando de Henares, in an oddly shaped plaza. We knocked at the door. A nun dressed in black opened the gate and asked what we wanted.

My mother said nothing but held out the letter from the central offices. The nun waved us in and took us to the Mother Superior while she went to find Isabel and Ana.

The Mother Superior said, "Your daughters are very well-behaved. We've taught them to be good wives and mothers. Spain needs children and new life to overcome all the deaths."

We didn't answer. The nun seemed uncomfortable in our silence but continued to smile.

The door opened, and Ana's voice resounded. "Mom!" They ran to each other, and Isabel to me, all of us weeping and hugging first one, then the next, then all at once in incredulous joy.

"I wish you all the best," the Mother Superior said after a while, putting an end to our time in the orphanage.

We walked out under a blue sky so intense it reminded me of holidays in Madrid many years ago when we would walk the streets of our beautiful city.

"Where's Dad?" Isabel asked hesitantly.

Mom looked at her, preparing her throat and mouth to say the dreaded words. "He's no longer with us." She made her voice as gentle as possible for the horrible news.

My sisters stopped short, mute and unsure how to respond, until Ana began to cry and cling to Mom again. Isabel joined in, and then all four of us were once more a mess of tears and arms. I felt the hairs all over my body standing on end. Love can be experienced physically, and my body was responding to what it had longed for

for so long. We walked to the bus stop holding one another's hands. Our train would leave from Atocha Station, and we didn't want to stay in Madrid one moment longer than necessary.

My mother carried my sisters' light bags and I carried the suitcase Angelines had packed for us, much larger and heavier, full of everything the good woman knew we would need. We looked for the train on the platform and waited impatiently for the departure time to come. We'd be traveling overnight.

"Jacinto reserved an entire compartment for us," Mom said. She was grateful to be able to spend those first few hours of being together again without other people around us. Our reunion felt incomplete, and it always would, even though we carried our father in our hearts.

Isabel sat on one side of Mom and Ana on the other, as close as they could. It made me happy to see them snuggled up together. I felt like as long as we were all there at the same time and touching one another, no one could separate us again.

"Mom, we were scared no one would ever come get us. Those nuns treated us well enough, though we had to work all day long. They said it was to teach us a trade, but I think they were just making a profit off our labor," Isabel said.

"You've got your brother to thank. He fought long and hard for us to all be together again."

Their eyes remained sad, but Isabel and Ana beamed at me. Soon they fell asleep leaning against our mother. I watched the countryside go by until it grew dark. The train made several stops, and the metaphorical parallel with life jumped out at me. Each of our experiences over the past few years had been a stop on the ride; the main difference is that in life we never know which stop will actually be the last. Madrid, San Martín de la Vega, Valencia, Barcelona, Perpignan, Bordeaux, Veracruz, Morelia, Mexico City, Lisbon, Bilbao, and Miranda de Ebro had been some of our train stations during those terrible years. I had left part of myself at each place and had learned something as well. At that moment, as I looked at my incomplete family, I felt like the long road had been worth it.

At midnight, the train stopped at the border. The customs agents didn't bother us, perhaps because we had a private compartment. I was both relieved and sad when we crossed the dividing line between countries. That mixture of ambivalence has stayed with me for decades: my heart always divided in half, never knowing which is my true self.

We arrived in Lisbon the next morning. The city was more beautiful than the first time I'd seen it. People were moving from one place to the next, all in a frenzy. Though Portugal was also ruled by a dictator, we didn't detect the same kind of gut-wrenching sadness that was so palpable in Spain.

In the port, a huge transatlantic steamer was waiting to take us back to Mexico. We got there just in time. We walked up the long gangway, left our luggage in the cabin, and went out onto the main deck. We looked out at the city and then at the people there to bid farewell to their loved ones, perhaps for a trip from which they would never return. My mother hugged us, and the rock-solid feeling of safety returned.

"Remember!" she said as the boat drifted away from land. "Remember, but don't hate. Remember, so the memory of what you are doesn't fade, so the nation you'll always belong to stays stuck to the bottoms of your feet. They've stolen our future and our beloved country, but they'll never be able to steal our memories."

Surrounded by the crystal waters, I thought of Dad. I recalled his mischievous smile, his ironic way of dealing with the world, his courage, and his self-possession. I swore that I would live as he had. I wanted to feel worthy of him and his sacrifice. I needed to be able to look at myself in the mirror in a few years and say that my life had been worthwhile; that the ideals of the dying Republic still resounded in my heart; that its ideals, for which so many had died, would one day turn my country into a place where justice and truth would shine like the dawn, spilling over the blood and tears of all who had given their lives to make this world a better place.

# Epilogue

The sun, the sea, and the flowers seemed to have stood still in time. My family settled in Mexico City after we left Spain. Mom found work in a theater and even earned a name for herself. We lived downtown, reconnected with Lisa, and studied at one of the schools for Spaniard immigrants. I went on to study law at a university but didn't finish my degree. I worked in a publishing house until I returned to Spain. For some reason, I just needed to see it again. Isabel studied medicine and Ana, journalism. They married Mexican men and never crossed the Atlantic again. The first thing I did before settling back in Madrid was visit my father's tomb in Miranda de Ebro. Since my mother and I had witnessed his death, this spared him the ignominy of being thrown into a mass grave as was the fate of so many. Arranging flowers over his simple grave marker, I recalled

347

the day of his death and marveled again at how fate toys with us like pawns on the chessboard of life.

I never married. A loner, I watched Madrid change little by little. My mother died in Mexico, and I didn't make it back to say a final goodbye. My sisters and I wrote often, but I hadn't met their children.

That day in November I learned of Franco's death. An era was over, leaving a wake of pain and suffering.

I got off the boat in Veracruz and walked through the chaotic city full of color and every imaginable contrast. When I arrived at the train station, I thought back to my first time there, experiencing everything through the eyes of a child. The world felt new to me right then, and every little thing, no matter how insignificant, brought me joy. I glanced down again at the piece of paper in my hand with María Soledad de la Cruz's address. I spent the whole trip to Mexico City thinking about how our reunion would be. I presumed she would be married and have a passel of children and grandchildren. Impatient, I walked through the city streets until I came to a small red villa in the shade of two huge trees.

I knocked at the door, and a maid led me to the living room. I glanced at the clock and waited, my hands jittery with nerves. Finally, I heard footsteps. The door opened and revealed a beautiful, mature woman with large, dark eyes. She smiled and said in her strong Mexican accent, "Well, hello there, little Spaniard gentleman. Welcome home."

For the second time in my life, I felt like I *had* come home.

# Clarifications from History

Remember Me is a work of fiction based on true stories. To discuss the period of the Second Spanish Republic and the Spanish Civil War is by definition to enter into controversy. Many of the events that occurred are interpreted differently by historians and the public in general, but everyone is in agreement that it was a human tragedy and a very sad and difficult period in Spanish history.

The Second Republic sprang up somewhat spontaneously and with the near unanimous approval of all the political forces and social classes in the country. The world was going through a serious economic crisis, not to mention the particular structural and social deficiencies of a backward, uneducated country. The Second Republic tried in a very short time to repair massive inequalities and to secularize the state. The conservative reaction did not delay. The burning of convents and the social revolutions in different parts of the country threatened the peaceful way of life, unleashing partisan violence that would result in one of the worst civil wars of the twentieth century.

Nor did the international political scene contribute to stability within the country. The triumph of the communist revolution in Russia and of fascism in Italy and Germany polarized Europe and questioned the viability of classic constitutional systems.

The description in this book of the city of Madrid prior to the war and at the time of the coup d'état of July 17–18, 1936, is based on real events. The exciting night and the arming of working-class civilians, the assault on the Montaña Barracks, and the killings that occurred in University City and Casa de Campo are real.

The bombings on Madrid are also real, as are the role of repressive chekas founded by some political groups, especially communists and anarchists, and the attempt to rescue the city's cultural heritage, in particular the Prado Museum.

The situation of towns on the outskirts of Madrid is also based on documents and testimony from survivors. Repression by the Nationalist or rebel band against teachers was brutal.

It is true that many Republicans fled to Valencia and that Spaniard children were evacuated to different countries in Europe and the Americas.

The stories of the Children of Morelia and their journey to Mexico are based on the testimonies of several of these children. The evacuation of between 450 and 470 Spaniard children (the exact number is difficult to determine) by boat from Bordeaux aboard the *Mexique* was carefully planned. The offer to provide protection came from Mexico at the insistence of the wife of President Lázaro Cárdenas and from the Ibero-American Committee for Aid to the Spanish Peoples. After the war, Mexico helped over twenty thousand Spaniards who found their second home in Mexico after they fled Franco's repression.

The portrayal of Morelia and the daily life of the Spaniard children while there, including their difficulties adapting to a country and to customs so different from their own, is realistic. Likewise based on real events are the attack on town churches, the death of a child through the school administration's negligence, the first director's degrading treatment of the children, the second director's militaristic approach, the abuses committed by older students against younger children, and the gradual changes that occurred at the Spain–Mexico School.

When the Spanish Civil War ended in 1939 and when Manuel Ávila Camacho assumed the presidency of Mexico in 1940, life for the Children of Morelia changed radically. Some were deported to Spain, and others were sent to convents or given to families in adoption.

The refuge homes in Mexico City, the conflict between Spanish Republicans and Francoists in Mexico City, the kidnapping of minors, and other events in Mexico relayed herein are also based on real events, though some liberties have been taken with chronology. The refuge on Alfonso Herrera Street opened in 1943, and Rubén Landa did not become director of the Luis Vives School until 1942.

The description of postwar Spain and the horrendous Francoist repression of Republicans is based on real testimonies and factual documents. There were over 108 concentration camps scattered throughout the country, most based on the design and function-ality of Nazi concentration camps. The camp at Miranda de Ebro was one of the longest functioning, not closing until 1947. Over the years, over sixty thousand people passed through that camp, many of them foreigners who had fought in the International Brigades. One of the camp's supervisors was the German Nazi Paul Winzer, who was an advisor to the camp's director.

The repression of Republican females was brutal. Many had their children taken from them to be given in adoption or forcibly placed in orphanages founded by Auxilio Social, the Social Aid department, or by institutions of the Catholic Church. By and large, children were treated very harshly in these orphanages. Besides enduring exploitation and abuse, they were often separated from living relatives and manipulated to forget their parents' ideologies.

Pardons for prisoners condemned to death became common starting in 1941, especially if the prisoners had not committed violent crimes.

The Alcalde family is fictitious, though I have based them on testimony from several families and the real events that occurred in their lives; thus, the story of the Alcalde family is based on events that really happened.

The teachers and caretakers of the Children of Morelia are real, though some names have been changed, as is also the case for most of the children mentioned in this book.

# Timeline

**July 17–18, 1936**

Military uprising against the Republican government, beginning in Morocco and spreading throughout the peninsula. The only victory for the rebel Nationalists in major cities was in Seville. One of the first measures taken in response by the Republic was the arming of workers.

**July 20, 1936**

Anarchists, leftists, and armed workers groups defeat the rebel military at the Montaña Barracks in Madrid.

**July 25, 1936**

Franco seeks aid from Hitler through Nazi contacts in Northern Africa.

**August 14, 1936**

Badajoz falls to the Nationalists, who massacre the population.

## August 27–28, 1936

Nationalist forces begin bombing Madrid.

## September 29, 1936

Franco is named head of government and highest commanding general (*Generalísimo*) of the Nationalist armies. From that moment, he directs all military operations and the course of the war.

## November 6, 1936

The Republican government moves from Madrid to Valencia.

## November 7, 1936

The Republic murders thousands of political prisoners in the area of Paracuellos del Jarama to eliminate the risk of potential traitors. The massacre discredits the democratic government and leads to increased violence on both sides of the conflict.

## November 8, 1936

The Siege of Madrid begins. With the help of the International Brigades, Madrid's citizens withstand the siege for twenty-eight months.

## November 1936

Artwork from the Prado Museum is transported to Valencia for safekeeping.

## November 20, 1936

Alicante José Antonio Primo de Rivera, the founder and leader of the fascist political party Falange Española, is executed in jail. Franco then becomes the undisputed leader of all rebel factions.

**January 1937**

> The population of Madrid is ordered to evacuate, but most remain in the city despite the bombings and scarcities. The people create the slogan, "They shall not pass."

**February 6, 1937**

> The Nationalist offensive against Jarama begins, with the aim of isolating Madrid.

**April 19, 1937**

> Franco decrees the unification of Falangists, Carlists, and the Juntas Ofensivas Nacionales Sindicalists (Committees for National Syndicalist Attack) under an umbrella party called the Falange Española Tradicionalista y de las JONS. Franco thus secures both full political and military power.

**May 15, 1937**

> Largo Caballero resigns. Juan Negrín replaces him and forms a more extreme Republican government.

**May 26, 1937**

> The expedition of Republican children going to Mexico leaves Bordeaux.

**June 7, 1937**

> Republican children are welcomed by large crowds at the port of Veracruz.

**June 10, 1937**

> The Republican children arrive in the city of Morelia.

## July 1937

France opens its borders with Spain to receive refugees of war.

## October 1937

Women between seventeen and thirty-five years old in Nationalist-occupied Spain are required to volunteer to serve with social services and aid programs.

## May 1938

The Vatican recognizes Franco's government as the only legitimate government of Spain.

## June 1938

France bows to international pressure and closes its border with Spain, leaving thousands of refugees trapped.

## September 1938

Internationally negotiated peace agreements between Republicans and Nationalists are rejected by Franco.

## January 1939

France reopens its borders to Spanish refugees.

## February 1939

France and Great Britain recognize Franco's government as the only legitimate government of Spain.

## March 28, 1939

Nationalist troops enter and occupy Madrid.

## March 31, 1939

Republican troops fall at Alicante, the last front of resistance against the rebellion, thus ending the armed conflicts.

## April 1, 1939

In his final wartime military dispatch, Franco declares the war to be over.

# Acknowledgments

Writing a book is always hard, lonely work. It's almost paradoxical that what you write all alone in your study is destined to be poured into thousands of souls in the farthest corners of the world. But this, as every project that's worth the effort, only comes about through the support and help of many people.

I want to thank Emeterio Payá Valera for his book *Los Niños Españoles de Morelia*. His sincerity and lucidity in relaying his difficult life provided inspiration for me on countless occasions.

I'm also indebted to Pedro Montoliú, who's spent a lifetime researching Madrid during the civil war and the hardships its population endured.

I would also like to thank Alicia González Sterling for her support as an agent but even more for her friendship.

My deepest admiration is due the booksellers of the Americas and of Spain. They keep fighting for books and are changing the world, even if they don't fully understand their impact.

# Acknowledgments

I would like to thank HarperCollins Español and HarperCollins Ibérica for transmitting through literature a bit of hope in this lost, confusing world.

Above all else, I'm grateful for readers throughout the world who read my books in over ten languages and cry with me in their hours of keeping watch over the fate of these characters.

# Discussion Questions

1. Before the war begins, Francisco and Amparo Alcalde are idealists devoted to a social cause. What changes and challenges them? How are their beliefs tested as the war unfolds?

2. The Alcaldes make a terrifically difficult decision when faced with the realities of war. If forced into a similar position, would you have chosen to send your children far away to safety? If not, what would you have done?

3. Describe how this novel reckons with notions of identity. How do Marco, Ana, and Isabel merge what they remember of their homeland with the realities of being "adopted children of Mexico"? How do the Alcalde children experience these notions differently?

4. How were the Spanish refugee children received by the citizens of Mexico? Had the Alcaldes fully understood the conditions under which their children would be living, do

you think they would have chosen to send them across the ocean?

5. Marco describes war as one of the primary causes of human degradation and suffering. In this story, and in your experience, how does war turn people into "unfeeling monsters"?

6. How much did you know about the Spanish Civil War before you read this novel? What did you learn, and what did the story teach you about the nature of civil wars in particular?

7. Describe a moment of heroism in this novel. What was striking about the moment you chose?

8. Though Morelia becomes an important place to Marco, he never stops missing his homeland of Spain. How do you define *home*, and how does this story define it?

9. What does this story tell you about the power of family? About the power of love and sacrifice?

10. The author based this novel upon the real Children of Morelia—many of whom never returned to Spain or reunited with their families. How does the truth of this story change the way you read and experience it?

Based on the true story of a brave German nurse tasked with caring for Auschwitz's youngest prisoners, *Auschwitz Lullaby* brings to life the story of Helene Hannemann—a woman who sacrificed everything for family and fought furiously for the children she hoped to save.

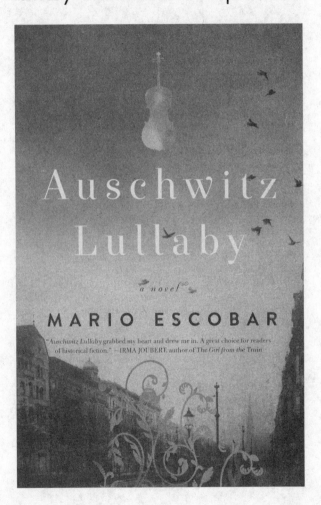

From international bestselling author Mario Escobar
comes a story of escape, sacrifice, and hope amid
the perils of the Second World War.

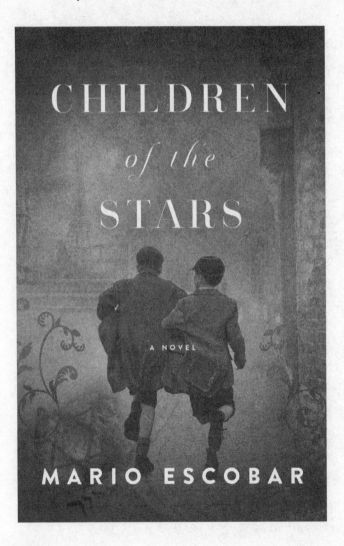

Through letters with a famous author, one French librarian tells her love story and describes the brutal Nazi occupation of her small coastal village.

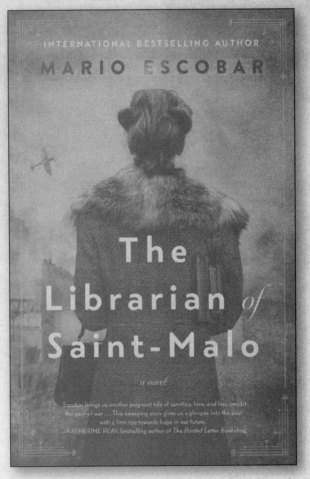

Available in print, e-book, and downloadable audio

# About the Author

Mario Escobar has a master's degree in modern history and has written numerous books and articles that delve into the depths of church history, the struggle of sectarian groups, and the discovery and colonization of the Americas. Escobar, who makes his home in Madrid, Spain, is passionate about history and its mysteries.

Find him online at marioescobar.es
Instagram: @marioescobar.oficial
Facebook: @MarioEscobarGolderos
Twitter: @EscobarGolderos

# About the Translator

Photo by Sally Chambers

Gretchen Abernathy worked full-time in the Spanish Christian publishing world for several years until her oldest son was born. Since then, she has worked as a freelance editor and translator. Her main focus includes translating/editing for the *Journal of Latin American Theology* and supporting the production of Bible products with the Nueva Versión Internacional. Chilean ecological poetry, the occasional thriller novel, and audio proofs spice up her work routines. She and her husband make their home in Nashville, Tennessee, with their two sons.